STRANGER THINGS

BY
MILDRED CRAM

Short Story Index Reprint Series

BOOKS FOR LIBRARIES PRESS
FREEPORT, NEW YORK

First Published 1923
Reprinted 1970

STANDARD BOOK NUMBER:
8369-3488-1

LIBRARY OF CONGRESS CATALOG CARD NUMBER:
78-121532

PRINTED IN THE UNITED STATES OF AMERICA

CONTENTS

STRANGER THINGS

STRANGER THINGS

WE were seated in the saloon of a small steamer which plies between Naples and Trieste on irregular schedule. Outside, the night was thickly black and a driving rain swept down the narrow decks.

"You Englishmen laugh at ghosts," the Corsican merchant said. "In my country we are less pretentious. Frankly, we are afraid. You, too, are afraid, and so you laugh! A difference, it seems to me, which lies, not in the essence, but in the manner."

Dr. Fenton smiled queerly. "Perhaps. What do any of us know about it, one way or the other? Ticklish business! We poke a little too far beyond our ken and get a shock that withers our souls. Cosmic force! We stumble forward, bleating for comfort, and fall over a charged cable. It may have been put there to hold us out—or in."

Aldobrandini, the Italian inventor, was playing cards with a German engineer. He lost the game to his opponent, and, turning about in his chair, came into the conversation.

"You are talking about ghosts. I have seen them. Once in the Carso. Again on the campagna near Rome. I met a company of Cæsar's legionaries tramping through a bed of asphodels. The asphodels lay down beneath those crushing sandals, and then stood upright again, unharmed."

The engineer shuffled the cards between short, capable fingers. "Ghosts. Yes, I agree; there are such things. Created out of our subconscious selves; mirages of the mind; photographic spiritual projections; hereditary memories. There are always explanations."

Dr. Fenton poked into the bowl of his pipe with a broad thumb. "Did any of you happen to know the English poet, Cecil Grimshaw? No? I'll tell you a story about him, if you care to listen. A long story, I warn you. Very curious—very suggestive. I cannot vouch for the entire truth of it, since I got the tale from many sources—a word here, a chance encounter there, and at last only the puzzling reports of men who saw Grimshaw out in Africa. He wasn't a friend of mine, or I wouldn't tell these things."

Aldobrandini's dark eyes softened. He leaned forward. "Cecil Grimshaw. . . . We Latins admire his work more than that of any modern Englishman."

The doctor tipped his head back against the worn red velvet of the lounge. An oil lamp, swinging from the ceiling, seemed to isolate him in a pool of light. Outside, the invisible sea raced astern, hissing slightly beneath the driving impact of the rain.

I first heard of Grimshaw (the doctor began) in my student days in London. He was perhaps five years my senior, just beginning to be famous, not yet infamous, but indiscreet enough to get himself talked about. He had written a little book of verse, "Vision of Helen," he called it, I believe. . . . The oblique stare of the hostile Trojans. . . . Helen coifed with flame. . . . Menelaus . . . Love. . . . Greater men than Grimshaw had written of Priam's tragedy. His audacity called attention to his imperfect, colourful verse, his love of beauty, his sense of the exotic, the strange, the unhealthy. People read his book on the sly and talked about it in whispers. It was indecent, but it was beautiful. At that time you spoke of Cecil Grimshaw with disapproval, if you spoke of him at all, or, if you happened to be a prophet, you saw in him the ultimate bomb beneath the Victorian literary edifice. And so he was.

I saw him once at the Alhambra—poetry in a top hat! He wore evening clothes that were a little too elaborate, a white camellia in his buttonhole and a thick-lensed monocle on a black ribbon. During the *entr'acte* he stood up and surveyed the house from pit to gallery as if he wanted to be seen. He was very tall, and the ugliest man in England. Imagine the body of a Lincoln, the hands of a woman, the jaw and mouth of Disraeli, an aristocratic nose, unpleasant eyes, and then that shock of yellow hair—hyacinthine—the curly locks of an insane virtuoso or a baby prodigy.

"Who is that?" I demanded.

"Grimshaw. The chap who wrote the book about naughty Helen. *La Belle Hélène* and the shepherd boy."

I stared. Every one else stared. The pit stopped

shuffling and giggling to gaze at that prodigious monstrosity, and people in the boxes turned their glasses on him. Grimshaw seemed to be enjoying it. He spoke to some one across the aisle and smiled, showing a set of huge white teeth, veritable tombstones.

"Abominable," I said.

But I got his book and read it. He was the first Englishman to dare break away from literary conventions. Of course he shocked England. He was a savage aesthete. I read the slim volume through at one sitting; I was horrified and fascinated.

I met Grimshaw a year later. He was having a play produced at the Lyceum—*The Labyrinth*—with Esther Levenson as Simonetta. She entertained for him at her house in Chelsea, and I got myself invited because I wanted to see the atrocious genius at close range. He wore a lemon-coloured vest and lemon-yellow spats.

"How d'you do?" he said, gazing at me out of those queer eyes of his. "I hear that you admire my work."

"You have been misinformed," I replied. "Your work interests me, because I am a student of nervous and mental diseases."

"Ah! Psychotherapy."

"All of the characters in your poem, 'The Vision of Helen,' are neurotics. They suffer from morbid fears, delusions, hysteria, violent mental and emotional complexities. A textbook in madness."

Grimshaw laughed. "You flatter me. I am attracted by neurotic types. Insanity has its source in the unconscious, and we English are afraid of looking inward." He glanced around the crowded room with an amused and cynical look. "Most of these people are as bad as my Trojans, Dr. Fenton. Only they conceal their madness and it isn't good for them."

We talked for a few moments. I amused him, I think, by my diagnosis of his Helen's mental malady. But he soon tired of me and his restless gaze went over my head, searching for admiration. Esther Levenson brought Ellen Terry over, and he forgot me entirely in sparkling for the good lady—showing his teeth, shaking his yellow locks, bellowing like a centaur.

"The fellow's an ass," I decided.

But when *The Labyrinth* was produced I changed my mind. There again was that disturbing loveliness. It was a story of the passionate Florence of Lorenzo the Magnificent, and Esther Levenson drifted through the four long acts against a background of Tuscan walls, scarlet hangings. oaths, blood-spilling, dark and terrible vengeance. Grimshaw took London by the throat and put it down on its knees.

Then for a year or two he lived on his laurels, lapping up admiration like a drunkard in his cups. Unquestionably Esther Levenson was his mistress, since she presided over his house in Cheyne Walk. They say she was not the only string to his lute. A Jewess, a Greek poetess, and a dancer from Stockholm made up his amorous medley at that time. Scandalized society flocked to his drawing-room, there to be received by Simonetta herself, wearing the blanched draperies and tragic pearls of the labyrinth he had made for her. Grimshaw offered no apologies. He was the uncrowned laureate and kings can do no wrong. He was painted by the young Sargent, of course, and by the ageing Whistler—you remember the butterfly's portrait of him in a yellow kimono leaning against a black mantel? I, for one, think he was vastly amused by all this fury of admiration; he despised it and fed upon it. If he had been less great he would have been utterly destroyed by it, even then.

I went to Vienna and lost track of him for several years. Then I heard that he had married a dear friend of mine—Lady Dagmar Cooper, one of the greatest beauties and perhaps the sternest prude in England. She wrote me, soon after that unbelievable mating: "I have married Cecil Grimshaw. I know you won't approve; I do not altogether approve myself. He is not like the men I have known—not at all English. But he intrigues me; there is a sense of power behind his awfulness—you see, I know that he is awful! I think I will be able to make him look at things—I mean visible, material things—my way. We have taken a house in town and he has promised to behave—no more Chelsea parties, no dancers, no yellow waistcoats and chrysanthemums. That was all very well for his 'student' days. Now that he is a personage, it will scarcely do. I am tremendously interested and happy. . . ."

Interested and happy! She was a typical product

of Victoria's reign, a beautiful creature whose faith was pinned to the most unimportant things—class, position, a snobbish religion, a traditional morality and her own place in an intricate little world of ladies and gentlemen. God save us! What was Cecil Grimshaw going to do in an atmosphere of titled bores, bishops, military men, and cautious statesmen? I could fancy him in his new town house, struggling through some endless dinner party—his cynical, stone-grey eyes sweeping up and down the table, his lips curled in that habitual sneer, his mind, perhaps, gone back to the red-and-blue room in Chelsea, where he had been wont to stand astride before the black mantel, bellowing indecencies into the ears of witty modernists. Could he bellow any longer?

Apparently not. I heard of him now and then from this friend and that. He was indeed "behaving" well. He wrote nothing to shock the sensibilities of his wife's world—a few fantastic short stories touched with a certain childish spirituality, and that was all. They say that he bent his manners to hers—a tamed centaur grazing with a milk-white doe. He grew a trifle fat. Quite like a model English husband, he called Dagmar "my dear," and drove with her in the Park at the fashionable hour, his hands crossed on the head of his cane, his eyes half closed. She wrote me: "I am completely happy. So is Cecil. Surely he can have made no mistake in marrying me."

You all know that this affectation of respectability did not last long—not more than five years; long

enough for the novelty to wear off. The genius or
the devil that was in Cecil Grimshaw made its re-
appearance. He was tossed out of Dagmar's circle
like a burning rock hurled from the mouth of a crater;
he fell into Chelsea again. Esther Levenson had
come back from the States and was casting about for a
play. She sought out Grimshaw and with her presence, her grace and pallor and seduction, lured him
into his old ways. "The leaves are yellow," he said
to her, "but still they dance in a south wind. The
altar fires are ash and grass has grown upon the
temple floor—I have been away too long. Get me
my pipe, you laughing dryad, and I will play for you."

He played for her, and all England heard.
Dagmar heard and pretended acquiescence. According to her lights, she was magnificent—she invited
Esther Levenson to Broadenham, the Grimshaw place
in Kent, nor did she wince when the actress accepted.
When I got back to England, Dagmar was fighting
for his soul with all the weapons she had. I went to
see her in her cool little town house, that house so
typical of her, so untouched by Grimshaw. And,
looking at me with steady eyes, she said: "I'm sorry
Cecil isn't here. He's writing again—a play—for
Esther Levenson, who was Simonetta, you remember?"

I promised you a ghost story. If it is slow in
coming, it is because all these things have a bearing
on the mysterious, the extraordinary things that
happened.

You probably know about the last phase of Grimshaw's career—who doesn't? There is something fascinating about the escapades of a famous man, but when he happens also to be a great poet, we cannot forget his very human sins—in them he is akin to us.

Not all you have heard and read about Grimshaw's career is true. But the best you can say of him is bad enough. He squandered his own fortune first—on Esther Levenson and the production of *The Sunken City*—and then stole ruthlessly from Dagmar; that is, until she found legal ways to put a stop to it. We had passed into Edward's reign, and the decadence which ended in the war had already set in—Grimshaw was the last of the "pomegranate school," the first of the bolder, more sinister futurists. A frank hedonist. An intellectual voluptuary. He set the pace, and a whole tribe of idolators and imitators panted at his heels. They copied his yellow waistcoats, his chrysanthemums, his eye-glass, his bellow. Nice young men, otherwise sane, let their hair grow long like their idol's, and professed themselves unbelievers. Unbelievers in what? God save us! Ten years later most of them were wading through the mud of Flanders, believing something pretty definite.

One night I was called to the telephone by the Grimshaws' physician. I'll tell you his name because he has a lot to do with the rest of the story—Dr. Waram, Douglas Waram—an Australian.

"Grimshaw has murdered a man," he said briefly.

"I want you to help me. Come to Cheyne Walk. Take a cab. Hurry."

Of course I went, with a very clear vision of the future of Lady Dagmar Grimshaw, to occupy my thoughts during that lurching drive through the slippery streets. I knew that she was a Broadenham, holding up her head in seclusion.

Grimshaw's house was one of a row of red brick buildings not far from the river. Dr. Waram himself opened the door to me.

"I say, this is an awful mess!" he said, in a shocked voice. "The woman sent for me—Levenson, that actress. There's some mystery. A man dead— his head knocked in. And Grimshaw sound asleep. It may be hysterical, but I can't wake him. Have a look before I get the police."

I followed him into the studio, the famous Pompeian room, on the second floor. I shall never forget the frozen immobility of the three actors in the tragedy. Esther Levenson, wrapped in peacock-blue scarves, stood upright before the black mantel, her hands crossed on her breast. Cecil Grimshaw was lying full length on a brick-red satin couch, his head thrown back, his eyes closed. The dead man sprawled on the floor, face down, between them. Two lamps made of sapphire glass swung from the gilded ceiling. . . . Bowls of perfumed, waxen flowers. A silver statuette of a nude girl. A tessellated floor strewn with rugs. Orange trees in tubs. Cigarette smoke hanging motionless in the still, overheated air. . . .

I stooped over the dead man. "Who is he?"

"Tucker. Leading man in *The Sunken City*. Look at Grimshaw, will you? We mustn't be too long——"

I went to the poet. The inevitable monocle was still caught and held by the yellow thatch of his thick brow. He was breathing slowly.

"Grimshaw," I said, touching his forehead, "open your eyes."

He did so, and I was startled by the expression of despair in their depths. "Ah!" he said; "it's the psychopathologist."

"How did this happen?"

He sat up—I am convinced that he had been faking that drunken sleep—and stared at the sprawling figure on the floor. "Tucker quarrelled with me," he said. "I knocked him down and his forehead struck against the table. Then he crawled over here and died. From fright, d'you think?" He shuddered. "Take him away, Waram, will you? I've got work to do."

Suddenly Esther Levenson spoke in a flat voice, without emotion: "It isn't true! He struck him with that silver statuette. Like this." She made a violent gesture with both arms. "And before God in heaven, I'll make him pay for it. I will—I will—I will!"

"Keep still," I said sharply.

Grimshaw looked up at her. He made a gesture of surrender. Then he smiled. "Simonetta," he said, "you are no better than the rest."

She sobbed, ran over to him, and went down on her knees, twisting her arms about his waist. There was a look of distaste in Grimshaw's eyes; he stared into her distraught face a moment, then he freed himself from her arms and got to his feet.

"I think I'll telephone to Dagmar," he said.

But Waram shook his head. "I'll do that. I'm sorry, Grimshaw; the police will have to know. While we're waiting for them, you might write a letter to Lady Dagmar. I'll see that she gets it in the morning."

I don't remember whether or not the poet wrote to Dagmar then. But surely you remember how she stayed by him during the trial—still Victorian in her black gown and veil, mourning for the hope that was dead, at last! You remember his imprisonment; the bitter invective of his enemies; the defection of his followers; the dark scandals that filled the newspapers, offended public taste and destroyed Cecil Grimshaw's popularity in an England that had worshipped him!

Esther Levenson lied to save him. That was the strangest thing of all. She denied what she had told us that night of the tragedy. Tucker, she said, had been in love with her; he followed her to Grimshaw's house in Chelsea and quarrelled violently with the poet. His death was an accident. Grimshaw had not touched the statuette. When he saw what had happened, he telephoned to Dr. Waram and then lay down on the couch—apparently fainted there, for he did not speak until Dr. Fenton came. Waram perjured himself, too—for Dagmar's sake. He had not, he swore, heard the actress speak of a silver statuette,

or of revenge before God. . . . And since there was
nothing to prove how the blow had been struck, save
the deep dent in Tucker's forehead, Grimshaw was
set free.

He had been a year in prison. He drove away
from the jail in a cab with Dr. Waram, and when the
crowd saw that he was wearing the old symbol—a
yellow chrysanthemum—a hiss went up that was like a
geyser of contempt and ridicule. Grimshaw's pallid
face flushed. But he lifted his hat and smiled into the
host of faces as the cab jerked forward.

He went at once to Broadenham. Years later,
Waram told me about the meeting between those two
—the centaur and the milk-white doe! Dagmar received him standing, and she remained standing all
during the interview. She had put aside her mourning for a dress made of some clear blue stuff, and
Waram said that as she stood in the breakfast-room,
with a sun-flooded window behind her, she was very
lovely indeed.

Grimshaw held out his hands, but she ignored them.
Then Grimshaw smiled and shrugged his shoulders
and said: "I have made two discoveries this past
year: that conventionalized religion is the most shocking evil of our day, and that you, my wife, are in love
with Dr. Waram."

Dagmar held her ground. There was in her eyes
a look of inevitable security. She was mistress of
the house, proprietor of the land, conscious of tradition, prerogative, position. The man she faced had
nothing except his tortured imagination. For the

first time in her life she was in a position to hurt him.
So she looked away from him to Waram and con-
firmed his discovery with a smile full of pride and
happiness.

"My dear fellow," Grimshaw shouted, clapping
Waram on the back. "I'm confoundedly pleased!
We'll arrange a divorce for Dagmar. Good heaven,
she deserves a decent future. I'm not the sort for
her. I hate the things she cares most about. And
now I'm done for in England. Just to make it look
conventional—nice, Victorian, *English,* you understand—you and I can go off to the Continent together
while Dagmar's getting rid of me. There'll be no
trouble about that. I'm properly dished. Besides,
I want freedom, a new life, beauty, without having to
buck up against this confounded distrust of beauty,
sensation, without being ashamed of sensation. I
want to drop out of sight. Reform? No! I am
being honest."

So they went off together, as friendly as you please,
to France. Waram was still thinking of Dagmar;
Grimshaw was thinking only of himself. He
swaggered up and down the Paris boulevards, showing his tombstone teeth and staring at the women.
"The Europeans admire me," he said to Waram.
"May England go to the devil." He groaned. "I
despise respectability, my dear Waram. You and
Dagmar are well rid of me. I see I'm offending you
here in Paris—you look nauseated most of the time.
Let's go to Switzerland and climb mountains."

Waram *was* nauseated. They went to Salvan and there a curious thing happened.

They were walking one afternoon along the road to Martigny. The valley was full of shadows like a deep green cup of purple wine. High above them the mountains were tipped with flame. Grimshaw walked slowly—he was a man of great physical laziness—slashing with his cane at the tasseled tips of the crowding larches. Once, when a herd of little goats trotted by, he stood aside and laughed uproariously, and the goatherd's dog, bristling, snapped in passing at his legs.

Waram was silent, full of bitterness and disgust. They went on again, and well down the springlike coils of the descent to Martigny they came upon the body of a man—one of those wandering vendors of pocket-knives and key-rings, scissors and cheap watches. He lay on his back on a low bank by the roadside. His hat had rolled off into a pool of muddy water. Dr. Waram saw, as he bent down to stare at the face, that the fellow looked like Grimshaw. Not exactly, of course. The nose was coarser—it had not that Wellington spring at the bridge, nor the curved nostrils. But it might have been a dirty, unshaven, dead Grimshaw lying there.

Waram told me that he felt a shock of gratification before he heard the poet's voice behind him: "What's this? A drunkard?" The doctor shook his head and opened the dead man's shirt to feel for any possible flutter of life in the heart. There was none. And he thought: "If this were only Grimshaw! If the whole miserable business were only done with!"

"By Jove!" Grimshaw said. "That chap looks like me! I thought I was the ugliest man in the world. I know better. . . . D'you suppose he's German, or Lombardian? His hands are warm. He must have been alive when the goatherd passed just now. Nothing you can do?"

Waram stayed where he was, on his knees. He tore his eyes away from the grotesque dead face and fixed them on Grimshaw. He told me that the force of his desire must have spoken in that look, because Grimshaw started and stepped back a pace, gripping his cane. Then he laughed. "Why not?" he said. "Let this be me. And I'll go on, with that clanking hardware store around my neck. It can be done, can't it? Better for you and for Dagmar. I'm not being philanthropic. I'm looking, not for a reprieve, but for release. No one knows this fellow in Salvan —he probably came up from the Rhone and was on his way to Chamonix. What d'you think was the matter with him?"

"Heart," Dr. Waram answered.

"Well, what d'you say? This pedlar and I are social outcasts. And there is Dagmar in England, weeping her eyes out because of divorce courts and more public washing of dirty linen. You love her. I don't. Why not carry this fellow to the *rochers* tonight after dark? Tomorrow, when I have changed clothes with him, we can throw him into the valley. It's a good thousand feet or more. Would there be much left of that face for purposes of identification? I think not. You can take the mutilated body back to England and I can go on to Chamonix, as he would have gone"——Grimshaw touched the pedlar with his foot——"free!"

That is exactly what they did. The body, hidden near the roadside until nightfall, was carried through the woods to the *rochers du soir,* that little plateau on the brink of the tremendous wall of rock which rises from the Rhone valley to the heights near Salvan. There the two men left it and returned to their hotel to sleep.

In the morning they set out, taking care that the proprietor of the hotel and the professional guide who hung about the village should know that they were going to attempt the descent of the "wall" to the valley. The proprietor shook his head and said: *"Bonne chance, messieurs!"* The guide, letting his small blue eyes rest for a moment on Grimshaw's slow-moving hulk, advised them gravely to take the road. "The tall gentleman will not arrive," he remarked.

"Nonsense!" Grimshaw answered.

They went off together, laughing. Grimshaw was wearing his conspicuous climbing clothes——tweed jacket, yellow suede waistcoat, knickerbockers, and high-laced boots with hobnailed soles. His green felt hat, tipped at an angle, was ornamented with a little orange feather. He was in tremendous spirits. He bellowed, made faces at scared peasant children in the village, swung his stick. They stopped at a barber's shop in the place, and those famous hyacinthine locks were clipped. Waram insisted upon this, he told me, because the pedlar's hair was fairly short and they had to establish some sort of a tonsorial identity. When the floor of the little shop was thick with the sheared "petals," Grimshaw shook his head, brushed off his shoulders, and smiled. "It took twenty years to create that visible personality—and behold, a Swiss barber destroys it in twenty minutes! I am no longer a living poet. I am already an immortal— half-way up the flowery slopes of Olympus, impatient to go the rest of the way. Shall we be off?"

"By all means," Waram said.

They found the body where they had hidden it the night before, and in the shelter of a little grove of larches Grimshaw stripped and then reclothed himself in the pedlar's coarse and soiled under-linen, the worn corduroy trousers, the flannel shirt, short coat, and old black velvet hat. Waram was astounded by the beauty and strength of Grimshaw's body. Like the pedlar, he was blond-skinned, thin-waisted, broad of back.

Grimshaw shuddered as he helped to clothe the dead pedlar in his own fashionable garments.

"Death," he said. "Ugh! How ugly—how terrifying—how abominable!"

They carried the body across the plateau. The height where they stood was touched by the sun, but the valley below was still immersed in shadow, a

broad purple shadow threaded by the shining Rhone.
"Well?" Waram demanded. "Are you eager to
die? For this means death for you, you know."

"A living death," Grimshaw said. He glanced
down at the replica of himself. A convulsive shudder
passed through him from head to foot; his face
twisted, his eyes dilated. He made a strong effort
to control himself, and whispered: "I understand.
Go ahead. Do it. I can't. It is like destroying me,
myself. . . . I can't. Do it——"

Waram lifted the dead body and pushed it over the
edge. Grimshaw, trembling violently, watched it
fall. I think, from what Dr. Waram told me many
years later, that the poet must have suffered the
violence and terror of that plummet drop, must have
felt the tearing clutch of pointed rocks in the wall
face, must have known the leaping upward of the
earth, the whine of wind in his bursting ears, the dizzy
spinning, the rending, obliterating impact at last. . . .

The pedlar lay in the valley. Grimshaw stood on
the brink of the "wall." He turned, and saw Dr.
Waram walking quickly away across the plateau
without a backward glance. They had agreed that
Waram was to return at once to the village and report
the death of "his friend, Mr. Grimshaw." The body,
they knew, would be crushed beyond recognition—a
bruised and broken fragment, like enough to Cecil
Grimshaw to pass whatever examination would be
given it. Grimshaw himself was to go through the
wood to the high road, then on to Finhaut and Cha-

monix and into France. He was never again to write to Dagmar, to return to England, or to claim his English property. . . .

Can you imagine his feelings—deprived of his arrogant personality, his fame, his very identity, clothed in another man's dirty garments, wearing about his neck a clattering pedlar's outfit, upon his feet the clumsy boots of a peasant? Grimshaw—the exquisite futurist, the daffodil, apostle of the æsthetic!

He stood for a moment looking after Douglas Waram. Once, in a panic, he called. But Waram disappeared between the larches, without, apparently, having heard. Grimshaw wavered, unable to decide upon the way to the high road. He could not shake off a sense of loneliness and terror, as if he himself had gone whirling down to his death. Like a man who comes slowly back from the effects of ether, he perceived, one by one, the familiar aspects of the landscape—the delicate flowers powdering the plateau, the tasselled larches on the slope, the lofty snow-peaks still suffused with rosy morning light. This, then, was the world. This clumsy being, moving slowly towards the forest, was himself—not Cecil Grimshaw, but another man. His mind sought clumsily for a name. Pierre—no, not Pierre; too commonplace! Was he still fastidious? No. Then Pierre, by all means! Pierre Pilleux. That would do—Pilleux. A name suggestive of a good, amiable fellow, honest and slow. When he got down into France he would change his identity again—grow a

beard, buy some decent clothes. A boulevardier . . .
gay, perverse, witty. . . . The thought delighted
him, and he hurried through the forest, anxious to
pass through Salvan before Dr. Waram got there.
He felt extraordinarily light and exhilarated now,
intoxicated, vibrant. His spirit soared; almost he
heard the rushing of his old self forward towards
some unrecognizable and beautiful freedom.

When he struck the road the sun was high and it
was very hot. Little spirals of dust kicked up at his
heels. He was not afraid of recognition. Happening to glance at his hands, he became aware of their
whiteness, and, stooping, rubbed them in the dust.

Then a strange thing happened. Another herd
of goats trotted down from the grassy slopes and
spilled into the roadway. And another dog, with
lolling tongue and wagging tail, wove in and out,
shepherding the little beasts. They eddied about
Grimshaw, brushing against him, their moonstone
eyes full of a vague terror of that barking guardian
at their heels. The dog drove them ahead, circled,
and with a low whine came back to Grimshaw, leaping up to lick his hand.

Grimshaw winced, for he had never had success
with animals. Then, with a sudden change of mood,
he stooped and caressed the dog's head.

"A good fellow," he said in French to the goatherd.

The goatherd looked at him curiously. "Not
always," he answered. "He is an unpleasant beast

with most strangers. For you, he seems to have taken a fancy. . . . What have you got there—any two-bladed knives?"

Grimshaw started and recovered himself with: "Knives? Yes. All sorts."

The goatherd fingered his collection, trying the blades on his broad thumb.

"You come from France," he said.

Grimshaw nodded. "From Lyons."

"I thought so. You speak French like a gentleman."

Grimshaw shrugged. "That is usual in Lyons."

The peasant paid for the knife he fancied, placing two francs in the poet's palm. Then he whistled to the dog and set off after his flock. But the dog, whining and trembling, followed Grimshaw, and would not be shaken off until Grimshaw had pelted him with small stones. I think the poet was strangely flattered by this encounter. He passed through Salvan with his head in the air, challenging recognition. But there was no recognition. The guide who had said "The tall monsieur will not arrive" now greeted him with a fraternal "How is trade?"

"Very good, thanks," Grimshaw said.

Beyond the village he quickened his pace, and easing the load on his back by putting his hands under the leather straps, he swung towards Finhaut. Behind him we heard the faint ringing of the church bells in Salvan. Waram had reported the "tragedy." Grimshaw could fancy the excitement—the priest hurrying towards the "wall" with his crucifix in his hands; the barber, a-quiver with morbid excitement; the stolid guide, not at all surprised, rather gratified, preparing to make the descent to recover the body of that "tall monsieur" who had, after all, "arrived." The telegraph wires were already humming with the message. In a few hours Dagmar would know.

He laughed aloud. The white road spun beneath him. His hands, pressed against his body by the weight of the leather straps, were hot and wet; he could feel the loud beating of his heart.

His senses were acute; he had never before felt with such gratification the warmth of the sun or known the ecstasy of motion. He saw every flower in the roadbank, every small glacial brook, every new conformation of the snow clouds hanging above the ragged peaks of the Argentières. He sniffed with delight the pungent wind from off the glaciers, the short, warm puffs of grass-scented air from the fields in the Valley of Trient. He noticed the flight of birds, the lazy swinging of pine boughs, the rainbow spray of waterfalls. Once he shouted and ran, mad with exuberance. Again he flung himself down by the roadside and, lying on his back, sang outrageous songs and laughed and slapped his breast with both hands.

That night he came to Chamonix and got lodging in a small hotel on the skirts of the town. His spirits fell when he entered the room. He put his pedlar's pack on the floor and sat down on the narrow bed, suddenly conscious of an enormous fatigue. His feet burned, his legs ached, his back was raw where the heavy pack had rested. He thought: "What am I doing here? I have nothing but the few hundred pounds Waram gave me. I'm alone. Dead and alive."

He scarcely looked up when the door opened and a young girl came in, carrying a pitcher of water and a coarse towel. She hesitated and said, rather prettily: "You'll be tired, perhaps?"

Grimshaw felt within him the tug of the old personality. He stared at her, suddenly conscious that she was a woman and that she was smiling at him. Charming, in her way. Bare arms. A little black bodice laced over a white waist. Straight blonde hair, braided thickly and twisted around her head. A peasant, but pretty. . . . You see, his desire was to frighten her, as he most certainly would have frightened her had he been true to Cecil Grimshaw. But the impulse passed, leaving him sick and ashamed. He heard her saying: "A sad thing occurred today down the valley. A gentleman . . . Salvan . . . a very famous gentleman. . . . And they have telegraphed his wife. . . . I heard it from Simon Ravanel. . . . It seems that the gentleman was smashed to bits—*brisé en morceaux. Épouvantable, n'est ce pas?*"

Grimshaw began to tremble. "Yes, yes," he said irritably. "But I am tired, little one. Go out and shut the door!"

The girl gave him a startled glance, frightened at last, but for nothing more than the lost look in his eyes. He raised his arms, and she fled with a little scream.

Grimshaw sat for a moment staring at the door. Then, with a violent gesture, he threw himself back on the bed, buried his face in the dirty pillow, and wept as a child weeps, until, just before dawn, he fell asleep. . . .

As far as the public knows, Cecil Grimshaw perished on the "wall"—perished and was buried at Broadenham beneath a pyramid of chrysanthemums. Perished, and became an English immortal—his sins erased by his unconsicous sacrifice. Perished, and was forgiven by Dagmar. Yet here was the victory —he belonged to her at last. She had not buried his body at Broadenham, but she had buried his work there. He could never write again. . . .

During those days of posthumous whitewashing he read the papers with a certain contemptuous eagerness. Some of them he crumpled between his hands and threw away. He hated his own image, staring balefully from the first page of the illustrated reviews. He despised England for honouring him. Once, happening upon a volume of the "Vision of Helen"— the first edition illustrated by Beardsley—in a book-stall at Aix-les-Bains, he read it from cover to cover.

"Poor stuff," he said to the bookseller, tossing it down again. "Give me 'Arsène Lupin.'" And he paid two sous for a paper-covered, dog-eared, much-thumbed copy of the famous detective story, not because he intended to read it, but in payment for his hour of disillusionment. Then he slung his pack over his shoulders and tramped out into the country. He laughed aloud at the thought of Helen and her idolators. A poetic hoax. Over-ripe words. Seductive sounds. Nonsense!

"Surely I can do better than that today," he thought.

He saw two children working in a field, and called to them.

"If you will give me a cup of cold water," he said, "I'll tell you a story."

"Gladly, monsieur."

The boy put down his spade, went to a brook which threaded the field, and came back with an earthenware jug full to the brim. The little girl stared gravely at Grimshaw while he drank. Grimshaw wiped his mouth with the back of his hand.

"What story shall it be?" he demanded.

The little girl said quickly: "The black king and the white princess and the beast who lived in the wood."

"Not that one," the boy cried. "Tell us about a battle."

"I will sing about life," Grimshaw said.

It was hot in the field. A warm, sweet smell rose from the spaded earth and near by the brook rustled through the grass like a beautiful silver serpent. Grimshaw sat cross-legged on the ground, and words spun from his lips—simple words. And he sang of things he had recently learned—the gaiety of birds, the strength of his arms, the scent of dusk, the fine crystal of a young moon, wind in a field of wheat. . . .

At first the children listened. Then, because he talked so long, the little girl leaned slowly over against his shoulder and fell asleep, while the boy fingered the knives, jangled the key-rings, clipped grass stalks with the scissors, and wound the watches one after the other. The sun was low before Grimshaw left them. "When you are grown up," he said, "remember that Pierre Pilleux sang to you of life."

"*Oui, monsieur,*" the boy said politely. "But I should like a watch."

Grimshaw shook his head. "The song is enough."

Thereafter he sang to any one who would listen to him. I say that he sang—I mean, of course, that he spoke his verses; it was a minstrel's simple improvisation. But there are people in the villages of southern France who still recall that ungainly, shambling figure. He had grown a beard; it crinkled thickly, hiding his mouth and chin. He laughed a great deal. He was not altogether clean. And he slept wherever he could find a bed—in farmhouses, cheap hotels, haylofts, stables, open fields. Waram's few hundred pounds were gone. The poet lived by his wits and his gift of song. And for the first time in his remembrance he was happy.

Then one day he read in *Le Matin* that Ada Rubenstein was to play *The Labyrinth* in Paris. Grimshaw was in Poitiers. He borrowed three hundred francs from the proprietor of a small café in the

Rue Carnot, left his pack as security, and went to Paris. Can you imagine him in the theatre—it was the Odéon, I believe—conscious of curious, amused glances—a peasant, bulking conspicuously in that scented auditorium?

When the curtain rose he felt again the familiar pain of creation. A rush of hot blood surged around his heart. His temples throbbed. His eyes filled with tears. Then the flood receded and left him trembling with weakness. He sat through the rest of the performance without emotion of any sort. He felt no resentment, no curiosity.

This was the last time he showed any interest in his old existence. He went back to Poitiers, and then took to the road again. People who saw him at that time have said that there was always a pack of dogs at his heels. Once a fashionable spaniel followed him out of Lyons, and he was arrested for theft. You understand, he never made any effort to attract the little fellows—they joined on, as it were, for the journey. And it was a queer fact that after a few miles they always whined, as if they were disappointed about something, and turned back. . . .

He finally heard that Dagmar had married Waram. She had waited a decent interval—Victorian to the end! A man who happened to be in Marseilles at the time told me that "that vagabond poet, Pilleux," appeared in one of the cafés, roaring drunk, and recited a marriage poem—obscene, vicious, terrific. A crowd came in from the street to listen. Some of them laughed. Others were frightened. He was an ugly brute—well over six feet tall, with a blond beard, a hooked nose, and a pair of eyes that saw beyond reality. He was fascinating. He could turn his eloquence off and on like a tap. He sat in a drunken stupor, glaring at the crowd, until some one shouted: *"Eh bien,* Pilleux—you were saying?" Then the deluge! He had a peasant's acceptance of the elemental facts of life—it was raw, that hymn of his! The women of the streets who had crowded into the café listened with a sort of terror; they admired him. One of them said: "Pilleux's wife betrayed him." He lifted his glass and drank. "No, *ma petite,"* he said politely, "she buried me."

That night his pack was stolen from him. He was too drunk to know or to care. They say that he went from café to café, paying for wine with verse, and getting it, too! At his heels a crowd of loafers, frowsy women, and dogs. His hat gone. His eyes mad. A trickle of wine through his beard. Bellowing. Bellowing again—the untamed centaur cheated of the doe!

And now, perhaps, I can get back to the reasons for this story. And I am almost at the end of it. . . .

In the most obscure alley in Marseilles there is a café frequented by sailors, riffraff from the waterfront, and thieves. Grimshaw appeared there at midnight. A woman clung to his arm. She had no eyes for any one else. Her name, I believe, was Marie —a very humble Magdalen of that tragic backwater

of civilization.   Putting her cheek against Grimshaw's
arm, she listened to him with a curious patience, as
one listens to the eloquence of the sea.

"This is no place for thee," he said to her.   "Leave
me now, *ma petite.*"

But she laughed and went with him.   Imagine
that room——foul air, sanded floor, kerosene lamps, an
odour of bad wine, tobacco, and stale humanity.
Grimshaw pushed his way to a table and sat down
with a surly Gascon and an enormous negro from some
American ship in the harbour.

They brought the poet wine, but he did not drink
it; he sat staring at the smoky ceiling, assailed by a
sudden sharp vision of Dagmar and Waram at Broadenham, alone together for the first time, perhaps on
the terrace in the starlight, perhaps in Dagmar's
bright room, which had always been scented, warm,
remote.

He had been reciting, of course, in French.   Now
he broke abruptly into English.   No one but the
American negro understood.   The proprietor shouted:
"Hi, there, Pilleux——no gibberish!"   The woman,
her eyes on Grimshaw's face, said warningly: "Ssh!
He speaks English.   He is clever, this poet!   Pay
attention."   And the negro, startled, jerked his
drunken body straight and listened.

I don't know what Grimshaw said.   It must have
been a poem of home, the bitter longing of an exile for
familiar things.   At any rate, the negro was touched
——he was a Louisianian, a son of New Orleans.   He
saw the gentleman, where you and I, perhaps, would

have seen only a maudlin savage. There is no other explanation for the thing that happened. . . .

The Gascon, it seems, hated poetry. He tipped over Grimshaw's glass, spilling the wine into the woman's lap. She leaped back, trembling with rage, swearing in the manner of her kind.

"Quiet," Grimshaw said. And her fury receded before his glance; she melted, acquiesced, smiled. Then Grimshaw smiled too, and, putting the glass to rights with a leisurely gesture, said: "Cabbage. Son of pig," and flipped the dregs into the Gascon's face.

The fellow groaned and leaped. Grimshaw didn't stir—he was too drunk to protect himself. But the negro saw what was in the Gascon's hand. He kicked back his chair, stretched out his arms—too late. The Gascon's knife, intended for Grimshaw, sliced into his heart. He coughed, looked at the man he had saved with a strange questioning, and collapsed.

Grimshaw was sobered instantly. They say that he broke the Gascon's arm before the crowd could separate them. Then he knelt down by the dying negro, turned him gently over, and lifted him in his arms, supporting that ugly bullet head against his knee. The negro coughed again, and whispered: "I saw it comin', boss." Grimshaw said simply: "Thank you."

"I'm scared, boss."

"That's all right. I'll see you through."

"I'm dyin', boss."

"Is it hard?"

"Yessir."

"Hold my hand. That's right. Nothing to be afraid of."

The negro's eyes fixed themselves on Grimshaw's face—a sombre look came into their depths. "I'm goin', boss."

Grimshaw lifted him again. As he did so, he was conscious of feeling faint and dizzy. The negro's blood was warm on his hands and wrists, but it was not wholly that. He had a sensation of rushing forward; of pressure against his ear-drums; a violent nausea; the crowd of curious faces blurred, disappeared—he was drowning in a noisy darkness. . . . He gasped, struggled, struck out with his arms, shouted, went down in that suffocating flood of unconsciousness. . . .

Opening his eyes after an indeterminable interval, he found himself in the street. The air was cool after the fetid staleness of that room. He was still holding the negro's hand. And above them the stars burned, remote and calm, like beacon lamps in a dark harbour. . . .

The negro whimpered: "I don't know the way, boss. I'm lost."

"Where is your ship?"

"In the Vieux Port, near the fort."

They walked together through the silent streets. I say that they walked. It was rather that Grimshaw found himself on the quay, the negro still at his side. A few prowling sailors passed them. But for the most part the waterfront was deserted. The ships lay side by side—an intricate tangle of bowsprits and rigging, masts and chains. Around them the water was black as basalt, only that now and again a spark of light was struck by the faint lifting of the current against the immovable hulls.

The negro shuffled forward, peering. A lantern flashed on one of the big schooners. Looking up, Grimshaw saw the name, *"Anne Beebe,* New Orleans." A querulous voice, somewhere on the deck, demanded: "That you, Richardson?" And then angrily: 'This damned place—dark as hell. . . . Who's there?"

Grimshaw answered: "One of your crew."

The man on deck stared down at the quay a moment. Then, apparently having seen nothing, he turned away, and the lantern bobbed aft like a drifting ember. The negro moaned. Holding both hands over the deep wound in his breast, he slowly climbed the side ladder, turned once to look at Grimshaw, and disappeared. . . .

Grimshaw felt again the rushing darkness. Again he struggled. And again, opening his eyes after a moment of blankness, he found himself kneeling on the sanded floor of the café, holding the dead negro in his arms. He glanced down at the face, astounded by the look of placid satisfaction in those wide-open eyes, the smile of recognition, of gratification, of some nameless and magnificent content. . . .

The woman Marie touched his shoulder. "The fellow's dead, m'sieur. We had better go."

Grimshaw followed her into the street. He

noticed that there were no stars. A bitter wind, forerunner of the implacable mistral, had come up. The door of the café slammed behind them, muffling a sudden uproar of voices that had burst out with his going. . . .

Grimshaw had a room somewhere in the Old Town; he went there, followed by the woman. He thought: "I am mad—mad!" He was frightened, not by what had happened to him, but because he could not understand. Nor can I make it clear to you, since no explanation is final when we are dealing with the inexplicable. . . .

When they reached his room Marie lighted the kerosene lamp and, smoothing down her black hair with both hands, said simply: "I stay with you."

"You must not," Grimshaw answered.

"I love you," she said. "You are a great man. *C'est ça.* That is that! Besides, I must love some one—I mean, do for some one. You think that I like pleasure. Ah! Perhaps. I am young. But my heart follows you. I stay here."

Grimshaw stared at her without hearing. "I opened the door. I went beyond. . . . I am perhaps mad . . . perhaps privileged . . . perhaps what they have always called me—an incorrigible poet." Suddenly he jumped to his feet and shouted: "I went a little way with his soul! Victory! Eternity!"

The woman Marie put her hands on his shoulders and pushed him back into his chair again. She thought, of course, that he was drunk. So she at-

tempted a simple seduction, striving to call attention
to herself by the coquetries of her kind. Grimshaw
pushed her aside and lay down on the bed with his
arms crossed over his eyes. Had he witnessed a
soul's first uncertain steps into a new state? One
thing he knew—he had himself suffered the confusion
of death, and had shared the desperate struggle to
penetrate the barrier between the mortal and the
immortal, the known and the unknown, the real and
the incomprehensible. With that realization, he
stepped finally out of his personality into that of the
mystic philosopher, Pierre Pilleux. He heard the
woman Marie saying: "Let me stay. I am unhappy." And without opening his eyes, simply making a brief gesture, he said: *"Eh bien."* And she
stayed.

She never left him again. In the years that
followed, wherever Grimshaw was, there also was
Marie—little, swarthy, broad of cheek and hip, un-
imaginative, faithful. She had a passion for service.
She cooked for Grimshaw, knitted woollen socks for
him, brushed and mended his clothes, watched out for
his health—often, I am convinced, she stole for him.
As for Grimshaw, he didn't know that she existed,
beyond the fact that she was there and that she made
material existence endurable. He never again knew
physical love. That I am sure of, for I have talked
with Marie. "He was good to me," she said. "But
he never loved me." And I believe her.

That night of the negro's death Grimshaw stood
in a wilderness of his own. He emerged from it a

believer in life after death.   He preached this belief
in the slums of Marseilles.   It began to be said of him
that his presence made death easy, that the touch of
his hand steadied those who were about to die.
Feverish, terrified, reluctant, they became suddenly
calm, wistful, and passed quietly as one falls asleep.
"Send for Pierre Pilleux" became a familiar phrase
in the Old Town.

I do not believe that he could have touched these
simple people had he not looked the part of prophet
and saint.   The old Grimshaw was gone.   In his
place, an emaciated fanatic, unconscious of appetite,
unaware of self, with burning eyes and tangled beard!
That finished ugliness turned spiritual—a self-
flagellated æsthete.   He claimed that he could enter
the shadowy confines of the "next world."   Not
heaven.   Not hell.   A neutral ground between the
familiar earth and an inexplicable territory of the
spirit.   Here, he said, the dead suffered bewilder-
ment; they remembered, desired, and regretted the
life they had just left, without understanding what
lay ahead.   So far he could go with them.   So far
and no farther. . . .

Personal immortality is the most alluring hope
ever dangled before humanity.   All of us secretly
desire it.   None of us really believes in it.   As you
say, all of us are afraid and some of us laugh to hide
our fear.   Grimshaw wasn't afraid.   Nor did he
laugh.   He *knew*.   And you remember his eloquence
—seductive words, poignant, delicious, memorable
words!   In his Chelsea days, he had made you sultry

with hate. Now, as Pierre Pilleux, he made you believe in the shining beauty of the indestructible, the unconquerable dead. You saw them, a host of familiar figures, walking fearlessly away from you towards the brightness of a distant horizon. You heard them, murmuring together, as they passed out of sight, going forward to share the common and ineffable experience.

Well. . . . The pagan had disappeared in the psychic! Cecil Grimshaw's melancholy and pessimism, his love of power, his delight in cruelty, in beauty, in the erotic, the violent, the strange, had vanished! Pierre Pilleux was a humanitarian. Cecil Grimshaw never had been. Grimshaw had revolted against ugliness as a dilettante objects to ugliness. Having become aware of it, he was a potent rebel. He began to write in French, spreading his revolutionary doctrine of facile spiritual reward. He splintered purgatory into fragments; what he offered was an earthly paradise—humanity given eternal absolution, freed of fear, prejudice, hatred—above all, of fear—and certain of endless life.

Now that we have entered the cosmic era, we look back at him with understanding. Then, he was a radical and an atheist.

Of course he had followers—seekers after eternity who drank his promises like thirsty wanderers come upon a spring in the desert. To some of them he was a god. To some, a mystic. To some, a healer. To some—and they were the ones who finally controlled his destiny—he was simply a dangerous lunatic.

Two women in Marseilles committed suicide—they were followers, disciples, whatever you choose to call them. At any rate, they believed that where it was so simple a matter to die, it was foolish to stay on in a world that had treated them badly. One had lost a son, the other a lover. One shot herself; the other drowned herself in the canal. And both of them left letters addressed to Pilleux—enough to damn him in the eyes of authority. He was told that he might leave France, or take the consequences —a mild enough warning, but it worked. He dared not provoke an inquiry into his past. So he shipped on board a small Mediterranean steamer as fireman, and disappeared, no one knew where.

Two years later he reappeared in Africa. Marie was with him. They were living in a small town on the rim of the desert near Biskra. Grimshaw occupied a native house—a mere hovel, flat-roofed, sunbaked, bare as a hermit's cell. Marie had hired herself out as *femme de chambre* in the only hotel in the place. "I watched over him," she told me. "And, believe me, monsieur, he needed care! He was thin as a ghost. He had starved more than once during those two years. He told me to go back to France, to seek happiness for myself. But for me happiness was with him. I laughed and stayed. I loved him —magnificently, monsieur."

Grimshaw was writing again—in French—and his work began to appear in the Parisian journals, a strange poetic prose impregnated with mysticism. It was Grimshaw sublimated. I saw it myself, although at that time I had not heard Waram's story. The French critics saw it. "This Pilleux is as picturesque as the English poet, Grimshaw. The style is identical." Waram saw it. He read everything that Pilleux wrote—with eagerness, with terror. Finally, driven by curiosity, he went to Paris, got Pilleux's address from the editor of *Gil Blas,* and started for Africa.

Grimshaw is a misty figure at the last. You see him faintly—an exile, radically featureless, wearing a dirty white native robe, his face wrinkled by exposure to the sun, his eyes burning. Marie says that he prowled about the village at night, whispering to himself, his head thrown back, pointing his beard at the stars. He wrote in the cool hours before dawn, and later, when the village quivered in heat fumes and he slept, Marie posted what he had written to Paris.

One day he took her head between his hands and said, very gently: "Why don't you get a lover? Take life while you can."

"You say there is eternal life," she protested.

"N'en doutez-pas! But you must be rich in knowledge. Put flowers in your hair, and place your palms against a lover's palms and kiss him with generosity, *ma petite.* I am not a man; I am a shadow."

Marie slipped her arms around him and, standing on tiptoe, put her lips against his. *"Je t'aime,"* she said simply.

His eyes deepened. There flashed into them the

old, mad humour, the old vitality, the old passion for beauty. The look faded, leaving his eyes "like flames that are quenched." Marie shivered, covered her face with her hands, and ran out. "There was no blood in him," she told me. "He was like a spirit— a ghost. So meagre! So wan! Waxen hands. Yellow flesh. And those eyes, in which, monsieur, the flame was quenched!"

And this is the end of the curious story. . . . Waram went to Biskra and from there to the village where Grimshaw lived. Grimshaw saw him in the street one evening and followed him to the hotel. He lingered outside until Waram had registered at the bureau and had gone to his room. Then he went in and sent word that "Pierre Pilleux was below and ready to see Dr. Waram."

He waited in the "garden" at the back of the hotel. No one was about. A cat slept on the wall. Overhead the arch of the sky was flooded with orange light. Dust lay on the leaves of the potted plants and bushes. It was breathless, hot, quiet. He thought: "Waram has come because Dagmar is dead. Or the public has found me out!"

Waram came immediately. He stood in the doorway a moment, staring at the grotesque figure which faced him. He made a terrified gesture, as if he would shut out what he saw. Then he came into the garden, steadying himself by holding on to the backs of the little iron garden chairs. The poet saw that Waram had not changed so very much—a little grey hair in that thick, black mop, a few wrinkles, a rather stodgy look about the waist. No more. He was still Waram, neat, self-satisfied, essentially English. . . . Grimshaw strangled a feeling of aversion and said quietly: "Well, Waram. How d'you do? I call myself Pilleux now."

Waram ignored his hand. Leaning heavily on one of the chairs, he stared with a passionate intentness. "Grimshaw?" he said at last.

"Why, yes," Grimshaw answered. "Didn't you know?"

Waram licked his lips. In a whisper he said: "I killed you in Switzerland six years ago. Killed you, you understand."

Grimshaw touched his breast with both hands. "You lie. Here I am."

"You are dead."

"Dead?"

"Before God, I swear it."

"Dead?"

Grimshaw felt once more the onrushing flood of darkness. His thoughts flashed back over the years. The "wall." His suffering. The dog. The song in the field. The negro. The door that opened. The stars. His own flesh, fading into spirit, into shadows. . . .

"Dead?" he demanded again.

Waram's eyes wavered. He laughed unsteadily and looked behind him. "Strange," he said. "I thought I saw——" He turned and went quickly across the garden into the hotel. Grimshaw called once, in a loud voice: "Waram!" But the doctor did not even turn his head. Grimshaw followed him, overtook him, touched his shoulder. Waram paid no attention. Going to the bureau he said to the proprietor: "You told me that a Monsieur Pilleux wished to see me."

"*Oui, monsieur.* He was waiting for you in the garden."

"He is not there now."

"But just a moment ago———"

"I am *here*," Grimshaw interrupted.

The proprietor brushed past Waram and peered into the garden. It was twilight out there now. The cat still slept on the wall. Dust on the leaves. Stillness. . . .

"I'm sorry, monsieur. He seems to have disappeared."

Dr. Waram straightened his shoulders. "Ah!" he said. "Disappeared. Exactly." And passing Grimshaw without a glance, he went upstairs.

Grimshaw spoke to the proprietor. But the little man bent over the deck, and began to write in an account book. His pen went on scratching, inscribing large, flourishing numbers in a neat column. . . .

Grimshaw shrugged and went into the street. The crowds paid no attention to him—but then, they never had. A dog sniffed at his heels, whined, and thrust a cold nose into his hand.

He went to his house. "I'll ask Marie," he thought. . . . She was sitting before a mirror, her hands clasped under her chin, smiling at herself. . . . She had put a flower in her hair. Her lips were parted. She smiled at some secret thought. Grimshaw watched her a moment; then with a leap of his heart he touched her shoulder. And she did not turn, did not move. . . .

He knew! He put his fingers on her cheek, her neck, the shining braids of her coarse black hair. Then he walked quickly out of the house, out of the village, towards the desert.

Two men joined him. One of them said: "I have just died." They went on together, their feet whispering in the sand, walking in a globe of darkness until the stars came out—then they saw one another's pale faces and eager, frightened eyes. Others joined them. And others. Men. Women. A child. Some wept and some murmured and some laughed.

"Is this death?"

"Where now, brother?"

Grimshaw thought: "The end. What next? Beauty. Love. Illusion. Forgetfulness."

He clasped his hands behind his back, lifted his face to the stars, walked steadily forward with that company of the dead, into the desert, out of the story at last.

THE YELLOW ONE

AT Waululu there was a white man, the only white man nearer than Pago-Pago, which was thirty miles across the warm sea, due south.

This man was tall and thin. By his look you would have said that he was always in pain. A thought dwelt behind his eyes—a screen between him and the world.

His world, what he saw of it, was beautiful enough to suit any dreamer of dreams. Coco-palms picketed the island about, and beyond, a coral reef foamed milk-white where the slow rollers broke. His house was not fifty feet from the lagoon where for the price of the mere desire there was swimming in water as clear and as green as liquid emeralds.

But this white man was queer. He never left his house except on the first day of every month, when he shambled to the beach, boarded his sailing-boat and vanished down the glittering sea towards Pago-Pago. He always went alone and returned alone, bringing a supply of canned goods, calico, beads, tinware and umbrellas. This was his "stock." Patiently, without enthusiasm, he carried it across the strip of blazing coral beach to his house and disappeared therein for another month.

He was storekeeper at Waululu. He had come in his sailing-boat—the *Miriam*—all the way from Meader, Massachusetts. So he said. Alone in a catboat on the open Pacific—God knows how he had made the traverse! He was burned nearly black by exposure to the sun, and his hair was tow-colour, stiff as hay, singed. His eyes were the only cold thing about him—they were ice-blue, and had a curious diagonal streak though the centres, like twin moon-stones set in copper.

He never explained himself. The natives came shyly down, with soft gossip and conjecture, to watch him land his sea-chest and a box of books. He indi-cated that he had come to stay. And when he had built his house—a single room and an out-shed—he painted the glass-paned window, glory of Waululu, black, to shut out any ray of sunlight that might try to enter his place of exile.

For it seems that he was troubled by something and hated the light of day. He had done something or had seen something which drove him to darkness. He slung a hammock indoors, made a trip to Pago-Pago for supplies, and, setting up a few shelves and a rough counter, went into that strange and terrible voluntary confinement. He spent most of his day sprawled in the hammock, while through the open door barefooted natives came and went, passing from the glare of sunshine into the damp shadows of the "store" and quickly out again. Chickens scratched and cackled on the sill and a pig usually grunted in some dark corner, searching for empty tins flavoured with sardines or cheap meats. The white man was motionless but not asleep. He was a fixture in that hammock. He had no friends and he seemed to have no enemies. No one knew whether he ate or drank. The simple folk of Waululu called him the Yellow One. But his name was Denny.

This he confessed to Herz, who came over from Pago-Pago in a launch to find out for himself what manner of man it was who had set about committing suicide in Waululu, when he might have done it more expeditiously in Meader, Massachusetts.

Herz was curious but not sympathetic. He had seen too many tag-ends of life washed up on these pink beaches. Once upon a time he had gathered them up and set them on their frayed pins again—out of his own pocket. But that was long ago, in Herz's youth, when a coconut-palm and a boozy beachcomber had spelled romance. Nothing was left except curiosity.

A tale had gone around through official and commercial circles at Pago-Pago—a very intriguing story indeed about a ghost of a 'Melican man in dirty duck who appeared in the streets on the first day of every month, who came in a catboat and departed again, without having uttered a word. This was neither natural nor proper. He was a white man, and his boat was called the *Miriam* and hailed from Meader. Something decidedly queer about it, Herz thought.

One day he hopped into his tiny launch and pursued that peeling Massachusetts craft across thirty miles of purple sea.

Then he walked in on the stranger, with fifty naked natives gaping at his heels.

"Howdy," he said, polite but on his guard.

Denny was stocking his shelves. He had a dozen or so soup and meat cans and a roll of purplish calico. He arranged everything very neatly, as if he had heard nothing. Then he turned and stared at the intruder with those queer eyes of his. "I'd be obliged if you'd get out," he said. He whispered, but there was a terrible ferocity behind his restraint.

Herz was accustomed to hysteria. "What's the idea? Fugitive? Suicide? Or nut?"

The Yellow One staggered over to his hammock— he was as weak as a boneless shad—and stretched himself full length with his bare feet higher than his head and his two hands dragging on the floor. Herz thought he had died. But even death failed to move Herz. He went outside to question the natives. And to his surprise he found that the man from Massachusetts had made himself popular—the brown people spoke of him with soft voices, their great eyes liquid with love. The Yellow One was sad. He never laughed. He sat alone with his God. But he was kind. He was as a child. He never cheated. Or lied. Or raised his hand in anger. . . .

Herz went back into the dark store. He stood with legs straddled, puffing at a cigar, staring down at the wreck of a man in the hammock. He judged him to be thirty-five—not more. A face sensitive and humiliated, as if stamped with some unforgettable

shame. A body emaciated, the colour of a corpse.
Dirty. Weak. A prisoner in his own skull. . . .

"I'll tell you what," Herz said suddenly. "If
you'll come back to Pago-Pago I'll get a man's job for
you. I don't trust you. I've seen your kind before.
Some girl. Some love twist. Some damn fool sex
notion. Your brain is addled like a bad egg. Get
up. For God's sake, face the light of day, you coward! Nothing is so dirty it can't be washed clean if
you leave it out in the rain or drop it in the ocean.
How many years have you been playing mushroom in
this cellar?"

"Three."

"You make me sick and ashamed for men. Think
of the poor devils behind bars who'd give half a life
for your chance!"

The Yellow One sat up. He made a clawing gesture with both hands and gasped for breath.

"I'm after a man. Some day he's coming here.
He'll walk through that door. And I'll kill him. I'll
kill him! By God, I'm only waiting."

Herz laughed. "Well, now I know. It's a nut
you are, after all. That's the damnedest confession
I ever heard, and I've heard many."

Then Denny told him, as Herz knew he would, the
whole story. Herz was a talented collector of such
tales; he had hundreds on file in his memory—stories
of cunning and failure, treachery, love, desperation
and death, a saga of those bright seas and blazing
coral strands, of wanderers, adventurers, fools, and
saints.

This was a story of the weaker and stronger, the Friend plot, second only in pathos to the Cinderella theme. It was a story of two men.

It began at Meader, a town on the coast of New England, chill, prim, and profane, a place of salt marshes and shipyards, flavoured with a sticky saltiness and the odour of pitch. It was destined to finish at Waululu in the warm Pacific.

A long traverse.

These two men were born on the same day, and from the first raucous squall of release and beginning, they were destined, they were doomed, to be friends.

They were born on a sultry day in August when great yellow thunderheads toppled on the horizon and the receding tide left ribbons of dirty foam along the shore. An evil day when the roads were hot and trees wilted like uprooted weeds.

Denny was born frail, with funny little blue hands, wrinkled, folded in, helpless. No one would have believed that he would one day do with them what he did do.

Hopper was born protesting. He kicked and struck out. Then they put him in a clothes basket and for a time forgot him, since his mother had just died.

As children they played together. As boys they adventured together. As young men they loved and hated together. Hopper was boss. He was that kind.

When he was no more than a baby he discovered that he had a secret way into Denny's imagination;

he could torment and delight him, he could dismay and disturb him, he could terrify him. He was Denny's god. Whatever he said, Denny believed. Whatever he did, Denny tried to do.

At eighteen they had been in more mischief than any two boys in Meader. Hopper was one of those rascals who manage to get themselves loved for their rascality. He stood six-foot-three and weighed two hundred and twenty pounds. His smile was the kind to melt down hearts as a flame consumes a tallow candle.

Denny found him terrible and fascinating. He couldn't keep away from him. He had tried and he had failed.

There was only one place where Denny could be alone. He used to go by the marsh road to the beach, and pace the sand wrestling with his great trouble. The slippery kelp would tangle about his feet and his hair would be drenched with spray from the breakers that rode in like sea horses with flying manes.

Nature had set her mark upon him—he was a dreamer of dreams who fancied himself weak. But on the beach he stood upright, knotting his hands behind his back, fancying himself to be the spitting image of Hopper, a rascal, a devil of a fellow. And then Hopper would come lounging across the marsh in pursuit, swinging his shoulders and bellowing a song. "What you doing here, Denny? Come on back."

"Don't want to."

"The Weymans have got a visitor. Girl from Bedford. Purty as an apple. You wait and see. I'll take a bite out of her cheek before sundown."

Denny sagged like a body without a soul and went along, his feet dragging in the sand.

No, Denny hadn't a soul of his own, only a sort of pseudo soul, a penetrating inner voice, a conscience. With this voice he conversed, holding himself up to ridicule, an object of his own contempt. Hopper was no good; Denny knew him for a blackguard, doing what he pleased and hang the consequences. And if there was a failure it was Denny, the shadow, who was blamed.

The case of the girl with cheeks like ripe apples was no different from the rest. Hopper was successful with women, perhaps because he cared nothing for any of them. He had a wide and impartial taste.

"Wait till you see her Denny! Lovely. Round and ripe. And crazy about me already."

A shaft of disgust entered that part of Denny which was still himself. But he said nothing.

This girl was destined to run through the fabric of their lives like a bright thread across a dark tapestry. When Denny saw her he loved her, and in the same breath surrendered her. But not before Hopper had noticed the quivering of Denny's lips, the flash of recognition in his eyes. He had waited and watched for this avowal.

Now, half of Miriam's beauty may have been her youth and half of it Denny may have put there out of his own queer imagination, his crooked, romantic, prisoned inner self, his jealous self no one ever saw or knew.

He sat on the Weyman's porch whittling a stick and not looking at her again, while Hopper made himself fascinating.

"Now here's Denny, and here's me," he said. "Denny's my friend. Share and share alike. Don't you calculate to fall in love with me, unless you calculate to include Denny!"

She laughed. "I don't calculate to love either of you," she said.

"You'll love *me*. They all do!"

Denny's face was expressionless. He had a way of shutting himself off as if he closed a door upon an intruder. He whittled the stick into a smooth, round wand, thick at one end, tapering at the other. Now he set about carving an elaborate design, an intricate pattern of leaves, fruits, and coiled snakes. He worked very fast; his fingers had a cunning, a precision, a frugal and crafty delicacy. He put his tongue in his cheek. You would have thought that he heard nothing. But he heard everything— Miriam's laughter, like a wren's, and Hopper's baritone guffaw. The battle that went on behind him, all for his benefit! He knew when Hopper possessed himself of Miriam's waist, and when he bit softly at that round cheek with his big, white teeth. Denny broke the stick into three pieces.

He hated.

"What did I tell you?" Hopper demanded on their way home. *"Mmm*—sweet's an apple!"

Denny loved her. But he was the weaker. He grinned, and all the while he hated. He snickered, and all the while he itched to rub Hopper's face in the dust, to wipe out the flavour of that kiss in ignominy.

"Well, by gum, why didn't you?" Herz demanded.

The Yellow One flung his dirty duck-clad arms over his face.

He couldn't. He hadn't the nerve. Maybe he was hypnotized.

People pitied him because he was the weaker, and popular suspicion had it that Hopper was charitable to boot—he permitted the dour Denny to bask in his own amazing popularity.

It couldn't be said of Hopper that he tried to keep Miriam to himself. Whenever he wooed her on the Weymans' porch, with laughter and loud talk and serene, bland looks out of his baby-blue eyes, Denny always sat near by whittling that everlasting stick of his.

Now here is where the story turns and something must be made clear.

Denny could do anything with his hands; they were strong as steel and facile as the hands of the devil. All his wit was in his finger-tips; all of his quaint, strangled dreams were translated into carvings and drawings; he could copy anything. But who knew this? No one but Hopper, who had the fat and helpless hands of a baby; characteristically, he ignored Denny's skill.

"I think Denny's wonderful," Miriam said one

day, bending down so that Denny felt her breath warm on his cheek, and his heart leaped in his breast. "See what he's made!"

Hopper looked, scorn gathering in his eyes, his smile paternal. "Oh, Denny's always pottering around, wasting his time. Now what's that? Abraham Lincoln?"

"Why, it's perfect."

"Is it?"

Hopper flushed and Denny felt an unholy joy welling up in himself like a gorgeous spring of intoxicating liquor. He held the copy at arm's length and squinted at it, and Miriam's head almost touched his shoulder, she leaned so close to him.

"One thing I bet you *can't* do," Hopper said.

"What's that?"

"Bet you a hundred. That's fair."

"What, then?"

"Bet you can't copy a silver dollar—bet you can't make one—bet you can't fool old Doc Gordon with one. Bet you a hundred."

Denny turned his head. "But that's not honest."

"You're not going to *use* it. Are you? *Are* you?"

"Why, no."

"Then what's the harm? Now, see here—here's a silver dollar. Think you can make one?"

Denny turned the bright disc over and over in his palm, while Miriam leaned down, so near, so near! She was dark and tinted a warm rose and soft as a bird, a little, fluttering bird, warm and tremulous in your hand. He could hear her breath, short and sharp.

"Oh, Denny, do!"

He pocketed the coin and shut himself away from her with that sudden, contemptuous drop of his lids. "All right," he said.

Denny lived alone in a rickety, wooden house on a terrace behind the town. Three tall elms stood in a row before the door, like formal bouquets. The sheds and outhouses, storehouses for the miscellaneous and mysterious collections of four generations, straggled up the slope in the rear; the furthermost of these draughty sheds was Denny's workroom. Here, like an alchemist, he worked in a light that fell dimly through cracked panes festooned with webs and knotted strands of dead flies, moths, and the dainty skeletons of many spiders, fragile, empty houses tangled in dust. All day there was a gnawing in the walls, and fieldmice made tentative excursions sniffing, palpitating, noiseless as little velvet ghosts on runners. . . .

"I think you were a damn fool," Herz remarked, shooing a cackling fowl out into the white sunlight of Waululu.

The Yellow One spread out his arms and stared with those eyes full of pain and confusion.

"I've always been a damn fool," he answered. "I'm no good."

"You're welcome to the idea," Herz said cheerfully. "It's your own. I'd be the last one to contradict you. . . . Like to knife me, wouldn't you? Like to squeeze my windpipe till I choked black as a stove! That's a healthy emotion. Well, swallow your rage and go on. I'm interested. Did you make that dollar?"

He did. He had to. Not for the money, not to win the bet, but to recapture the triumph—oh, the fragile, slender, evanescent triumph!—of that moment on the Weymans' porch when Miriam had leaned her head down to whisper: "Oh, Denny, do!"

The poor soul of him was bedazzled; his conscience, which was all the brain he had, was dumb.

He worked day and night carving his silver dollar. He did not stoop to make an imprint. This was to be no sleight of hand, but a veritable copy, an eye for an eye, an eagle for an eagle, properly made in reverse, just deep enough, delicate and beautiful. He failed and tried again. In his forge, an iron pot thrust into a charcoal bed, he melted up all the silver he could find, spoons, teapots, and trays, filched from an old treasure chest in the garret. Denny's mother had preferred hand-painted crockery and souvenir spoons to the antique remnants of the family's better days—what were sea captains' treasures to the hideous gleanings of Boston shops and her own wedding presents? Denny rifled the garret. He would not make one dollar but a dozen, to string into a necklace for Miriam. He could fancy it lying, cool and bright, on the warm brownness of her throat, lifted by her breath—his gift. At the thought his face flushed and his lips trembled. He was clumsy! Confound the tools! Confound his fingers! How was it done?

When he went out people questioned him: "Don't see you 'n' Hop together these days. Mad? Mad, are you?"

"No," he said shortly.

And then, one night, the work was done. Perfect, beautiful—twelve silver dollars! He slipped them through his fingers one by one, locked the door on his triumph, and took the old road to the beach. It was a night sultry and dark; fireflies flickered in the marsh grass. Down on the wet sand, packed smooth by the outgoing tide, he found Miriam—a white dress shining in the darkness with an incandescent, a phosphorescent glow, a white face, and white hands groping for his!

"Denny! Denny!"

They walked together, close to the water, away from the town, as if they had met by some tacit conspiracy. Denny was too startled to know how or why she had come there. As always, a subtle transformation had taken place in him—here, he was master of himself.

"I finished the dollar, Miriam."

She held out her hand. "Let me see."

"No. You wait till tomorrow. I've got a surprise for you."

"For me?"

"I love you, Miriam."

How had he come to say that?

She leaned against him, his arm went about her, and they paced slowly through the warm darkness, little waves hissing at their feet, their footprints vanishing behind them.

"I didn't know, Denny," she said.

Then for a precious hour they made love, those two, and Denny promised her everything under the shining sun. Finally and for ever, he thought, he was done with Mr. Hopper of the baby-blue eyes, his very good friend. This was a dizzy sense of freedom, and Denny boasted very loud. They would leave Meader for ever and sail to Bedford in his catboat. Already he had painted out the name *Ariel* and had substituted the precious syllables *Miriam*. Oh, they would be happy! And Hopper could go to the devil.

"He's not so bad, Denny."

"You don't love him, Miriam?"

She shook her head. "I love you, Denny. You're my silly darling. My boy." She caught one of his hands and kissed the clever fingers.

Then they heard some one running behind them.

"Denny! Oh, Denny!"

Denny felt his heart grow cold. His knees sagged. His lips were dry. And his voice had no life in it; it was like a cracked bell.

"Hop! He's after me!"

"After you, Denny?"

Hopper appeared in the darkness, a blur, a shadow, with long arms that gesticulated.

"Reckon you'd better come back with me, Denny. They want you."

Then he saw Miriam and, reaching out, swung her to his side: "And I reckon you'd better stay with me. You don't want to be seen with Denny."

"Why not?" she pleaded. "Why not? What's Denny done?"

"Passed a bad dollar at Staples' this afternoon."

"That was the dollar you gave me!" Denny cried.

"My dollar? Hear him! It was one of the bad dollars he's been making. Staples got the sheriff and they fetched me and we've been up to Denny's place. Regular mint. Regular counterfeit plant. . . ." He broke off. "You'd better come back. They're after you."

"But you put him up to it!" Miriam cried. "Denny, say something! It was a bet between him and you. I was there. A joke! A bet! Denny, why don't you say something?"

"I made them for Miriam," Denny explained, all the lustre gone from his voice. He withdrew from them, there in the dark, and seemed to wander back, mysteriously, to hover, disembodied, featureless. . . .

"For Miriam! Silver dollars to give a girl! Covering up your own crookedness. . . . You'd better come."

"I'll come."

Suddenly, like a fury, Miriam tore away from Hopper and hurled herself at Denny; she clung to his arms, his shoulders, his neck, pulling his face down to her eager lips. She tried to give her own life to him.

"Denny—Denny! I'll tell the truth. They'll believe me."

"No," Denny said patiently, "they'll believe Hop!

They always do." He got her fingers loose and pushed her away. It was Hopper's arm that caught and held her.

"Well," Herz said, after a pause, "what then?"

"Ten years in a stinking jail. Ten years away from the sea. Ten years behind bars. Ten years, hating and hating. Ten years planning to kill. It made rot of my soul."

"I thought you didn't have any."

"Get out, damn you!" the Yellow One said petulantly. "I've told you enough."

"Not yet."

Herz flicked his cigar at a runting pig. A shadow fell across the doorway, and a naked brown native of Waululu stalked in with the graceful slow gait of his kind.

"One fella boat," he said. His great eyes shone in the shadows. He spoke the *bêche-de-mer* of other distant islands. A chief's son, with a flower behind his ear. "One fella boat belong Pago-Pago come, mahrster."

The Yellow One stiffened. He made a terrible effort and rolled sideways out of the hammock, somehow striking a precarious balance on his naked feet.

"*Hopper!*" he said, in a sort of squeak.

Herz laughed. "Things like that don't happen."

He went to the door and squinted at the sea. A small white speck flecked the purple of that wide expanse. It was a mere dot in Herz's eye. But unquestionably a boat, a motor-launch, headed for this island of Waululu, this dirty, beautiful little hoop of coral and coco-palms, this forgotten second-rate Paradise, this crust of loneliness and desolation. . . . Herz wondered. . . . Behind him, he heard a miserable sniffling and chattering, as if the Yellow One had been seized with a chill.

"A boat all right," Herz said.

"*Hopper!*"

"What makes you think so?"

Whereupon, sitting upright in his hammock, like a terrified skeleton, Denny finished his story.

It was brief enough. And as Herz listened he got the impression that he was hearing again the tale of Dr. Faustus and the Devil, only that Denny had had no payment of any sort for his soul. He saw this man, this Hopper, fat, benign, smiling, genial, and unctuous, with thick, wet lips and bland eyes, mild as a milk-fed god on Olympus. And Denny, starved and wolfish, thin as a slat, prowling down Meader's main street on his way home from prison. The prison pallor on his skin. The prison look in his eyes. Guilt and shame written there like a tattoo indelible and hideous. And the idea an established fact, his weakness a screen between himself and the actual world. The world distorted, ugly—a place where human hearts withered and demons ruled. Sky empty. Flowers withered. Laughter mocking. No reason to live except to kill. . . .

He stood for a long moment at his own gate, the dust of the journey thick upon his shoulders. No good. No good. No good except to kill! He would kill that night and then get away in his boat—the *Miriam,* blistered, peeling, leaky, but still afloat—through the Neck, over the bar and straight out to sea!

The empty house echoed and creaked as he moved about. He found a rope and fashioned a slip-knot. Then he went into the orchard (where the grass was knee-deep) and swung the lasso over branches, stumps, fence-posts, rocks. The sun was sullen in a whirl of hot vapours. The clover smelled sweet, heady as honey-wine. Oh, what a world! And Denny, with his tongue in his cheek, coiled and swung, coiled and swung, over and over, until the sweat rained down his cheeks, until dusk blurred the outline of things and the hour had come. He slipped the coil of rope under his jacket and went towards the town.

The marshes smelled flat and brinish; a pink moon floated up.

Who should he meet, of course, but Hopper in white ducks and a straw hat, swinging a cane! Coming to meet his enemy, on a dark road, with no gun, no knife, nothing, mind you, save his infernal nimbus, his halo of evil—the fires of damnation seemed to play about him as he swaggered forward, an unearthly glow of fireflies and sullen moonlight, while before him a swollen shadow capered and danced.

" 'Lo, Denny!"

Denny stood there shivering, and the rope came

uncoiled from beneath his coat and wriggled down to his feet like a dead snake.

"What you got there?"

"A noose."

"To hang me with?"

His voice changed. "Well, why don't you?"

"I can't!"

And he couldn't. He turned and ran to the river anchorage, waded out to the *Miriam*, scrambled aboard and poled her over the bar out to sea.

Herz dropped his cigar and stepped on it.

"This girl. . . . What became of her, you very bad egg?"

The Yellow One shivered. "She waited. She believed. She is still waiting, back there."

"And that wasn't enough? Oh, you blistering blighter! You solid streak of sanguinary ochre! So you ran away?"

Denny lifted his head; his face froze to attention. "Listen!"

In the lagoon a sharp *chug-chug* seemed to splinter the silence. A chorus of excited voices rose from the beach, and, as if startled by these detonations, a cackle and screaming of fowls and birds broke out like an explosion.

Herz went to the door and the Yellow One tottered after to stare with light-dazzled eyes over his shoulder.

A motor-boat, recognizable as a semi-official and

public craft of Pago-Pago, approached the beach across the shining and polished surface of the lagoon. A man stood upright in the bow, holding an open umbrella over his head. There was something in his attitude of the self-ordained monarch, a grotesque and pompous dignity. His girth was prodigious. And on his head he wore, at a certain rakish angle, the latest thing in straw hats.

"Hopper?" Herz inquired. "Is it your arch-demon, Denny? Does life work this way? And why? What's he doing here on this blister in mid-ocean?"

"Oh, my God!" the Yellow One said. "Now I shall kill him."

Herz sat him down on the bench by the door and kindled another cigar. "Do so, Mr. Denny. I'm all attention. But how?"

Hopper landed and his boxes were put ashore after him. He looked about with a well-pleased air. The island lay in the sea, at that hour of sunset, like an open flower in a crystal bowl, scented and lovely. The simple savages made a lane for him as, with his umbrella still held aloft like a banner, he crossed the coral beach. Not such a rogue, to all appearances. He had a china-blue eye and a cheek as soft as a baby's. As he came through the brief shadow of the coco-grove, his huge self a target of targets, Herz winced away and aside from an unexpected spurt of flame from the door of the Yellow One's mud and straw house.

But the evil one came on, untouched.

"I am looking for a man called Denny," he said politely, and, furling his umbrella, removed that dazzling straw hat to mop his brow.

"Right here," said Herz, holding his breath.

"Here?"

They both stared, Herz with a gingerly turn of his head, Hopper leaning forward, blinking his eyes.

The Yellow One lay crumpled on the sill. He had fainted away.

Herz lingered a while to talk to Hopper. He found him an abysmal fool. As a demon, he failed to register. But you never know.

"Now these natives," he said, wagging his fat hands. "Greasy niggers, I call 'em. Lower than the brutes. Look at 'em! Ding-blasted apes with posies in their ears!"

"Really," said Herz.

"Meaning, you don't agree with me? Quite so. Most white men lose their pride of race when they come down here. Next to *going* native, like my poor friend Denny, *thinking* native is as low as a civilized man can fall."

"Well, really—"

Hopper mopped his brow. "I intend to make them stand around. I've never failed to dominate. I *am* superior. I behave accordingly. And the inferior species crawls. Crawls.

"Why?" He glanced around at the silent circle of Waululuans, children of the reefs, and all those brown bodies seemed to quiver as leaves shaken by a little wind. "These people will fetch and carry for me. Superior mentality. Superior nerve. To-morrow they will be my slaves."

"What do you expect to do?" Herz asked.

Hopper glanced over his shoulder at the huddled shape of Denny, the Yellow One.

"He is my friend. What should I do?"

This was beyond Herz.

He tried again: "How did you happen to know," he demanded, "that you would find him here?"

"An American sailor, fellow from Meader, had seen him in Pago-Pago. He wrote me. And I don't mind saying he described the ditch Denny had fallen into. Was it or was it not my duty to fetch him away?"

"Is it true—was he in prison?"

"Oh, yes. My friend is no good. But I do my best. Superior. Magnanimous."

"Well," Herz said briskly, "I'll be going."

He hurried away from there without a backward glance. Herz had long ago abandoned his desire to be philanthropic. Denny would have to take care of himself. And if he couldn't, better that he should be devil-ridden to the horrible day of his death. For it is given to men to win their own battles, and if they are strong enough, desirous enough, persistent enough, of sufficient candour, simplicity, and faith, they will win through to some substantial victory; whether it happens or no, makes little difference. But if they are flaccid, witless, frightened, and sorry, if they weep for their own sins and apologize for their own mistakes, they will pass down and out one way or the other. Only now and then are there miracles, when a miserable, skulking soul turns on itself in rage and scorn, shedding its skin like a wretched snake, with travail, for ever.

Herz went back to Pago-Pago. The last he saw of Denny he was sitting in a sort of stupid agony on the bench by the door, watching Hopper move in.

"Here you! You black swine! Get my boxes in! Hurry, now! I'll bash your black heads in. . . ."

A file of upright brown bodies moved from the store to the beach, slowly, with reluctance.

In the shadow of the coco-palms, enormous, pompous, bellowing, Hopper took command of Denny and of his new kingdom.

Herz followed the official launch, Hopper's barge, down a streak of copper light, to Pago-Pago. Then, very patiently, with a wisdom born of many disappointments, he waited for the *dénouement*. He had seen the stage set, the curtain raised, the actors assembled. Some day, he knew, he would witness the *finale*. In anticipation, very often, he smacked his lips. Life was slow-moving in Pago-Pago and he could afford to wait.

The end came in a strange way.

One day of cloudless sky and white-hot sun, there was a clatter on Herz's veranda, a loud bang at the inner door, and a bellowing voice that shouted:

"Herz! Anybody home?"

Herz had been asleep. He sat up, trying to link the voice to a half-forgotten impression. Then he padded in his stockinged feet to the door.

The man outside was tall and blond. He straddled and arched his chest. His arms, set athwart the door, were big around as mahogany branches.

"Yes?" said Herz politely, blinking.

"Hallo! I'm Denny, from Waululu. Thought I'd stop by and say howdy. Also so long. I'm leaving tomorrow on the Ward Line steamer for San Francisco."

"Glad to see you."

Herz said afterwards that he gasped for breath. He opened the screen, and that sinewy giant strode by into the shadows of the room. He had a swagger. He made Herz feel like a timid woman.

"Gosh! Hot! Hot's Hades! Got anything to drink? I'm dry. Dry's a bone. Give us something cool and lively."

Herz said that he very nearly salaamed. He found his grass slippers and got into his coat in a terrible hurry. Then he sought a certain bottle and two tall glasses. All the while he was spying on his visitor out of one corner of his astonished eye. This, Denny? This cock-o'-the-walk, the Yellow One? This—— Words failed him.

He tendered the glass. And all at once his eyes met those of his guest and a look flashed between them —a look full of humour, appreciation and devout questioning.

Denny drank. He tipped back his head and the cool liquor gurgled down his throat. It would have singed the soul of a weak man. But Denny only licked his lips and asked for more.

"Over from Waululu today?" Herz ventured, obliging.

"Today. I'm scorched. I'm parched as a desert. Give us another."

"No," said Herz firmly, "not until you tell me, soberly, how you dished your demon, and where, and why. If you burn, so do I—of curiosity. Come, now—I see you're Denny, but it's hard to believe."

"It is that." Denny set the glass aside, and doubling up his fists, looked with pride at the rippling muscles up and down his sunburnt arms. "There's a thing in the Bible. How does it go? *As a man thinketh so is he. . . ."*

"I understand. But the change, the pivot, the beginning. . . . Did you kill Hopper?"

Denny laughed. And the laugh of him was full-throated; it came from deep springs of content, like a geyser.

"Just you listen," he said, wiping his mouth with the back of his hand, "and I'll tell you.

"You'd gone. I heard the launch *chug-chugging* out to sea. I was alone with him. He was riding my soul, same as ever.

"'Think I'll stay awhile,' said he. 'I like the scenery. And I'm sick at heart for the state you're in. Demented. Poor Denny!'

"'Poor Denny!' he said. To me! 'Poor Denny!' And him as fat and as soft as a clam, only I didn't know it. And me as strong as a baby hippo, only I didn't know it. If the bird knew it could fly, would it let itself be swallowed by the noble anaconda, do you think? Not on your life!

"Well, I cried and tied myself into bow knots, begging him to go away. But he moved in. Kicked the population in the seat of its pants——"

"Hypothetical," Herz interrupted.

"Any way you please," Denny agreed in his rough-and-ready manner. "The population was not flattered. There was no word said, but tears stood in the eyes of the Waululuans, and they looked to be terribly sorry for me. Now, they liked me. I was their Sick Man, their pet and favoured Sorrow. Only I didn't know this, either. I had missed everything; I had been a dark and suffering fool. . . .

"But that's neither here nor there. Deep in me was that piece of myself I told you about—a spark, a chip, a primeval bug. Æon? Atom? Planet? It was me! And it began to stir.

"That night Pifa—the big fellow with the hibiscus in his ear—came bringing food. Taro. Coconuts. A fowl. Some native messes served on leaves. He stood straight as a bamboo, and his eyes were melting and running over. 'For you,' he said in the native lingo, 'what the right hand bears. For the other, the fat Devil, what the left hand bears. It is poisoned. I was kicked,' he explained, 'where I sit down. And I am the son of a son of a chief's son, and then some.'

" 'Thanks,' I said, choosing carefully. The light broke. It flooded me. My shaking legs straightened out, my chest filled my shirt for the first time in fifteen years. 'Eat,' said I to Hopper; 'it's poisoned.

And good appetite to you. I'll bury you at dawn, any style, embalmed, burned or bleach-boned. The chief is fond of long-pig. And if I say the word. . . .'

"He sat there, staring at what Pifa put before him. A single candle flickered on the counter. Him and me danced on the ceiling like puppets on strings. The sweat stood on his brow, little cold drops that presently rolled off and down his nose.

" 'Poisoned,' he remarked, trying to laugh. 'That's pretty.'

" 'Not at all,' said I. 'You may not kick a Waululuan in his seat of dignity.'

" 'Niggers,' he said.

" 'Not so simple.' And cracking a chicken wing I buried my teeth in it. 'Eat—eat!' I said.

"But he tried to grab my portion. Pifa was quicker, and caught his wrists. Later, Hopper laughed and opened a can of sardines and sat him down to eat. 'Your simple savage,' he said, 'isn't too simple for me.'

"I hadn't thought of that. I lay on my face and cried. And Hopper slept that night in my hammock —slept and snored. And so must I, for in the morning the shelves were empty. Gone every blessed and beautiful tin! Every sick sardine and bloated bologna and resonant corned beef hash! Oh, man, I laughed.

"After that he didn't dare to eat, unless he cracked his own copyrighted coconut with his own innocent hand. Before my eyes he grew famished

and the fat fell on him in empty pouches.   Oh, he was
an ugly devil!

"But that wasn't all.   The chief was holding a
kava feast in the main tent, and Hopper ran amuck
and kicked over the ceremonial bowl.   After that he
was marked.   Only I didn't know.   I was slow to
learn.

"Whenever he went out some one would pitch a
knife at him or miss him by half an inch with a spear
or lay a snare of vines to trip him up.   They stole his
shoes.   His hat vanished.   His umbrella moved
down to the chief's house and became a throne-
canopy.

"Nor was that all.   They danced a dance of
death and vengeance, and all one night there was a
shuffling of bare feet, a beat of drums, a clapping
of palms, a hum, a wail, monotonous and threatening.
It made me shiver.   Even then I didn't know.   I sat
on the floor, watching Hopper.   He'd jump as if
bitten by a flea.   He'd listen.   He'd stare into
space.

" 'What's all that tomfoolery?   What are the
greasy topknots doing now, eh?   What's their game?
You'd better tell me.'

"I didn't know.

"Isn't it strange how slowly a man will find
himself?

"One day I caught him trying to steal away in the
Miriam.   She lay just off the beach in shallow
water.   And there was Hopper, a great hulk of white
flesh, waist-deep, wading out. . . . Then it was I

knew. He was afraid! I shouted: '*Sharks! Sharks, you fool!*' And back he came, tossing up a foam, his face as grey as an oyster.

"Then I anchored the *Miriam* farther out and cherished mine enemy. He slept no more in my hammock, but on the floor with the fowl. Where he belonged—not I. I was tasting new wine—the red, swift blood of me. It ran through my veins hot and electric. Look at me. There's life in me. Day by day I found it out, and day by day Hopper died, like an octopus that is hauled up on the reef and left in the sun. He dared not eat for fear of poison. He dared not drink. The grove was infested with evil brown children who laughed and tormented him. He bellowed. He threatened. He swaggered. But I was the core of his hate. As I grew stronger he collapsed, like a balloon that is pricked with a pin.

"The day came when he had a fever; he was parched and terror-ridden. He came to me. I was whittling a god for the chief. Out of a thick vine trunk I made it, all twisted and horrible, a snake with Hopper's face atop. This was the demon of demons.

" 'What's that?' he asked, licking his lips.

" 'You,' said I. 'Tonight there's a feast. They'll roast you on hot stones and put this on your cooking-place. *In memoriam.* The simple savage,' I explained, 'is civilized in certain artless ways. He never leaves a grave unmarked.'

"Oh, then he went down on his knees, and he gave me back my soul. 'For God's sake! I'm your

friend. We were born on the same day. For old
time's sake, speak to these people and tell them I'm
going away. For ever!'

"'I'll tell them you're flavoured with garlic and
tough as shoe-leather. Get up. Get up, you coward,
you no-good, you slobbering liar!' I said more, but
it's too hot for speech, and my throat's parched.
Give us another."

Herz obliged.

"That girl——" he began.

"She's waiting."

Denny stretched himself and flexed his muscles.
Then, with a jerk at his belt and a hitch of his
shoulders, he went to the door.

"So long."

Herz said afterwards that he followed almost
timidly. This was such a brave and eager fellow.

"Where," Herz asked, "is Hopper?"

The Yellow One jerked a thumb. "Oh, I left
him at Waululu. He's valet to Chief Oku. Run
and fetch. Day and night. For a coconut and a
raw fish. . . ."

THE DRYAD

MRS. MARRIOTT put a scarf over her shoulders and went down into the garden. If she walked slowly she would be just in time to meet them at the inner gate—Major Bulkley and his friends, the Stovers. They had wired that they were coming out from London by train, and she had sent a motor to bring them from the station. But she did not want these guests to have their first impression of the place from the carriage drive— better to let them come on foot across the fields, through the orchard into the rose-garden, where they could look straight up at the house itself. Mrs. Marriott knew the value of her background, and Major Bulkley had written that the Stovers were fastidious.

She had heard of the Stovers often enough. Stover himself—Hal, the Major called him—was an explorer, one of those scientists who become famous because, for mysterious reasons of their own, they choose to live in outlandish places and to disappear for years at a time.

"I ran into the Stovers in British Guiana," Major Bulkley had written, "just back from some delectable adventures in the jungle. We hit it off rather well down there. Now I have encountered them again—

here in London, of all places! Did I tell you that Mrs. Stover always travels with him? Let me bring them down to you. Beauty will do them good after five years of jungle ooze, monkeys, naked savages, and fever."

Beauty. Well, she could give them that! Mrs. Marriott had a deep sense of beauty, although it frightened her to be alone with it. In this garden, for instance. She seldom came here unless there happened to be some one with her, some one to fend off her consciousness of flowers, sunshine and the singing of birds. She felt somehow safer indoors, or on the terrace, aloof from things that stirred her to the heart. Time enough for beauty when she ceased to be beautiful herself; now, the wonderful old house and the poignant loveliness of the gardens were simply a part of her own charm, what she was pleased to call her "aura."

She hurried a little in spite of herself. She would get to the inner gate too soon, and they would think her eager. Perhaps she was. She wanted to hear voices and laughter, to be looked at, appraised and admired. For more than a month she had been alone, watching the death of summer with a sort of inward shudder of the spirit, as if summer would never come again. Out beyond the terrace the wheat fields had blazed warm gold in the sun, and the downs were all dusted over with the same radiance—a sort of pollen, only that it was made of the intangibility of light!

Autumn! Mrs. Marriott sensed it in the cool wind

that came at sundown. On the lawn, where gardeners raked during the day, there were always a few crisp leaves, rattling up and down with a dry little whisper. And in spite of the hot sun it was cool in the flecked shadow of the orchard and along the yew walk near the greenhouses. Mrs. Marriott stayed in the sunny room which faced the "view" towards the hills, and wrote letters in a big flourishing hand, or played the cottage piano, or read novels. A month. Quite enough.

She was glad that Bulkley had asked to bring the Stovers. It was just like him—taking her hospitality and her interest for granted. And, smiling a little, she thought: "Bulkley will ask me to marry him. I don't love him. But I may—it would be an experience."

Her marriage to Marriott had been an experience, too. An unpleasant one. Five years of feverish gaiety in European capitals. One year of darkness, when Marriott fought death with all the stubborn tenacity with which he had pursued life. Then release, and the strangeness of belonging to herself again, being mistress of all this beauty, with no Marriott to laugh at her love of it. But she had never quite found herself again. One part of her was still Marriott's—perhaps always would be. . . .

She went through the rose-garden into the orchard. The sun was on the rim of the high downs, balanced there like a juggler's ball. When she crossed the field, knee-deep in the grass, the great gold disk slipped out of sight and the fragrant coolness of twilight stole over the land like a palpable mist. She felt, somehow, that she herself had been overtaken by a sort of twilight of the spirit—not resignation, but calm, as if nothing could ever happen beyond the tranquil perfection of her days. Stopping to pick a daisy that was blooming quite out of season, she thought: "I wonder if Marriott spoiled me for peace? Is it wildness I want, after all? Bulkley isn't wild. He'll watch out for me and see that nothing hurts me and suffer when I am indifferent. Then one day I'll discover that it is too late—I will be too old for madness."

She put the daisy in her belt and reflected with a smile that she must look very cool and "civilized." Her dress was a clear yellow, made of floating chiffon and gathered over her narrow hips; the colour matched her amber hair and the tawny, tiger-yellow of her eyes. She wore pearls—a lustrous string wound twice about her throat—but no rings, because she was proud of the whiteness of her hands and the shapely perfection of her fingers.

She heard the motor before she reached the inner gate. After all, she would have to hurry. . . . The driver saw her and brought the car up with a screech just as she reached the roadside.

"I came across the fields to stop you," she said, and looked from Major Bulkley at the Stovers, who sat together on the back seat, smiling at her. Mrs. Stover was a little brown thing with an atrocious hat. Stover himself jumped up and bared his head. He was a big, dishevelled man with fair hair.

"Mrs. Stover, Margaret. And Captain Stover."

She found herself smiling at the explorer, and, reaching up, gave her hand into his big grasp. "If you aren't too tired, we'll walk over to the house. I am rather anxious that you should see it first from the garden."

Mrs. Marriott led the way with Stover, Major Bulkley following with the little brown woman.

Strange, that she had not felt the beauty of the field when she came through it alone! The glow filled the sky where the sun had been. And there came from the orchard the scent of ripe apples and fallen leaves.

"Beautiful!" Stover said.

She looked up at him, conscious that he had been staring, not at the landscape, but at her. And something within her felt suddenly alive and joyous.

"Major Bulkley says that you've been away from England a long while."

"Four years." His eyes still held hers. "Too long, I'm beginning to think. I'd forgotten this country of ours. Larches, bracken, the scent of burning wood, wild meadows like this, and larks! There's nothing finer!"

"Not even the jungle?"

"Oh, that's different. The jungle touches your imagination. This is a part of you, like blood in your veins—like breath."

Conscious of Major Bulkley's voice behind them, Mrs. Marriott hurried a little. She was aware of her small waist and the way her hair blew across her cheeks. Stover was looking at her as if he could not get enough; and she thought: "I suppose his wife is a frump—and he knows the difference." Twisting her long white fingers in the double strand of pearls, she said: "I'm glad you like the country. Then you won't be sorry Major Bulkley brought you."

"I'm happier than I have any right to be. I ran away from lecture engagements—all sorts of stupid duties. I have a manager—a young Jew. I gave him the slip this morning in the Strand. Saw him a block away and jumped into a taxi and hid. He had booked me for tonight. Some banquet or other. But I couldn't face it."

Mrs. Marriott laughed. She liked his face—ugly and arresting, with a high, narrow forehead from which the hair grew back in two points, like horns, twisted and heavy. His skin was dark—burnt, she supposed, by exposure to tropical sunlight—and his eyes, strangely ice-blue beneath the thick blond brows, stared at her with a sort of hunger. They entered the orchard side by side, silenced for a moment by the shadows beneath the intricate branches burdened with fruit. It seemed to Mrs. Marriott that Stover, too, heard with impatience Major Bulkley's voice behind them—a cheerful, matter-of-fact voice.

"Hal tells me that you're going out to South America in November," he said.

Mrs. Stover's answer was inaudible. And Mrs. Marriott, closing her eyes to hide the look of curiosity she knew must be in them, opened them again and asked: "Is it true? Are you leaving England?"

"I'm not certain. I thought so. But I have a new appetite for this sort of thing."

Mrs. Marriott smiled. They came out of the orchard into the rose-garden, and above them the house appeared, silhouetted against an amber sky— a long, simple façade with slender windows and a beautiful cornice. Lights went up behind the French doors, and they saw a servant moving about. He drew a curtain across and disappeared like an actor in a pantomime.

They began to mount the terraces, slowly, for Mrs. Marriott saw the look on Stover's face— ecstatic, absorbed, as if he were waking from a dream to find it true. And she wondered what he was going to mean to her—something more, surely, than a casual encounter. Already she could remember every aspect of his face—his curious, oblique eyes and his smile—like a faun's. It amused her to think that he might be a faun, come into this shadowy garden from the wild meadow, from his hiding-place near the stream which skirted the grove of young larches. A faun who had seen her wandering alone, sad and enticing, beyond reach until one day he dared to stretch out his brown hand and touch her. She thought of the days that had just passed; she remembered her loneliness, her fear, her coldness—how could she have doubted life? Now she felt kindly, courageous, eager; there was a faint excitement in her heart, because something in this stranger's eyes had challenged her.

"This is my house," she said, a little breathlessly, as they entered the hall from the terrace.

Major Bulkley and Mrs. Stover entered, too, and in the warm light of the shaded lamps Mrs. Marriott saw the face beneath the atrocious hat—a thin, burnt face with solemn eyes, not pretty, but wistful and very innocent. Mrs. Stover looked about the big hall, at the soft rugs and deep chairs and flowers, the tranquil perfection of those grey walls, the stairway sweeping up to the gallery, the long vista of rooms like some manifold reflection of loveliness. Then she glanced quickly at her husband.

"This is better than a mud hut, isn't it?" Hal Stover demanded.

Mrs. Stover said simply: "Yes."

"England! Home! By Jove, how I love it!"

Mrs. Marriott smiled at them. Conscious again that the explorer was looking, not at the hall, but at her, she said: "Bennett will take you up. Your rooms face the downs. After dinner, I'll show you the English moon."

Then, and only then, did she glance at Major Bulkley, with veiled eyes that told him nothing.

She did not remember when she had been so happy at dinner. She had sat alone at the big square table for so long. And she had no taste for solitude, since Marriott had filled every waking hour with boisterous companionship. It had been ghostly, eating in silence, while the servant tiptoed behind her chair and the cool breeze stole in the open windows and leaned the candles down. This was different. Now she had an audience, and she was beautiful. Her white shoulders, polished and flawless, gleaming against the dark blue of the chair. Her amber hair. Her remoteness, that mistiness, cool and tranquil, which had fascinated Marriott. The feeling, too, that she faced men who valued her charm. Major Bulkley stared at her like a worshipping dog. Stover drank too much wine, and watched her eyes where the candles struck sparks in them. No, she was not even on the skirts of autumn. There was warmth in her. It was not over, as she had feared it might be—her capacity for life. She had not had enough.

She caught herself wishing that Stover had changed for dinner; he still wore his dusty tweeds and a lock of that thick gold hair, thick as molasses, fell over his eyes. He brushed it back, laughed and closed his eyes while he drank. He talked; the others listened —Bulkley with an amused smile, a sort of shame-faced pleasure in the man's exaltation. Mrs. Stover watched, too. She was browner than ever without the hat—her cloudy hair was combed straight back and knotted in the nape of her neck. She looked as if the sun had burned away whatever loveliness she might have had. Only her eyes were young, in that weather-scarred, lined, watchful face. And her dress! A shabby affair with unfashionable sleeves and a bit of lace at the throat. . . . Mrs. Marriott, surprised by a feeling of solemn pity, looked down at her own white arms and at her fingers twirling the green stem of the wineglass so that a little emerald light danced on the tablecloth. . . .

Stover talked well. He was a poet, and an ardent lover of the world. He had never suffered from surfeit of adventure, as other men had suffered for lack of it. There was always one more mountain range to cross, one more river of doubt, one more forgotten city tangled in jungle creepers. If he had any appetite, it was for strangeness. When he spoke of places across the globe—high-flung plateaux, lakes in the clouds, flowery fields touching ice-blue glaciers—there was greediness in his eyes. It was impossible to imagine him tied down to anything—he had had glimpses beyond the horizon and hankered for more. He was not a philosopher; a lover never is. He talked with passion of remote beauty. Suddenly you saw him—appealing, attractive, a desirable friend. Then he vanished, and you felt that you had glimpsed a faun, had stumbled on an ugly, wild fellow who fled before your stare. He had a way of putting his chin on his hands and looking sideways with a humorous lift of his mouth at the corners. Mrs. Marriott, listening with her head bent, thought: "Poor mortals. Bulkley and that little woman. And perhaps me. What does he think of us?"

After dinner they walked on the terrace and the moon she had promised them came out of the clouds and floated through a clear sky devoid of stars. Mrs. Marriott stood with Bulkley, who puffed at a cigarette and blew the smoke of it into the face of the moon. Through the back of her head she was conscious of Stover prowling up and down the terrace with his wife; the murmur of their voices grew loud, diminished, increased again as they passed, but she did not once look round at them. Presently she knew that Stover had come up behind her, and she thought, with a leap at her heart: "Clumsy of him!"

Yes, there he was, watching her with those strange eyes which were both roguish and desirous. Quite as if he had forgotten the little brown woman standing beside him, he said: "Bulkley says you play. Will you play for me now?"

Mrs. Marriott nodded and went in, leaving the others in the moonlight. The piano had been put near the doors, because she had liked to play looking into the garden. She sat there for a moment, her fingers idle on the keys, her head bent, wondering what she should play that would bring him in to her, clumsy again because he was too simple to resist.

She began to play Chopin's First Nocturne, and stopped.

"Go on," Major Bulkley called.

"Not that," she said, "tonight." And, seized by a daring perversity, she began *L'Après-midi d'un Faune*. While she played she saw herself, gleaming white, standing in a little round temple on the shores of a lake. There were yellow trees overhead, and the water of the lake broke in exhaustless ripples against a flight of marble steps. Then she saw Stover standing in the doorway, his face changed, rather terrifying.

He came over and leaned against the piano, gazing at her. When she had finished he said: "Strange. But not you. You are the Schumann *Carnival,* seductive and cool. Will you play it?"

She shook her head.

"Chopin, then. The Third Ballade."

But she preferred *Clair de lune.* She played it with gravity, as if she were caught by the sweetness of that fainting music. She could see the moon through the open doorway and the blurred figures of Bulkley and Mrs. Stover, standing apart out there. What had Stover said? Seductive and cool. . . .

She looked up at him. "Tell the others to come in. Let's talk. I want to hear about orchids and monkeys and armadilloes."

A fire was lighted and they sat before it—Stover on the floor at Mrs. Marriott's feet, so close that when he tipped his head back she could have put her hand on his thick hair. Bulkley smoked and crossed his thin legs and swung one patent-leather shoe and, crinkling up his eyes, laughed at Stover's exuberance. Mrs. Stover sat a little out of the fire-light, her rough hands folded in her lap.

With a pang of jealousy Mrs. Marriott thought: "She is married to him. She can go away with him —tonight, tomorrow—down the world." And suddenly she hated her own possessions—the house, the pictures, the garden, even the double string of pearls around her neck. Then, looking down, she saw that Stover, leaning back and away from the heat of the log-fire, had rested his hand on the train of her dress where it curled around her slippered feet. The others could not see, but she saw that his fingers caressed the satiny stuff, as if, coming from the discomfort and hardship of an outlandish wilderness, the touch of beauty had transformed him. . . .

Three days of gold; summer had been caught and held fast by some enchantment. Bees droned in the bushes. The sun was hot, ripening the apples and drawing from the earth the odour of grass and ferns and gorse. A mist lay over the downs that was part haze and part the smoke of burning leaves. Gardeners raked on the lawns, gathering little heaps of crimson and yellow and russet.

Mrs. Marriott and Stover walked over the fields, where cattle waded knee-deep in the grass, and, crossing the stream, climbed the hills beyond. There, sitting in the fragrant sunshine, they watched the checkerboard fields below and the toy-like villages set in hollows among Noah's Ark trees.

Mrs. Stover would not come. "That awful little chap, the manager," had found out where the explorer was and had sent telegrams and letters which must be answered. Mrs. Stover stayed indoors to answer them. She sent Stover away, like a mother watching out for the happiness of her child. And Stover went, gay, singing, "drunk on beauty," he said.

"I wonder whether I'm cruel?" Mrs. Marriott thought.

She wore her prettiest dresses and hats. Bulkley, watching all this with his dog's eyes full of pain, said: "I'll ride, if you don't mind. I'm not awfully good at climbing about." And went off, every day, mounted on one of Mrs. Marriott's hunters. Once he said to her: "Hal's a strange chap, eh, Margaret?"

And Mrs. Marriott, conscious that she did not want to lose him, yet stirred to the heart by the very mention of Stover's name, answered lightly: "Yes, strange. Not quite human. He belongs in mythology."

She knew how deeply Major Bulkley cared for her. He was the sure prop, the wall against which she could lean in moments of faintness. If she married him, the future would be safe. Security. Ah! that was what she ought to have—yet somehow she did not want it. If she married him, they would spend eight months of the year in the country, four months in London or Paris. He would hunt, because he liked it. He would be kind, impeccable, understandable. No mystery about Bulkley. Sleek of hair, well put together, just thin enough, with those kindly brown eyes that crinkled at the corners when he laughed. Life with him would be a succession of calm tableaux, a faultless record of the English tradition. No more. Safety. The long tranquillity of Indian summer, and the sun declining towards a comfortable winter. . . .

Why had he, of all men, brought Stover to the Orchards? For Stover, she knew, had forgotten everything in his eagerness for this new beauty. When he spoke to the little brown woman his eyes were on Mrs. Marriott. It took all her self-assurance to protect herself, and him, before the others. When she was alone with him his audacity frightened her.

"Beautiful—beautiful—beautiful!" he said once, touching her hair, her cheek, her shoulder with the tips of his fingers. When she drew back, pretending to frown, he laughed. "Are you afraid of being beautiful? It won't last for ever, you know. No longer than this false summer."

Among the quivering groves of larch, on the brilliant slopes of the hills, sun-bathed, dreaming, bewitched, she was seized with doubts of herself, of him, of everything. The turmoil in her heart was more pain than happiness. She almost wished that she had never seen him. Yet she was afraid to let him go. One afternoon in the orchard, when they were coming back from the village, he stopped short and held out his hands. "Margaret," he said, "love me." She went straight to him, put her hands on his shoulders and kissed him.

"Now," she thought, "I've done it. That poor little woman!"

She felt his hands on her hair. She saw his eyes, full of mischief and pleasure, not at all repentant. He begged her to meet him that night. "Here. I'll wait for you."

"Perhaps," she said.

He let her go and they walked very staidly up to the house, through a luminous twilight that blurred the rose-trees and the hedges into violet shadows. They heard a flutter of sleepy birds close by. Above them, the lighted windows of the drawing-room cast two shafts of yellow light across the terrace, and they saw the little brown woman standing there, motionless.

"Letters all done?" Stover asked lightly.

"Quite," said Mrs. Stover. "Eisenstein wired again. He wants you to come tomorrow."

"Put him off, my dear!"

Mrs. Marriott smiled in the dark. That funny little person and Stover! Impossible that there could be love between them.

"You must stay as long as you can," she said aloud, trying to throw into her voice an impersonal kindliness. She felt kindly, just then. Kindly and sorrowful, elated and fearful. She wondered whether her ecstasy had stamped itself on her face, and quickly put her hand over her mouth as if to hide the kiss she had given and received. . . .

She dressed for dinner, with ceremony, staring at her unfamiliar face in the mirror. She wore a white gown and white sandals with a strap around the ankle. She had bought a laurel wreath of gold somewhere in Italy, and had never worn it. Now she took it out of its box and put it on her hair, astonished by the beauty it gave to her straight brows and her eyes. Marriott would have stared at her with lifted brows. "Goddess?" he would have said. "Ridiculous, my dear. You're a woman, and a damn pretty one."

Putting the thought of him aside with a little shudder, she went to the window and leaned out. The moon was rising, pale, with a large bite taken out. And there was a dry rattle of leaves in a wind that seemed suddenly chilly.

She went down to dinner holding her head high. The table had been set with coloured glass and a forest of candles burned in tall candelabra. In that relentless light the little brown woman was plainer than ever. She wore a black dress embroidered with butterflies, a funny, dowdy little dress that accentuated her pallor and the grave innocence of her eyes.

Stover glanced at her. "The butterfly dress," he said. "I haven't seen that since the night of Graham's dinner."

Mrs. Stover smiled. "At Kalacoon! You remember?"

"Rather." Stover turned to Mrs. Marriott again. "You should go out there. A wilderness. And right in the heart of it Graham's house. Not a primitive place, mind you. A real house with screened porches and waxed floors and comfortable chairs."

"And bath-tubs," Mrs. Stover added.

"Amazing!"

Mrs. Stover nodded. "Yes, it was. Amazing." She turned to Bulkley. "We had been travelling two weeks, walking straight away from the last outpost of civilization. They had told us that Graham's place would astonish us. But when we saw it we could not believe our eyes. Luxury in the wilderness!" She glanced around the table. "Well, not this—not beauty. But Graham dressed for dinner. And I'll never forget his low patent shoes and silk socks. Quite correct. Even out there."

"Heroic," Bulkley said, crinkling his eyes.

Stover leaned towards his wife. "I couldn't match Graham's elegance," he said, "but you could! I remembered how gratified I was when you came in wearing the butterfly dress."

"I dare say Graham didn't notice it."

"Perhaps not. But I did. You looked very pretty."

There was a brief silence, while Stover and Bulkley both stared at the little brown woman. Mrs. Marriott, staring too, became aware of mischief in those innocent eyes, a sort of lilt, a dancing that had not been there before. Stover must have seen it, for his look kindled.

And suddenly the memory of that moment in his arms besieged Mrs. Marriott—the wild sweetness of her abandonment. With a feeling that he was eluding her, she said: "You haven't seen my farm at Barncastle, Captain Stover. We'll drive over tomorrow and have tea there."

Stover did not seem to have heard. He answered with tempered enthusiasm and went on with the soup. A remoteness had come into his eyes. He listened to Mrs. Marriott as if his mind were straying to the conversation between Major Bulkley and the little brown woman. He looked that way, furtively, with a sort of shamefaced, secret longing. Mrs. Marriott shivered. Was there no lasting happiness? No captured and enduring rapture? No dream? Only glimpses, and then the shutting down of reality across

the vision? Sun on the hills; shadows in the valley.
Illusion. And autumn.

After a while she began to hear, in spite of herself, what Mrs. Stover was saying. Leaning a little
forward, with her elbows on the table and her eyes
shining, the little brown woman was telling Bulkley
about some forest—in America, perhaps—where she
and Stover had spent a summer. "Just wandering,"
she explained. "Riding all day; camping at night,
wherever we happened to be."

Mrs. Marriott listened inwardly, striving to hold
Stover's attention with the magic of her whiteness,
what he had called her cool audacity. And the story
of that delectable adventure pierced her consciousness like stabs of pain. The little brown woman had
lived Stover's life. She had let herself be burnt by
the sun, roughened by wind, buffeted by that world
Stover loved. She had learned to suffer what he
suffered, to go where he went, to face danger, loneliness, ugliness, or whatever glory there happened to
be. With a sort of eager jealousy Mrs. Marriott
thought: "She is angling for him." But her inner
consciousness corrected that: "She is dancing away
from him. And he will follow, because she is a
midget, a gnat, a wild little dryad always just out of
his reach."

What was she talking about now? Waterfalls,
drifting down from great heights. Canyons carved
like Assyrian temples. Icy lakes. The smell of pine
boughs. Trails through some gigantic forest where

she and Stover had seemed to be "minnows lying quiet at the bottom of the sea. Even the sunlight was pale, striking down through that unfathomable green."

Stover interrupted. "We'll go back there! Next year, or the year after, on our way home. What d'you say, my dear?"

There was passion in his voice, an eagerness, a plea for forgiveness, perhaps. The little brown woman shivered. She turned her head slowly and gave Stover a look so lost and rapturous that Bulkley, stirred by an emotion he could not understand, said in a loud voice: "It must be jolly—travelling about together. But don't you ever get tired of it?"

"No," Mrs. Stover said. "Never."

After dinner Stover prowled about the bookshelves until he found an atlas—a huge affair bound in red leather. He carried it over into a circle of firelight, and putting it on the floor, drew his wife down beside him to turn the pages. Her cheek brushed his shoulder as she knelt there.

"We'll go here," he said, "and here, and here."

Mrs. Marriott, smiling, touched with the tips of her fingers the wreath of laurel which crowned her amber hair.

Stover glanced up. "Play for us," he said.

"Yes," Bulkley urged. "Do! Something gay."

Mrs. Marriott went to the piano. She could see the moon—that chilly moon with the bite taken out —just touching the rim of the downs. She began, wearily, to play the *Orfeo* of Gluck. And presently

Bulkley came over, crinkling up his eyes at her. "Are you going to marry me?" he asked quietly.

Mrs. Marriott could see his hand resting on the top of the piano. She thought: "An English gentleman. Security."

Aloud she said: "Yes." And added: "Will you close the door, my dear? It's rather cold."

ANNA

THE three men seated around the small table on the club-house veranda were not alike, outwardly at least. Field was small and dark with a nearly bald head and flashing teeth; Holmes was stout and blond; Parker, very tall, with an ugly, arresting face and eyes steady beneath thatched brows. Yet they were strangely similar, with the similarity bestowed upon men by a common social experience.

Behind them the veranda was empty, dimly lighted by a few electric globes around which went on an unceasing dance of moths. The lawn and the links beyond were dark and smooth, like a calm sea. A waiter in a white coat lounged in a doorway, his sleepy eyes fixed on these three men who seemed never going to move. He had served them coffee and cigarettes, and now they sat talking, a little pushed back from the table, relaxed, smiling.

"Here we are again," Holmes was saying, striking a match that for a moment illuminated his florid face. "After three years. Unchanged. At least—well, a few pounds lost or gained."

Parker shrugged his shoulders. "It's one of those eternal mysteries—how little impression life makes on our bodies, after all. We suffer like the devil, enjoy ourselves, go through all sorts of inner complications and readjustments—grow, if you like—and then some one says: 'How well you're looking! Haven't changed in all these years, by George!'"

Field ran his hand over that smooth, brown baldness. "I haven't a sorrow in the world—and look at me!"

"Not a sorrow?"

"Not one. I've got everything I want. Mary and the children and all the decencies. I never did have extravagant desires." He laughed. "I'm not like you, Parker—always running off after rainbows. What do you do when you disappear into the rest of the world. . . . ? I've envied you more than once." He looked at Parker with a sudden amiable curiosity. "You come and go—doing pretty much what you please—and we stay here, domesticated, unquestioning, kowtowing to our little household gods. Who knows which of us has the essence of living, the heart of the thing, the elusive—what shall I call it—fragrance of existence?"

Parker leaned back, touching the table-top with his broad, square-tipped fingers. Just then his eyes were hidden, but there was a queer smile on his lips.

"You two——" he began.

"Yes—we two!" Holmes interrupted. "You're contemptuous of us, you nomad *de luxe*, you footloose gentleman of leisure! Don't deny it! You come back to these meetings of ours with just a little pity in your heart for our bland security."

"Oh, no."

"Be honest." Holmes's plump hand rested for a

moment on Parker's arm. "It is an old belief that unhappy men like to involve others in their own unhappiness. Well, perhaps. What I'm trying to say is that America's a good country—a bit raw, but in the makin'—and American women are real women; and happiness—good God, don't involve me in Polyanna." Holmes tossed his cigarette over the railing—a little comet flash of sparks. "I suppose you're going off again," he remarked dryly, "to New Guinea or Santo Domingo or Kalamazoo. . . ."

Parker did not answer for a moment. His fingers were still pressed against the surface of the table, his eyes in shadow.

"I suppose you mean," he said finally, "that I'm wasting my time knocking around the globe. I ought to marry and settle down. I'm not exactly young enough to expect to overtake the rainbow!" He raised his eyes and regarded his friends with a look that was both challenging and apologetic. "The truth is—I'm off again next week. Russia."

"Russia? But I thought——"

"I've just come back from there. I know. I'm going back for a purely romantic reason. At my age!"

"A woman," Field said sharply.

Parker nodded. "Isn't it always a woman? You want me to stay here, don't you, to marry a purely hypothetical creature, some one who would be 'good for me,' fill the deficit in my heart, make me contented with mediocrity! Excuse me. I'm finding it hard to be polite because I appreciate your—your affection. Both of you. But it just happens——"

He was silent again. A warm scent of clover came from the darkness on the breath of a wandering, erratic summer wind. A group of people moved across the veranda—women with smooth, sleek hair, brilliant wraps, high-heeled, buckled slippers. There was a ripple of laughter. Some one began to play a piano, rather well, making loveliness out of a seductive dance measure. . . .

"Well," Holmes said sharply, "I'm sorry, Parker. . . ."

"You needn't be sorry. I'll be coming back here some day. Sure to. For just such a dinner as this. . . . Unchanged."

"No younger."

"No. But don't fancy that I'm cheating this hypothetical wife you're offering me. Or cheating myself. You see——" Suddenly he stared at them, his face a little twisted. "You see—I'm married already."

Field answered after an embarrassed silence. "We didn't guess. Of course, that makes it different!" And he offered his hand.

Parker did not seem to see. He was twisting his coffee-cup between his fingers. "Funny," he said, smiling again, "but I've never acknowledged it before, not even to myself. I'm a bit startled, hearing myself say: 'I'm married.' As if I could take your hand over it and drink with you and let the fact of it warm my heart—as I suppose Mary must warm yours, Field, and Miriam yours, Jo. Mine wasn't that sort of marriage. No welkin, or flowers, or old slippers.

Only horror." He spread out his hands. "You accused me of going after the rainbows! And I came back with this—nothing! The inevitable end of all rainbow-chasing, perhaps. I'll tell you about it. First of all, because you two will understand, if any one will, the peculiar quality of my suffering. You know me well enough to take my selfishness for granted. I believe in individualism—life for me, my way, bad or good." He pushed the cup away. "And that's that!"

Holmes, turning half-way in his chair, beckoned to the lounging waiter. "Here—more coffee, if you please. Hot milk. And matches." When these things were put before them, Parker began:

"I had been in France with the Red Cross—that you know about. Towards the end of the War I was sent to Venice, and with the Armistice into Austria; then to Rumania and Serbia, and from there to Russia, where there was still fighting, of course. You will forgive me if I succumb to the malicious temptation of mentioning again your reason for disapproving of me—there weren't many rainbows during those two or three years! Typhus. Hunger. Whole nations gone blind with despair, cheated of security, betrayed by their rulers, given over to starvation and brutality. If I had fallen in love with mankind during the War, I fell out of it again in Rumania and Serbia. Why save the beasts? You understand, there isn't anything picturesque about dirty peasants, cringing before the scythe-sweep of death, going down by the tens of thousands. . . . And mud. Dirt. A shuddering vileness. Why, there were times when life itself, not death, seemed unreal, when a living person was a curiosity.

"The air seemed full of poison-tipped arrows, so that people walked through the villages with scared, furtive eyes—dodging invisible missiles, as it were. I myself stopped one of these—javelins, in Belgrade. And I assure you it would have been easier to die than it had been to live. I remember thinking: 'Now I can rest.' But it wasn't to be as easy as all that! I lived. And with the assumption of the old burden—at first it seemed unendurable—I was sent back to Paris and then to London, where I got used to the sight of healthy humanity.

"I'm telling you all this because you'll more readily understand why I went to Siberia with one of those purposeless, hurried expeditions sent out to the 're-lief' of Kolchak. I had been familiar with death—well, I wanted more of it. Morbid? Of course. My curiosity wasn't satisfied.

"I went first to Vladivostok and, after a time, joined the American Red Cross, where I really be-longed. And again I found myself in the thick of it—typhoid fever, typhus, dysentery. Only here there was more than a struggle with death; Russia, Siberia in particular, was engaged in a gigantic battle with an idea. The White leader represented to the people only another autocracy, yet he advanced with the blessing of the Council of Four—a wolf wearing the skin of a lamb. I found the zemstvo officials trying to erect a genuine democratic foundation for the future, the Americans were popular, there was hope of sanity. . . . Then Omsk, and all it stood for, rose like a cone of volcanic smoke, spread over the land, and a reign of lawlessness followed.

"I got into the middle of it. I knew very little about the revolutionary movement; Russian socialist party politics were a sealed book to me. These people were all insane—a madhouse visited by typhus! And all the while Allied troops kept arriving, and crowds of refugees and weary, hopeless, political prisoners, going they knew not where, punished by they knew not whom. I moved through that atmosphere of distrust, betrayal, terror, and persecution like a man protected by destiny. At that time the Americans were popular with both factions—the White army looked to us for support, and the zemstvos still had faith that America possessed the open sesame to political freedom in her Constitution. . . .

"I'm taking a long time to say this. After all, it was only a phase—gone now in the amazing onward rush of human affairs. Who cares about that crowd now? It was a woman I promised to tell you about. . . ."

Parker quenched his cigarette by digging it savagely into the polished surface of the table, as if the unaccustomed carelessness satisfied an inner impulse to make a savage gesture. His face was turned down, away from the light, but Field and Holmes saw the sudden twist of his mouth into a sort of smile that did not mask the anger or pain or disgust he felt.

"I saw her first in a military hospital in one of the

smaller Siberian cities. A prison-train had just arrived, and about four hundred men, women, and children had been herded into that overcrowded, filthy place. There was typhus, of course. And the Russian officials, childish and helpless said to me: 'Go. Do what you can. You Americans are omnipotent.' That, at least, was the purport of the polite shrug they gave.

"The hospital was in charge of an old surgeon— a man who might have been a great swell under the old régime. But the authorities suspected him of being a Bolshevik, and he was already in the shadow of Supreme Authority. He took me over the place.

" 'Most of these people are perfectly innocent,' he explained. 'At most, a hundred are guilty of petty offenses. I can do nothing for them. Typhus! And under these conditions. . . . You must contrive to get the convalescents away into barracks of some sort. Otherwise the whole population——' He spread out his thin old hands and sighed, not for himself but for those others, millions of them, who were perhaps to receive the poisoned arrows in their breasts. 'Typhus! My dear sir, look at them——'

"He opened a door. I saw a long, bare room, with humid walls of plastered stone, lighted by a few barred windows set too high to be opened or shut. Straw mats had been thrown on the wet floor. A few dirty beds. And everywhere, crouched together, lying in heaps like the victims of a massacre, the prisoners. The most seriously ill lay full length or sat against the walls, with their heads thrown back.

All of them turned their feverish eyes toward us as we came down the room, and there arose a subdued babble, moans and broken shouts for water, medicine, air, release. . . .

"Anna was sitting on the floor, holding a child in her arms. I stopped and spoke to her, and to my surprise she answered in French.

" 'The child is dead,' I explained, as gently as I could, for I thought it might be hers.

" 'I know. But I cannot bury it here,' she said."

Parker leaned forward to strike a match. He straightened slowly.

"I won't try to describe this woman to you, or why she touched my imagination—immediately, as she did. There was a look of brooding in her face. Her eyes were grey with a black iris, and her brows —like fine wings—almost met above the bridge of her nose. The mouth was too coarse, but set in inflexible lines, as if she had closed her lips upon a terrible secret. Even beneath the shawls and ugly wrappings of her peasant costume, you saw that her body was graceful and strong. Yet she sat motionless, calm as a sphinx—only her eyes seemed alive in that beautiful and terrible immobility.

"While the doctor went on down the cluttered aisle of the room, I questioned her. She answered with disdain, in an expressionless voice.

"She came, it seems, from a town near Omsk. Her father was a tradesman, a small shopkeeper. He lived with his wife and Anna in a house near the railway station. He loved Russia, but he was too old to take part in the revolution. Yet it was his fate to be drawn into it and to perish for it.

"Anna told me the story without a shade of difference in her voice—flatly—almost as if the recital bored her. I had not taken the child from her, and she held it tight between her strong arms, drawn up against her breast. There was nothing else for her to cling to, then. . . .

"Do you know anything about Omsk? It's the coldest place on God's earth—frozen and still, like a bad dream. On a December night—the twenty-second, I believe—there were riots in and about the town. The usual thing: workmen attacking a prison and releasing a few unimportant Bolsheviki. Anna's father got caught in the mob, and because his old legs were stiff, he was arrested, while most of the real instigators got clean away. There followed a merciless execution.

"Not anything as humane as hanging or shooting. That gang knew to a nicety the extreme limit of human endurance—the hair-line between life and death. Those of the rioters who had been arrested were stripped and driven naked through the streets. Anna ran beside her father, screaming and pleading. . . . It was night, and the breaths of the victims and the torturers rose above them in frosty clouds. There was something shocking, terrible, about those naked, white bodies, running stiffly, with bleeding feet, through the snow.

"The Supreme Ruler wanted the names of the

leaders in the rebellion. Naturally, Anna's father knew nothing. He kept turning his tortured eyes to her and groaning: 'Tell them I'm innocent.' But at last, she said, he straightened his pitiful body and screamed: 'I am one of them!'

"In the end the half-dozen wretches were placed in rows against a wall and shot. With other women, Anna grovelled in the trampled snow at the feet of the executioners, pleading for that precious life. She had wound herself around the legs of a big fellow in a sheepskin coat, striving to reach the knives in his belt—to kill him, or herself—she wasn't sure. But he kicked her, and fired over her body at her father.

"These are horrible details. Sitting here, on this club-house veranda, it's easy to believe that the thing never happened. We are going to slip very soon into our former security, if we don't watch out. . . . I was not as horrified when Anna told me the story as you are, hearing it from me, all these thousands of comforting miles away from the madness and the brutality of men like that. Her father's body— frozen now for good—was put with the others into a freight car.

"Anna went temporarily mad. She ran back through the town cursing the Supreme Ruler, proclaiming herself Bolshevik, simply offering herself up. She was capable of such heroic folly. I can imagine her, her face white and wild, her red mouth drawn into a grimace of hate, her step reckless and provocative—a young fury bent on self-destruction.

"They arrested her, of course. Her mother, too.

She was sent to this military hospital of mine. Her mother was shipped off in the opposite direction.

" 'Do you know where your mother is now?' I asked Anna.

"She shook her head. 'No. If I live, I will find her. That is all there is left to me.'

"I could not linger to talk to her longer. . . . I took the dead child away from her as gently as I could, loosening the desperate clutch of her fingers. Then I hurried after the doctor.

"Barracks, to serve as both quarantine and prison, were absolutely necessary. Besides, I had to have some sort of convoy for them, and, of course, a guard. There was cavalry in the city, the ragged remnant of one of the Little White Father's crack regiments, which had undergone many a sea-change. The old doctor sent me to their chief to beg for his protection and assistance. This young officer lived in the most substantial house in the place—occupied a whole suite of rooms to himself and put on style. I found him lounging before a fireplace in a big, faded drawing-room. He got to his feet when he saw my uniform and saluted smartly. Oh! he was a great swell. He waved me to a chair and he himself sprawled on a satin sofa with one highly polished boot dangling, and a pillow under his blond head. What did I want? He was glad to do anything for the Americans. Had I heard that the English were solidly behind the new administration? The French, too? And why were the American troops being kept in Eastern Siberia?

"I knew why, but I said polite things which did not in the least deceive him. I told him that the military prison was overcrowded, that typhus had broken out and that I must separate the prisoners at once, or the epidemic would get beyond control.

" 'Oh, I can give you barracks,' he said. 'There are some disused buildings in the suburbs.'

" 'I shall want a convoy for them,' I added. 'And a guard. These people are very sick, but they are prisoners, and I cannot take the responsibility of freeing them.'

"He smiled, showing those little white teeth under his gold moustache. 'My dear sir, I cannot lend my men for such purposes. Cavalry doing guard duty! Impossible!'

" 'Then there will be typhus in Siberia. Do you know anything about it, captain? It is no respecter of persons.'

"His eyes met mine. As he lay there, I assure you he looked like a comic-opera prince—his jacket was trimmed with astrakhan and unbuttoned, showing a silk shirt. He wore a gold bracelet on his wrist.

" 'Who are these people?" he demanded finally, in a different voice.

"I explained. He sat up, looking very eager, with a flush in his smooth cheeks upon which there was, I swear, the down of youth.

" 'I'll tell you what I'll do for you,' he said gaily. 'Hand over the whole four hundred, and in twenty-four hours there won't be a sick or well among them.

We mustn't take chances with typhus. Wipe it out now and have done with it.'

" 'Do you mean a wholesale execution of all these innocent people?' I demanded.

" 'Yes. Why not? They're dogs, traitors, and dangerous to public health, besides. I've a good mind to take it into my own hands. That old doctor is a Bolshevik himself.'

" 'Nonsense. There are Bolsheviki in his hospital, but you can't very well expect him to kill them off.'

"The young man said again, with maddening calm: 'Why not?'

" 'You know well enough why not. It is the White leader's boast that he is going to establish a free government in Russia on the firm basis of public trust. He is getting moral support from the Allies. Suppose it became known outside of Russia that mistakes are being made—I am putting it politely——'

"He looked at me with a frown between his baby-blue eyes; his mouth curled into a sneer. He got to his feet and saluted again, clicking his heels together. And while he dismissed me, he buttoned his Prince of Pilsen jacket up to the throat, as if he wanted to impress me with the faultlessness of his attire.

" 'My dear fellow, be careful what you say. You are, officially, a doctor, not an arbiter of Russia's political destiny. I will consider your request and let you know—later.'

"There was nothing for me to do but to go."

Parker, who had not touched his cigarette, now took a deep puff and, tipping back his head, watched the slow up-curling of the smoke that drifted under the veranda roof and was whisked suddenly sidewise out into the darkness.

"Well," Field asked finally, "what did the young devil do? And why didn't you cut his throat then and there?"

"And get my own cut? Hardly! I went back to the hospital and told the old doctor. He simply shrugged his shoulders and went on working. . . . Of course, I sought out Anna, because her face had haunted me, as the faces of the obsessed always do. She was working, too—the sleeves of her dress rolled up to the shoulders, showing her capable arms, flawless as marble. She had magnificent hands—not at all the hands of a peasant—broad, but finely modelled, with long, cool fingers. Her face was dead white, and when she saw me a flash of recognition came into her eyes that for a moment made my heart unsteady. But I soon saw that she looked upon me only as a possible means of gaining her own freedom and finding her mother. She had but one idea—it burned in her with a clear flame, comsuming every other emotion. There was no room in her for pity or love or fear. Only that thought, that intention, tragic and ruthless—to rescue the other loved one, no matter how. She credited me with divine powers. I was not a man—I was a weapon in her hand.

"I did not fall in love with her then; I can say this honestly. In spite of her French—learned from the

nuns at a rural school of some sort—she was as far
removed from my way of thinking as pole is from
pole. I'm not trying to defend my way of thinking,
you understand—only if we spoke to each other at all,
it must be across an abyss of differences. But I was
fascinated, as one is fascinated by a sleek tiger in a
cage. And, remember, I was far away from my
world of complex mondaines. This woman was mysterious because she was so magnificently simple.

"She whispered to me every time we met: 'You
must get me away. You can. You are powerful
here.'

"Powerful! My prestige was worth nothing, unless that cub of an officer chose to be impressed by it.
The wheels of authority began to revolve, and on the
morning following my unfortunate interview with the
cavalry chief he appeared at the hospital, in all his
glory, to make an inspection. The military commandant of the city, he told me, had authorized him to
choose fifty of the prisoners for execution—'as an
example.' Either this, or the whole lot must perish
together of typhus. He had a list of names, which
he consulted frequently, of the most dangerous 'cases.'
With the tired old doctor at his elbow, he went from
room to room, identifying them.

"You have probably guessed. Anna was one of
those who came under this wholly illegal and detestable ban. She received the sentence without a quiver
or a change of expression. Only the blood ebbed from
her face, leaving it whiter than ever.

" 'A pretty girl,' the cub said to me in English.

'Too pretty. They're the worst sort.' And he passed on, screwing a monocle into one baby-blue eye and squinting at the official list—which I am perfectly certain was not official at all, only a complete record of the prisoners' names which had been on file at the commandant's office. He went all through that reeking hospital, leaving behind him a trail of violet scent and stark, unreasoning horror. No one knew what he would do next. When he had gone, I went at once to Anna, finding her still standing upright with her hands clasped behind her. The look she gave me was full of a challenging hatred.

" 'They're going to shoot me,' she said. 'To-morrow. Before I have found my mother or avenged my father. And you say nothing! American? You are no better than the worst of these. What are you going to do?'

"I answered, looking at her steadily: 'Will you marry me? Now? I think I can fool these people. . . . It's worth trying.'

"Anna made a gesture with her head, weary and disdainful. 'I will do anything. I will promise anything. Only don't let me die now.'

"I believe I raised my voice angrily. She was so confoundedly cool about it! 'I'm not asking anything of you. If I get you out, you can go where you please, when you like. If you marry me, you become automatically an American citizen. I can threaten them with that, and before they've had time to think about it, you'll be in Vladivostok—safe away. Afterwards, I can take you to England—or wherever else you want to go. Only, please, don't speak to me of promises.'

"Suddenly she caught my hand and, going down on her knees, covered my fingers with kisses. That was the only sign of gratitude I had from her—then or later. I lifted her up and she stood before me, calm as a sphinx again, with her head thrown back and her hands behind her. Our eyes met with hostility, the glances of guilty conspirators. Love? I hated her then. . . . But the old doctor sent for a priest and we were married. Then I went to the commandant and bullied and threatened him. My wife was suspected by Captain Blank—I've forgotten the baby monster's name—and under sentence to be executed with forty-nine others in the morning. The execution of a citizen of the United States might cause the withdrawal of American approval and support—and all the rest of it.

"I stormed and clawed the air. I pounded the old chap's desk with a clenched fist. I painted a picture of his own dismissal and downfall. And in the end, with a shrug, the military commandant reached hurriedly for a pen and scratched off a pardon for Mrs. Waldo Parker, of the United States of America. . . . He tossed it to me and said: 'I am under the impression that both you and your wife are Bolshevik sympathizers. The Red Cross must not cloak traitors. I advise you to return to Vladivostok and leave the typhus epidemic to us Russians. We are more humane.'

"With that parting shot he dismissed me."

Parker looked at Field with a grim smile. "Cheerful, wasn't it? I went back to the hospital and worked all night with the old doctor, an *interné*, three Sisters of Mercy and Anna, who was as tireless as a machine. She lifted sick men in her arms as if they were children. I had no time to do more than tell her of the pardon. She said simply: *'Merci, monsieur.'*

"*Merci, monsieur!* And she was my wife! Well—that was part of it—I hadn't bargained for romance exactly. When dawn filtered in through those dirty, barred windows, we heard a clatter of cavalry in the courtyard. The condemned—some of them were seriously ill—stood together in a group, shivering and silent. The door opened and the baby monster came in, clattering, very zealous, with a flush in his cheeks. I showed him the commandant's pardon for Anna.

" 'But this is outrageous!' he shouted. 'The order calls for the execution of fifty persons.' He looked quickly around. 'I will take another.'

"The old doctor was standing with the group of condemned, his arm around one of them. The young officer's eyes widened and he motioned to the doctor to go with the others. The wonderful old fellow turned very pale, but he went, bowing first to Anna and saying quietly: 'A life for a life. And I am old.' She bent her head and, without flinching, watched him leave the room.

"Then she turned to me. 'I give you my word,' she said, 'that I will avenge him, too. And I give you my word that when it is safe for me to leave you,

I will do so.' There were no tears in her eyes, not a break in her voice! And, standing side by side, as remote as two strangers who have never exchanged a word, we heard the crackle of rifle-fire outside in the courtyard.

"That isn't quite all. I took her first to Vladivostok, and then, because we were both in very real danger, to England. I believed, and still believe, that Bolshevism would eventually prove to be nothing more than one means to an end, as yet unguessed— a sociological experiment, a political expedient, chaos in chaos. But to Anna, Lenin and Trotsky loomed as gods indeed—saviours, giants, omnipotent and unconquerable. And beliefs of this sort were not permissible in the wife of a Red Cross official. I told her so. She took the rebuff with dignity, only that there was comtempt in her eyes and her brows drew quite together. 'Very well. I will think, but I will not speak.'

"Of course, her one desire was to get back to Russia. She sat in our hotel drawing-room in London, staring down into the crowded streets with eyes that saw nothing. I knew that she was dreaming of that hopeless rescue, all the while the hate bit deeper into her heart. I was no more than the sword in her hand, nor had I fallen in love with her. I was in London, you see, on my own social ground again, in touch with familiar reality, in sight of those women of elegance with whom my life, so far, had been spent.

"If I felt anything, it was resentment against the cold, quiet girl who bore my name without pride or affection. By George, she got on my nerves! Her desire was so turned towards Russia that I began to pull diplomatic wires to get back there—in any capacity. The adventure would not be over, my responsibility not ended, until I had done what she expected of me. In the meantime, of course, we lived almost in hiding. That she would leave me, once we were in Russia, I knew; and I did not intend to regard our marriage as binding in case, in some distant future, I should meet that American wife you just offered me.

"We went nowhere, saw no one. As long ago as Vladivostok she had accepted money from me, enough with which to buy warm clothes and furs. Now, in London, I insisted upon more fashionable things for her—we must not be conspicuous, even in the obscure hotel where we waited.

"It did not make it easier for me, the discovery that she was beautiful—a desirable creature. I was haunted by her very human strength and health, repelled by her obsession, angered by her indifference. Once she said: 'I have nothing in me but hate. Take me back before I poison you, too.'

"And at last the opportunity came. We returned, this time by way of Germany. Kolchak had disappeared in the avalanche of the revolution. There seemed to be no one against whom Anna could direct the violence of her loathing. And where, in that disorganized welter of hopeless humanity, did she expect to find her mother? I questioned her. She only smiled. It was evident that she intended to hurl herself into the Bolshevik maelstrom. Remember, her father's last words had been: 'I am one of them!'

"And I was going into Russia on official business, taking with me a beautiful wife who was apparently a Frenchwoman! I can imagine how this must shock and disgust you. It may shock and disgust you more when I tell you that I felt some of Anna's desperate desire to wipe out the memory of those atrocious crimes, to speak once for Russia cleansed of bloody folly, to go through with the wild adventure to the end—no matter what the end might be."

Parker tossed the second cigarette away. He did not light another, but sat with his arms folded on the table and his head bent.

"It was like me," he said, "to fall in love with her, just as I was about to lose her. And there your accusation hits me hard—rainbow chaser! Exactly. . . . I had seen this woman every day for eighteen months, without guessing what was in her of gentleness and wit and generosity. I had let her feed upon hate, instead of offering her love. I had turned my back on her. I had shut her away from beauty, and she was made for beauty! With eyes like that, youth like that, and fire in her that could kindle the heart in any man!

"So, at last, it kindled mine and very nearly consumed me. Funny, wasn't it? I had the rainbow within reach and I couldn't grasp it if I would. The hardest thing I had to do was to preserve my ridiculous aloofness. She must be free to the last, because I had offered her nothing but freedom.

"There were dangers and difficulties in the crossing of Russia. It was bitterly cold. The trains were overcrowded and underheated when they ran at all. We were regarded with suspicion, held on absurd pretexts, questioned, forgotten, questioned again—it might have been the Czar's Russia, save that everywhere the New Russia was being proclaimed, and that there was very little food and no trustworthy public service. Russia was suffering what all the rest of the world is suffering—only a little more so.

"We arrived in Petrograd at night. It was snowing when we came out of the station and stood looking for a carriage to take us to our hotel.

"In the carriage Anna said: 'Russia. We are here!'

"Something in her voice made me turn to look at her. Her face was transformed, lighted by an inner radiance. And for the first time I saw her smile. She put her gloved hand through my arm 'Russia. And again, *merci, monsieur.*'

"Our eyes met. I thought: 'This is what you get for your knight-erranting. *Merci* and good-bye.' Aloud I said, in spite of myself: 'I love you, Anna.'

"She continued to look at me. The smile faded, leaving her eyes sombre and questioning. I felt her tremble. The snow drifted into the carriage and lay thick on our furs, like powdered crystal. And suddenly I knew that she wanted me as I wanted her— had all along, perhaps. Only there was such terrible pride in her, such unfaltering honesty! She held me away from her, as if she were trying to get at the truth, to read in my eyes whether I loved her or only pitied her. And then, with a sob, she gave me her lips. . . . I'm telling you this, because that was the end of it. A kiss—and between us the sort of love that happens once in a lifetime. There was no doubt that she was destined to be the one woman, all women. . . . No doubt, then or now.

"The carriage drew up before the lighted doorway of the hotel and she sank back out of my arms, her hand across her eyes. I asked her to wait, and went in to inquire about rooms.

"I must have been inside for five minutes—not more. When I went out again, with the porter—an ex-soldier in a frayed tunic—the carriage was still standing there. Snow lay on the driver's fur cap, on the horses' backs, on the luggage. I put my head inside and said: 'Anna?'

"She was not there.

"I might have known that she would do just this. More than she loved, she hated. . . . She was gone. Gone as completely as if I had imagined her there, wrapped in her furs, with her gloved hand over her eyes, waiting for me! Gone. Even her footprints were obliterated by the silent snow. The driver had seen nothing.

"The porter ran one way down the dark street; I ran the other, but there was no trace of her. Of course not. She had promised to go, and she had gone.

"I remained in Petrograd six months. But I never saw Anna again."

Parker pushed back his chair and stood up. "Shall we go in?" he asked, in a different voice. "It's rather late, and that waiter seems anxious to get rid of us."

"By all means," Field answered.

Holmes rose, too, slowly, staring at Parker with that amiable, affectionate curiosity of his. "Well, I'll be damned!" he said.

THE AMULET

PHILMORE CHAMBERS said, and he was one to know, that there "never had been and never would be any gold in the mountains back of Sunshine."

Sunshine straggled for a quarter of a mile across the dusty face of a blistering-hot plain. A picket fence of mountains hedged in the horizon. And if there was no gold in them, neither was there water. Men who had gone into their heart searching for the one died for lack of both, and there were sun-bleached skeletons marking the graves of dreamers who had perished of disappointment and thirst.

But one dream persisted to our day, and not a man in Sunshine or a chick or a child but hasn't heard of the Tarletons and their gold.

The first Tarleton passed through Sunshine in '50, when it was no more than a string of shanties. He rode a yellow horse and declared to be going farther west. He went no farther than those mountains you see over there, for in Sunshine he ran across a poor fellow, a consumptive, so they say, who had come down to die within earshot of the fiddle in Bailey's saloon. This fellow took a fancy to Tarleton, and on his death-bed plucked a lump of gold from out his bosom and put it into Tarleton's palm. First he'd cough and then he'd raise himself on his elbow and whisper and point and draw maps on the air with his thin forefinger.

So it was that the first Tarleton got wind of the thin trickle of water which threads the gully known today as Tarleton's Cut—first smelt gold, and first lost his soul.

He buried the consumptive fellow in a shallow grave, mounted the yellow nag, and went away telling no one where he was set for. He was looking for the dead man's claim. Under his shirt, sewed in a leather packet, he wore the lump of gold like an amulet. It was warm against his skin, alive, electric, delicious. There must have been something devilish about it; it was no larger than a man's thumb-nail, brilliant and pure, with marks on three sides that might have been made with a rude chisel. In our mountains, sir, there is nothing like it—never has been. Look at them—heaps of volcanic ash. No gold there! Scrap them all, from Mitchell to Nubble, and you'd not find enough gold to make a Lincoln penny.

You're down here to ask questions about the Tarleton boys, and you're not the first stranger that has been after the particulars. Joseph Tarleton could tell you—his life was ruined by that little lump of gold. Frank Hanscom's widow could tell you, only she wouldn't. I'll tell you, if you'll be patient enough to go back to that first Tarleton on the yellow horse. You can see him crossing the plain in the hot glare of white sky on white sand, like a figure moving within a crystal sphere. He probably wore a beard. The gold-fever was in his eyes. Now and again his hand went up to his breast to caress the amulet. Gone his vision of vineyard and garden in Spanish California—the homestead he was to have had if the hand of destiny had not reached out of the unknown to drag him into those mountains over there.

He found the consumptive fellow's gully and the trickle of ice-white water that threads it, slipping from stone to stone with a sound like voices heard far off—a sort of purposeless murmur. A stream like that would drive most men mad—it comes from nowhere, and on the rim of the plain drops out of sight, never to reappear. But old man Tarleton built himself a shack and scratched himself a vegetable patch and set out to match his three-squared bit of gold against Fortune and Chance.

This is a story of obsession, sir. Inherited madness—there was a gold tumour on the brain of every male Tarleton for three generations. Folk in this part of the country say that the old man was sociable enough. He used to come down to Sunshine and drop in at Bailey's for a drink now and then. And one night he ran off with one of the girls—jerked her up alongside of him on the yellow horse and took her back to the hills. Pretty place for a woman like that! She could walk just so far up the Cut and just so far down, keeping in the shadow. Beyond, there was nothing but sand, or lopsided, purple mountains, dry as bones, where the old man clawed and scratched for gold. She was a pretty thing, wild and devilish, with black curls. So they say.   He never brought her back to Sunshine, and folk who went out, curious a little, to see what he had done with the dance-girl in that God-forsaken place, never saw more of her than the tail of her red skirt vanishing through the shanty door.   Old man Tarleton kept her hidden away for two years.   Then she died, giving birth, unattended, to John Tarleton.   Old man Tarleton rode for the doctor after she was dead, carrying the baby, wrapped in a blanket, on his arm, the yellow horse sort of picking his way as if he knew.   Horses are sensitive creatures, sir.

John Tarleton was the father of Asa and Joseph. It's their story you want and their story I'm telling you.   It goes back to that red, squalling baby in a blanket, son of a "light" woman and man in whose eyes the gold-fever was already flickering like living flames.   A passionate belief in the existence of a fabulous vein somewhere near the gully was born in that baby, just as surely as he inherited a shock of curly black hair from his mother, and his father's stooped shoulders.   He grew up with it.   He believed, as you and I believe in the sun, the moon, and the stars.   His belief was all the religion he ever had, the only schooling.   His babyhood was spent watching his father honeycombing the crumbling flanks of the gulch, panning in the cool and indifferent stream, sitting at night with a tallow dip alight and the lump of metal a-glitter on the table, a malevolent, inscrutable god of Mammon withholding the secret of its being.   His baby fingers caressed it.   Once, when his father's back was turned, he kissed its smooth surface as he might have kissed his mother.

But there was no gold where the consumptive had said there would be. Attracted by the fable, many men went in, and very few of them came out alive. Hearing of this, old man Tarleton always laughed. His own claim was the key to the riddle. Every time his pick struck he expected to see a fortune in minted coins roll down the slope like money spilled out of a treasure-chest. In his mind the legend grew until the flinty walls of the gulch seemed to glitter in the noonday sun. He died when his son was sixteen, leaving him the shanty, the vegetable patch, the barren claim, and the baleful, yellow lump.

John inherited his father's methods of wooing along with his gold-madness. About the time most young fellows are pretending to scorn women he began to prowl about Sunshine looking for a wife. He'd come down once a week, sometimes oftener, brushed up, shaved. He was a tall, handsome boy, and had a proud way of walking, staring out of his eyes with a sort of disdain, as if he were a king in disguise.

In those days there was only one street in Sunshine, and that wasn't paved. When it rained, this boulevard of ours was pitted with footprints and hoofmarks and wheel-ruts; in dry weather horse and man went canopied with chalky dust. Society sat on Bailey's porch and spat into the road. What girls there were minced back and forth along this ugly quarter of a mile, wearing finery that had come across the plain by coach—bustles and kid gloves and little parasols and pill-box hats.

Anne Lincoln was the handsomest girl in Sunshine and the proudest. She had the air of not seeming to see the drunken fences, the sun-blistered houses; she floated, her hands always crossed over a lace shawl, a smile on her face, like a lady walking in your Bois at Paris or in the Prado of Madrid. Her father was a lawyer and had built himself that brick house yonder with the green blinds. Anne was "somebody." When she passed, the talk on Bailey's porch died like falling rockets—they gave her the homage of ashamed silence. She might and she might not have liked this.

Other girls paraded arm in arm, giving long looks, giggling, while Anne looked neither to right nor left and smiled her disdainful smile as if she saw nothing, or, better, as if she saw palaces and gardens. They said of her, "She might be sittin' in a carriage." There was a rustle and a perfume about her, an elegance, a strength. And there was not a man in Sunshine who would have raised his eyes to her except John Tarleton, down from the hills with his mad dream and his amulet. The loafers at Bailey's looked to see him frozen dead when he lifted his hat to her one day and stood aside to let her pass, but she glanced at him straight, lifting her head a little, and the look passed through his heart, sweet and painful, like an arrow dipped in honey. He stood staring after her, and his face flushed to the roots of his hair.

They must have met after that—sly meetings on the rim of the plain, out of sight of curious, sniggering onlookers. Or across the fence by moonlight, when he would lean forward, whispering to her of all that gold in Tarleton's Cut, *his* gold, the key to the wonders of the world. She must have been a fierce woman, elemental for all her perfumed rustle and her ivory skin. Her lips would part as he talked, as if she could taste the wine of life he was offering her. Perhaps he unhooked his amulet from about his neck and let her see the squat little god, let her hold it in the palm of her hand and rub it against her cheek.

The dusty street, white as snow in the southern moonlight, vanished completely, and she saw herself walking through the rippling light and shadow of some leafy promenade. With this man at her side? God knows, sir, if she thought at all of him! It was his dream she believed in, then.

Afterwards, they tell me, she was a splendid lover, jealous and fiery, cherishing her man.

The upshot of it was that she married this ragged fellow without so much as a wedding-guest to see it done, and rode away with him, sitting behind him on his horse and holding him tight around the waist with both arms. Like John's mother, she never came back to Sunshine. That was in '75. In those days Sunshine was an outpost of civilization, a backwater, a forgotten blister on the face of the desert. Twenty-five or thirty miles away, Anne Tarleton's new home was waiting for her—a two-room shanty set askew between the walls of the Cut, where day and night there was no sound save the murmur of water. In Sunshine she had had a pretty bedroom with muslin curtains at the windows, a clothes-press, and a high wooden bed with carved posts. She left her scents and powders, her lace shawls and beaded slippers in her father's house. She left him with his heart broken. So they say. I am inclined to believe that he suffered from chagrin and loneliness. It became the business of his life to discredit John Tarleton.

"My daughter was hypnotized," he used to say. "By a lie! By a lie! She thought she could better herself. And where is she now?"

She was probably sitting bareheaded on the steps of the shanty, smiling her scornful smile and dreaming her dreams. Her hair, which she had always worn in a brown silk net, streamed down her back; her feet were bare. She wore the lump of gold against her own flesh—where the neck of her dress turned back, you saw the rough cord; there should have been seed-pearls or topaz to match her yellow eyes. If any one went out there, as they rarely did, she wouldn't speak. After a year or so she hid herself away, even from her father. People weren't wanted.

"It's mighty queer," they said in Sunshine. "There must be gold. The place must be full of it. A woman like Anne Lincoln wouldn't stick to an illiterate ragamuffin if he didn't have something to offer her."

The legend spread. It became a conviction in the

town that Tarleton was hoarding treasure. Men and boys, fired by the mad idea, crept to the rim of the Cut and spied on the shanty. They saw nothing but the cold stream slipping through the purple shadows down there, and a man and woman sitting side by side with hands interlocked. One fellow, bolder than the rest, slid down the gully-wall, feet first, in a cloud of dust and a rattling of pebbles. John Tarleton, catching sight of him from the rear of the shanty, went very deliberately indoors, came out again carrying a rifle, and, taking aim with the coolness of a man firing at a marauding dog, shot twice. The bullets fanned the intruder's ears as he scrambled back to the rim and to safety.

The next day Tarleton appeared at Bailey's, carrying the rifle.

"Tarleton's Cut is Tarleton's claim," he said to the men on the porch. "I calculate to shoot at sight any but invited guests. Keep off."

A year later he rode in for Dr. Fairweather. And he was in a desperate hurry. Dr. Fairweather stood in his doorway stroking his chin to hide a smile and said, in a slow way he had, "Baby or no baby, Mr. Tarleton, I'm waiting for an invitation."

That was the only time a Tarleton ever bent knee to any man. The big fellow went down in the dust by the doctor's gate and begged him, for God's sake, to hurry. Anne Lincoln was alone at the shanty twenty-seven miles away.

"Wait a minute," the doctor said, snatching his

bag. "And get up. I beg your pardon. It isn't for God's sake that I'm going with you, but for that woman's."

This was in '82, and Joseph was born that night. He, I reckon, is the hero of this story. Only don't let any one in Sunshine hear you calling him a hero! We haven't a romantic point of view down here, and the Tarletons from first to last were romantic.

I believe that Anne Lincoln's love for John was a great love, an elemental love such as happens in one out of a hundred marriages. It fed on loneliness and false hope, poverty, and disappointment. John went enfolded in it, like a man wearing invisible armour. I remember his—loping into town with his rifle on his arm, always taciturn, suspicious, sensitive. Romantic!

Anne's father sent north for experts and paid for an expedition into the heart of that volcanic range over there. If there was gold—— But there wasn't. Copper. Of the more precious metal not a trace, not so much as an indication!

When the engineers came out, with a report that made several men in Sunshine millionaires, old Mr. Lincoln went to Tarleton's Cut and demanded to see Anne.

This time she came out of the shanty and confronted him with her baby in her arms.

"Father," she said, "I can't ask you to sit down, for we haven't any chairs."

He stared at her, forgetting his errand in his horror and amazement. His Anne, barefoot, a slattern! Even while he watched, the baby fumbled with fat hands in the neck of her dress and brought forth the charm that had bewitched her. Joseph cut his teeth on the baleful little lump, they say!

"I want you to come back with me," Mr. Lincoln said. "There isn't any gold in these mountains. I've got proof of it. You're wasting your life out here. You and that lazy scoundrel, your husband! If you'll come back, both of you, where you belong, I'll see that John gets something to do." And then, with a touch of wistfulness, he added persuasively: "Your room is just as you left it, and I have sent to New York for a silk dress for you. Mrs. Hanscom is bringing it."

Anne's eyes seemed to shine for a moment—she loved pretty things—and her father thought he had won her. But then he became conscious that John Tarleton had been standing all the while behind him, striking that light in his wife's eyes. She shook her head.

"It's jealousy," she said, "and fear. Go back and tell them so. All of them! We'll fight for what's ours with our lives."

"You mean this cinder-heap?" Mr. Lincoln demanded, making a wild gesture with both arms. "You're mad. Stark, staring mad! Both of you."

"Perhaps," she said.

He had to leave it at that. He never saw her again. His disappointment and chagrin became hatred, a fixed desire to drive both of them out of the country. This is where Ed Hanscom comes in. He was Mr. Lincoln's right-hand man—a sort of servant, secretary, and police dog, eager to serve a man whom he recognized to be his superior, but an upstart and a bombastic swaggerer at heart. He had wanted Anne Lincoln, and had cowered before that smile of hers long before John Tarleton ever set eyes on her. When she eloped, Hanscom married a common little vixen, pretty as paint, who adored him and gave him a son five years before Anne Lincoln's first child was born.

But Ed Hanscom never forgave Anne Lincoln for having understood him. And while he pretended to believe in the report of the "experts" from up north, in his secret heart he cherished a faith in that Tarleton gold. It haunted his imagination like Anne's mocking smile. Outwardly he scoffed. Inwardly he wasn't so sure.

You see how a fable like that takes hold of men. To this day there's not a man you know who wouldn't like to strike his wealth out of the earth with pick and shovel. In Hanscom's time Sunshine was a hitching-post for pioneers and prospectors—there was loud talk of wealth wherever there was talk of any sort. Men went haloed by hypothetical millions. It stuck in Ed Hanscom's crop, and stayed there, like an undigested meal, that Tarleton's Cut was lined inside and out with gold. He could picture Anne and John storing away the precious "dust" under the shanty floor or in some hiding-place in the rocks. He had a double motive for what he did.

I'm getting to that. Slowly, because there are several threads that must be gathered up.

Hanscom finally got himself elected sheriff, not because he was popular, but because a lot of people calculated to get rid of him that way. Sheriffs didn't often outlive their term of office in a town where life is notoriously cheap. Hanscom had kept his suspicion to himself. Whenever any one laughed at "those crazy Tarletons," he guffawed louder than the rest. Outwardly he left them alone, apparently satisfied with his pretty wife, his son, and his star of office. He killed John in '89, just before Asa was born. This way:

John Tarleton came into Sunshine one Monday morning with two live fowl which he sold for twenty-five cents apiece. On his way through the town he stopped at Bailey's for a drink. No one was there except Bailey and an Indian, who was fast asleep, with his head on a table and his moccasined feet hooked up on the rungs of his chair.

Bailey filled a glass and said:

"How's Missus Tarleton?"

"Well," John answered.

He stood there a moment, fingering the drink as if in doubt about tasting it, and Bailey went to the back door to speak to a nigger who was sweeping out the yard. When he came in both the Indian and John Tarleton were gone, and with them twenty dollars from the till behind the bar.

The Indian had pigeon-toed in a leisurely manner down Main Street and across the trackless plain.

But John Tarleton had passed in a cloud of dust, hell-bent like one pursued, leaving his drink untasted. Ten people had seen the Indian pause to gaze within the crown of his greasy hat and to scratch the calf of his leg. Twenty people had seen John Tarleton's going that afternoon. Ed Hanscom paused at Mr. Lincoln's gate long enough to say, 'Reckon I got him this time! Stole twenty dollars from Bailey. No doubt of it! I'm going out to the Cut to bring him in."

"Dead or alive, it's one to me," Mr. Lincoln remarked. "Only get him."

"I'll get him," Ed Hanscom said. He added, with a satisfied smile, *"Damn fool!"*

It was late when he arrived at the Cut. Have you been there? A natural fortress, if there ever was one —the shanty a sort of sentry-box, at the front door. Behind it, three miles of cañon floor and a way out into the mountains, known only to the Tarletons.

As Ed Hanscom approached, the glare of the setting sun fell straight into the mouth of the Cut, illuminating the shanty. John was nowhere about, but Joseph, a ragged seven-year-old was peeling potatoes on the steps.

"Where's your father?" Hanscom demanded.

Joseph had the Tarleton distrust of strangers. He scowled and jerked his head.

"Back yonder."

Hanscom rode along the river-bottom, a trail across hard, white sand, smooth as the palm of your hand. On either side the walls rose steep and sharp, pitted here and there by the Tarleton "diggings." It was a risky thing to do. But with that star of office shining on his breast, Ed Hanscom fancied himself inviolable—he moved under the protection of the law and his own egoism. He turned his head this way and that, sniffing the cool air. High above him, the rim of the Cut kindled in the red sunlight. John Tarleton saw the sheriff coming and, snatching up his rifle, ran forward to meet him. He was bearded and gaunt, with big bare feet that left zigzagging tracks on the sand as he ran.

Ed Hanscom pulled his horse sidewise to block the trail and said: "I've come to take you."

Nothing else. John made a quick move and the sheriff fired. He sat there on his horse watching the wounded man go down on his hands and knees, coughing and spitting, then fall forward and lie still. It was a neat shot clean through the heart. Darn fool! *Damn crazy idiot!*

Hanscom turned away at last to ride back to the shanty and give his news to Anne Lincoln. His smile had about it some of the quality of her own.

He had not gone a hundred feet when he felt a sharp blow, penetrating and violent as a viper's sting, between his shoulders.

"Not dead!" he shouted, with a look over his shoulder at Tarleton. "Damn fool!"

He fell out of the saddle and died while the sun was still red on the cañon rim. Both of them died, sir. And it was the sheriff's horse that wandered back to the shanty with that piece of news for Anne.

The following day the Indian, being a naïve thief, tried to spend his twenty dollars at Bailey's and was strung high, good and plenty, for his simplicity. While this was happening Anne Lincoln was burying John with her own hands. She was a proud, strange woman.

Seven months later little Joseph rode for the doctor, and Asa was born to Anne. The doctor said that she was indifferently glad. She lay with the baby on her arm, her head turned so that she could look out of the open door. She seemed to listen to the murmur of the water. When the doctor begged her to let him send a woman to help, she said: "Joseph will tend me."

Joseph tended her to the best of his ability. He was sturdy, but almighty small—a pint of cider with a big head and eyes that were always looking off. No one had taught him to read; he was more like a hairy little animal than a child. Asa had the Tarleton good looks.

The two of them grew up in the hut, ignorant, wild, mothered by a proud woman who never smiled any more and who went in rags with tangled hair. Grew up, if you will believe me, without books; often, for weeks at a time, without speech, and with one overwhelming desire, one passion—to possess a non-existent thing. Anne fed the flame. She was wild,

implacable, a whip at their heels. She suckled them
both on hate and avarice. She enacted the tragedy
of their father's death as you and I would play the
game of "three little bears in the wood."

For years the remnant of her beauty clung about
her, a very faint perfume of the old seduction. I remember seeing her when Joseph was eighteen and
Asa ten—I had clambered into the Cut from above
to spy on them, for they had a fabulous reputation
even then. I saw Anne distinctly as the three of
them knelt panning in the river—there wasn't a
thread of grey in her hair, and when at last she stood
up she seemed heroic and dauntless, with her feet
spread and firmly planted and her arms bare to the
shoulder. Joseph had a stubble beard and wore
calico trousers.

When Joseph was twenty he came to Sunshine to
do his wooing. There must have been some sort of
family tradition, or else Anne had inflamed him with
recitals of her own love. She gave him the amulet,
and for the first time he wore the flaming little god
next to his skin.

You've got to get a new picture of this town as it
was then—paved sidewalks, a frame hotel, and the
first sprawled buildings of the United Metal Company on the outskirts. Mr. Lincoln's house was
flanked by a drug-store, and there was no more
Bailey's—the swarm of miners and workmen, engineers and buyers hung around the porticoed stoop
of the new Patchfield House or sat in the barber-

shop. It was a man's town. The first settlers had become by rights of precedence "first families," but there was no society to speak of.

Ed Hanscom's son, Frank, was our most promising young man—destined to become prosecuting attorney —sharp, ambitious, sober, a hard worker. He was a furnace without heat—he burned, but there were no flames. At twenty-five his head was thrust forward like a battering-ram. He never smiled, and he was superbly contemptuous of obstacles. It was like him, I told myself with annoyance, to fall in love with Bertha, my sister, and the prettiest girl in Sunshine.

One afternoon she came to my office opposite the Patchfield House and said to me, "I am going to marry Frank Hanscom."

She had come in from the street, but she was cool and fresh as a carnation.

She leaned on the desk and smiled down at me. "I thought you'd be glad. Frank is doing awfully well. He is going to be district attorney some day."

"I suppose he told you so?"

"Don't be mean, or jealous."

"You can't possibly love him, Bertha."

"I admire him. That's better."

"You know about his father?"

Bertha shook her head.

"He was shot in the back by one of the crazy Tarletons over at the Cut. Anne Tarleton is rearing her sons for vengeance. Some day, if you marry Hanscom, your husband will be shot—in the back."

Bertha laughed. "I'm not afraid of two ignorant

ragamuffins and an old witch. Frank says that the Tarletons are a disgrace to this part of the country."

She lifted her head and looked beyond me through the partially screened window to the street, where Hanscom paced up and down waiting for my blessing. I called him in and gave it; gave my hand into his dry clasp and managed to slap him on the back.

The engagement began in the early spring. Bertha and her young man used to whisper on the front steps, leaving me anchored by the parlour lamp, irritated by their commonplace love-making. When he had gone, promptly at ten, Bertha would come indoors.

I am telling you this because one night she didn't come in at once after Hanscom had called his brisk "Good night!" from the gate.

Five minutes. No more. But I was curious enough to glance at her when she came. Her cheeks were flushed and she hesitated, one hand on the latch.

She paused by my chair, whispering:

"*Tell me about the Tarletons!*"

"Why?"

"I think I saw one of them just now. Short, with a black beard and funny eyes."

"Joseph."

She laughed.

"He stopped by the gate and stared at me—like a dog asking for a bone."

"Oh, *that's* why you stayed there! Watch out. The Tarletons get their wives over a fence, in the moonlight."

She gave me a startled glance. "He said so—just now."

"D'you mean he spoke to you?"

She nodded and, getting up hurriedly, I went to the door. Through the screen I could see Joseph leaning on the gate, staring straight up at me. His battered hat was held between both hands and he seemed to be begging, as Bertha had said, for a bone.

While I hesitated he straightened up and moved off in the dim moonlight, drifting down the street with the curious, catlike tread of men who go barefoot.

"He likes me," Bertha said with a shiver.

"Don't speak to him again. He's after you because you're engaged to Frank Hanscom."

"Oh, that!" she said.

I can't give my first hand what happened during the next month. The moon was gone; I was tired and busy; I forgot Bertha and her love affair. Long afterwards I got the details of Joseph's wooing of my sister. He came, in the manner of the Tarletons before him, ardent, persistent, persuasive, romantic—romantic, even in calico pants and a hat inherited from his grandfather! It seems that he always waited in the shadow of the house across the way until Frank Hanscom had gone, and then crossed to the glow of Bertha's white dress as a moth staggers into light. He had the face of an emaciated saint, the arms of a blacksmith, and the sensitive spirit of a child. All quiver and feeling, he was. It was as if the restlessness of that stream had got into him,

tormenting him.   Mixed up with it there were dark
hates, fostered by Anne—impulses not his own, but
bequeathed to him.   He wouldn't have hurt a fly, yet
he was bred to kill.   Even then his fate was in his
eyes.   Oh, my lord, he was ugly as sin!   Bertha used
to mock at him and tease him, keeping her side of the
fence, laughing a cool little laugh that was enough to
set a man's teeth on edge.   No woman ever listened
to such strange love-making.

One night he coaxed her all the way down to the
gate and showed her the lump of gold.   At first he
was wary of letting her touch it.   But her nearness
overpowered him—he succumbed to the subtle fragrance of carnation and gave his treasure into the
palm of her white hand.

"You can have it if you'll marry me."

"It's ugly.   It isn't worth a dollar.   Besides I'm
going to marry Frank Hanscom."

Joseph snatched his treasure back, hurting her
fingers.   His face was twisted with passionate fear.
He ran away from her through the darkness,
muttering.

And when she told Frank Hanscom—as at last
she did on the eve of her marriage—he urged her to
get possession of the amulet if it were offered to her
again.

"There may be more gold at the Cut," he said
seriously.   "My father believed so.   They killed
him, curse them!"

He apologized for swearing in her presence, but
she saw that his eyes were shining with some new

emotion and that his hands actually trembled. He left her earlier than usual, as if he sensed the presence of his rival in the shadows. And, sure enough, he had no sooner gone than that eccentric figure materialized, beckoning to Bertha from the gate. I am telling you, she hadn't any pity. She wanted to see the pretty lump of gold again. She hadn't meant to hurt his feelings. Was there really more of it? *Lots and lots of it?* Enough to buy Paris hats and dresses and a carriage? More? Enough to pave streets, to build houses, to make queens of beautiful women? Out came his fantastic dreams. He caught her hand and put it against his lips. Bertha felt her body grow cold with fear and repugnance, but she still begged for the little god. Presently Joseph gave it to her. Then he opened the gate and followed her up the path, torn between fear and a desire he couldn't understand.

She ran away from him and up the steps to the porch where the light from my lamp fell aslant, showing him her smooth black hair, the whiteness of her throat, and her two hands cupping his treasure. Something in his face made her say: "I'll keep it until I marry you."

At that he went on his knees and got hold of her dress, so that she had to reach down and unclasp the clutch of his fingers.

"Until we're married," she repeated. "Let me go now."

She tore herself free and ran indoors, slamming the door behind her.

"Look what I've got," she said. "Look what I've got! Oh, that silly man!"

I snatched it out of her hand and went to the door, but Joseph had gone, poor devil, believing himself betrothed.

In the morning Bertha and Hanscom were married and went away to spend their honeymoon in San Francisco, taking the Tarleton trophy with them. And I was left to deal with Joseph.

I made no excuses for Bertha. She was young. She was pitiless. She suffered as much, perhaps more than was necessary.

"You tell Joseph," Bertha had said. "It's a good joke. I didn't *have* to say I was going to be married in the morning! Did I?"

The last I heard was her light little laugh as she drove away towards the future.

Joseph came at ten o'clock. He was wearing a new shirt and had shaved his beard. I called to him; he shied like a wood-animal, then came through the gate, clutching his hat to his breast. I told him that Bertha had married and had gone away, but I took pains to assure him that Hanscom was not responsible for the "joke." I even promised to return the amulet to him when the honeymooners got back from San Francisco.

He listened, said nothing, and when I had finished made a single, awkward gesture with both arms, as if he cursed the stars. His face was twisted to one side, his eyes mad. He turned and ran, light-footed as a prairie-dog, away into the darkness.

The rest of the story is pure narrative.

I couldn't get the lump of gold away from Bertha and her husband. I don't pretend to say that there was magic in the thing, but the truth is that Hanscom became infected with the belief that some day enough gold would be washed out of the Cut to rebuild Babylon. It was the devil to find, but it was there! His father's dream was transferred to him, and, like his father, he cherished it in secret. But he was afraid of the Tarletons. He kept the amulet in a safe; I have no doubt that he often took it out to scan its brilliance and beauty, to whip his dreams into definite desires. It poisoned him, sir. He laid the plans of his life according to its false promise of easy wealth. And Bertha, her smile turning into a cool postponement of every day, seemed to wait for—for treasure. I have no other way to put it.

Strangely enough, Joseph never came to Sunshine again. Now Asa came, shy as a wild thing, furtive and ignorant. Joseph stayed in the hills with Anne.

Fourteen years. You must bridge it in your imagination, if you can—Sunshine no longer a single street, but a sprawling checkerboard of shanties and sheds, belching chimneys, picket enclosures, tracks. Where the stage-coach had swayed along in a funnel of dust, squawking flivvers and trucks stirred up a cloud that never settled. The vision of the Forty-niner had become Twentieth-century industry. Men scoured and pitted the mountains for metals and converted them into currency. Thirty miles away the Tarletons were forgotten save by a few "old-timers"

who never took the trouble to go out there. The
legend didn't appeal to the soda-water school of
youngsters. And when Asa rode in, as he did once
or twice a year, no one noticed him except perhaps
Frank Hanscom, peering out of the plate-glass
windows of his office.

Once I stopped Asa and inquired for Anne. He
reined in his horse and stared down at me with a
startled look.

"How's your mother?" I asked him.

He scowled. "Well," he said.

"Any luck?" He didn't seem to understand.
"Any gold?"

At that he fled. Fled as if I had threatened his
life.

I forgot him in the turmoil of war in 1917. But
Hanscom didn't. By this time he was prosecuting
attorney, with a sizable record of convictions, known
as a sharp-tongued, driving, fearless accuser—his
eyes levelled a pointed finger at innocent and guilty
alike. Men of his sort attract a following of people
who are afraid of them. He seemed always to have
something up his sleeve.

One day, in the middle of the draft turmoil, he
came to me in great excitement.

"How about this Tarleton fellow? Won't the
draft get him? The youngest one, I mean. He's
twenty-six."

It seemed absurd for a Government already glutted
with intelligent young men to reach into that forgotten cañon and drag out Asa Tarleton for service

in an army he had never heard of, for a cause he couldn't understand. "They're half animals, those Tarletons," I said. "You'd better leave them alone."

"Oh, I won't mix up in it," Hanscom assured me. "It's time somebody burned 'em out of their hole. darned sneaks! Asa's able-bodied, isn't he? Is there any reason why he *shouldn't* serve his country? He's making love to a girl who works at a peanut-stand near the plant. We'll catch him there. The girl's afraid of him."

Hanscom closed his eyes—a trick he had when he wanted to conceal his purposes. "I questioned her. She's a pretty, soft little thing—an Italian. Tarleton wants to take her out there——"

Suddenly remembering Bertha's part in the drama, he got up and hurried away.

Asa paid no attention to the draft notice—he probably couldn't read it, and if Anne did, she could not comprehend it.

The sheriff went out alone and saw Joseph—Asa was either in hiding or up in the mountains with pick and shovel. During the interview between the Government agent and the elder Tarleton, Anne Lincoln sat on the shanty steps, brushing her white hair out of her eyes with the back of her hand and laughing to herself.

"Don't you listen to him, Jo," she said. "It's a scheme. *War with Germany?* Germany's across the ocean, Jo. Don't you listen. Tell him we'll kill any one who comes here after Asa."

Two days later the sheriff went back with a posse.

They were fired on from the shanty before they entered the Cut. Asa got out through the back door while Joseph and Anne held the posse off. There was a way out of the Cut into the mountains, and then a chance to reach Mexico, if he could gain, say, half an hour. He hugged the walls, dropping now and then behind the big, flat boulders that fill the river-bottom. I wasn't there. I don't know exactly how it happened. They say that Joseph held the shanty for more than an hour. Then Anne must have persuaded him to follow Asa, for he made a break, firing as he ran, and this allowed the attackers to close in on Anne Lincoln. She was a tigress, that old woman! They say she fought until her calico dress was in ribbons. They left her to two men, while the others followed her sons along the cañon floor.

Joseph they wounded and captured at the foot of the "stairs." Asa led them into the heart of that range over there, doubling on his tracks like a puma. He had no idea what he was running away from or why. All he knew was what Anne had told him— the whole world coveted his invisible possession; war had been made; humanity was banded together against the three of them, to wrest the dream of gold out of their grasp. He fought for life.

It was perhaps the crowning irony that he was in sanctuary, on Mexican soil, when they brought him down. He stood silhouetted on the crest of a hill, judging the distance beneath him and weighing his chances if he should leap. He made a fair target in the flushed light of dawn, and his dead body fell forward as a plummet drops, fifty feet, to Mexican soil!

Joseph was tried and sentenced to life imprisonment. I saw him in the dock. He was like a wild creature looking out at its captors with eyes singularly innocent and pathetic. He knew nothing. He could neither read nor write. He had never heard of Germany. To the end he insisted that he was the victim of a conspiracy. But it is not likely that any one in the court-room will forget the look with which he met Frank Hanscom's prosecution. It was like witnessing the strokes of a cowhide across a sensitive skin—brutal and physical punishment. Two men of the sheriff's posse had died in front of the Tarleton shanty. That was enough for the purposes of the law. Perhaps justly.

The Italian girl testified that Asa had made love to her—had promised her riches.

Hanscom's eyes were closed during her testimony, as if he could not bear the brillance of the vision.

After the trial, in an effort to get control of the Tarleton claim, he went out there alone. I can do no more than outline the facts. He carried with him the original amulet and his automatic. He must have climbed up the natural "stairway" at the end of the Cut, that precarious exit to the mountains by which Asa had escaped. For when he was found, two days later, he had apparently lost his footing and had fallen headlong, his body striking with terrific force time and again as he rolled down the steep slope. He lay sprawled face down on the cañon floor, and like a trail behind him, like a brilliant comet's tail, we found a myriad three-squared lumps of solid gold—he was buried in them; his dead hands were full of them.

I do not pretend to understand. These strange nuggets legally were, of course, Anne Lincoln's. Like the amulet, they bore the marks of rude chiselling, but other than the shower of them unearthed by Hanscom's fall, no more have been found from that day to this.

Anne Lincoln is living in Paris. She is seventy years old and she is still beautiful, believe it or not. You can see her any day riding in the Bois in her carriage, wearing black silk and carrying a black-lace parasol. She looks out at the world with her old smile, disdainful, aloof, mysterious. It is as if the years between had been only a postponement of what she knew would be hers. Terrible woman! Magnificent woman! The shadow of the chestnut-trees ripples over her as her carriage passes swiftly with a little rattle and clink of silver harness. She seems to have forgotten—I believe she has—Asa buried in the burning sand, Joseph imprisoned, John asleep near the cold stream. She passes, in possession of her dream.

THE GAUDY LITTLE FISH

NOW that there's so much talk of the South Seas, I may as well tell you a funny story I happened across when I was a trader. A romance. A confounded queer story of love.

I first saw Archer in Papeete. Twenty years ago, at least. Then, he was a big lean chap with fair hair and a sort of stoop. I should have called him a swell, a gentleman with something confounded ungentlemanly in his past. His face was full of tracks where bad feelings had come to the surface and run across it; he was a living map of dissipations. His eyes looked out at you, sceptical and ashamed. Yet he never explained himself to any one. He wasn't that kind.

One day he came down to see my schooner, the *Anne Beebe*.

"I hear you're going into the Low Archipelago," he said. "I want to go along."

I didn't want a passenger on the *Anne Beebe*, and said so. But later I agreed to take him. He had no particular destination. He was willing to drift with us, three months or more, from island to island, from atoll to atoll, while we discharged our cargo of flour, canned goods, lumber, and calico, picked up copra, and ferried natives from one place to another.

Before the volcanic cones of the Societies had dropped behind, I found myself wondering about him. Fifteen days later, poking in and about the Paumotu reefs, I was still wondering. It occurred to me that this young gentleman-beachcomber from Papeete was seeking a place of exile, a place remote from his own particular tragedy, where no echo of Piccadilly and Trafalgar Square could penetrate, a place beautiful, desolate, and everlastingly his own.

I was right. One dawn the *Anne Beebe* rode down a path of light towards an island whose name I've forgotten—a large half-moon of pink coral, perhaps eight miles long and two or three miles through its centre. It lay on the sea like the blade of a scimitar. A fringe of surf broke clear around, where the long combers crashed on the reef. From the masthead you could see beyond to the lagoon, polished as green glass.

Archer came on deck in his pyjama trousers, displaying his thin, stooped body to the waist. He stood staring off, shading his eyes with his hand.

"What place is this?" he asked with a sort of exultation in his voice.

I told him. In Polynesian, the name meant Sea Bird or Cloud of Spray. Some such fanciful calling. It couldn't have been too fanciful to suit Archer. He nodded his head several times, turned on his heel, and went below.

That afternoon he appeared on deck again, shaved and dressed up like a Tahitian dandy. He had on an immaculate suit, a violet tie, silk socks, canvas shoes and, to top it, a green-faced helmet. He went ashore in a native outrigger canoe, sitting up stiff and fault-less between two naked Paumotuan pearl divers. It gave me a funny feeling to see him, running away from whatever it was, into that blazing hot lagoon where he didn't belong and never would belong.

At sunset one of the natives came out to the *Anne Beebe* bearing a note scribbled in pencil on the back of an envelope:

"I am staying here. Send my things ashore.

"ARCHER."

"Damn his impudence!" I said.

But the boxes and bags went ashore in the whale-boat. Archer received them, non-committal and aloof, standing with folded arms and legs planted well apart as if he were breasting the tide of naked savages that pressed around him. Old women and little pot-bellied babies, diving boys and round-legged, broad-backed men of the reefs—they babbled and stared at this elegant apparition in silk socks, this incompre-hensible dandy from beyond the horizon. Behind them again, a cluster of palm-thatched huts, a row of staggering palms and a vast arch of sky flooded with orange light. . . .

Oh, this was the tag-end of the world! Thirty days and more from Tahiti, a long cruise from Nukuhiva.

"Very few traders call here," I explained to Archer. "You'll maybe regret staying."

"I like it," he said. And then he made his first and only explanation: "I want to be alone!"

"You'll be alone, all right," I answered him.

We left him there, magnificently alone—the only white man on a coral atoll that supported not more than a hundred people.

I did not see him again for two years. Then I took flour, lumber, and canned goods out to him from Papeete. There was, besides, a slim packet of letters.

I was not prepared for what I found.

As before, the *Anne Beebe* approached the atoll at dawn. It was a boisterous daybreak. The sea was deep blue, shot with metallic light. A flotilla of canoes broke through the reef and danced towards us, in their lead a lone man paddling with swift, powerful strokes. He shot under our bow and skimmed along side, raising a sun-blackened face, and shouting: "Hallo, there!"

It was Archer. He came aboard, naked as your hat save for a scarlet loin-cloth. His hair was brushed, parted in the middle. He was shaved. But there was no more stoop, and he had the body of a Kanaka savage. His muscles rippled under smooth brown skin. He was, if you'll excuse my saying so, the damnedest sight I've ever seen, with that slicked yellow hair and those ice-blue eyes and that unconscious nakedness!

"I've got your stuff," I told him.

He showed his teeth in a sort of smile, went to the side and babbled at the islanders in their own lingo.

In their own lingo, mind you! Then he turned to me again.

"I hope you'll have dinner with me tonight." He pointed. "That's my place. In the grove to the right."

It was on the tip of my tongue to tell him that I couldn't wait—I was already a hundred miles out of my course. But curiosity stayed me and I nodded. "Thanks. I will."

His canoe had drifted a little away. Archer slipped into the water and overtook it, swimming in the native fashion with incredible ease and speed. He had not even asked me for his mail!

I took it ashore myself that night, turning up for dinner, at seven-thirty, quite as if I were in San Francisco or London. Archer's "place" dominated the native village. He had a palm-thatched house with corrugated iron walls, a wide veranda, and beyond, in the grove, a little group of outbuildings. A neat shell path led to his door. It all seemed very habitable and civilized. And Archer himself, waiting on the veranda to greet me, called through the darkness: "Ah, Captain! Glad to see you. Come in!" There was a swinging lamp behind him, and I saw, with a shock of surprise, that he was wearing an orthodox dinner jacket, silk socks, and low patent shoes! Out there! In that outpost of silence, that stepping-off place, that crust of pink coral in a forgotten sea! A dinner jacket! I stammered when I took his hand: "I've got letters for you."

"Very good of you." He put the letters in his

pocket without glancing at them, and waved me to a place at his table.

I tell you, my eyes popped out of my head. He had made a centre-piece of shrubs planted in an empty tin can. A candle burned in an inverted coconut shell. It was quite gay and somehow distinguished. A golden-skinned girl with streaming black hair served the meal of raw fish, pork, and coconut salad. There was black coffee, but no sugar and no wine.

I talked. That mysterious fellow listened, smoking cigarettes and swinging one patent shoe. Do you imagine that he explained where he had got the lamp, the coffee, the iron walls of his house? Not he! Do you think I asked? Not I! I preferred to choke on my unspoken questions. His face was polite and graven. His eyes seemed to say: "I know I'm buried out here and it's deuced queer, but I'm not explaining. Take me or leave me."

In the end, of course, I left him. But before I went I had a glimpse, fleet and tantalizing, behind the mask. We were sitting on the veranda, reduced at last to monosyllables, a little heap of quenched cigarettes in a dish between us. Out beyond the lighted enclosure a blue moonlight rimmed the palms and made strange beauty of the tossing spray on the reefs beyond the lagoon. The thunder of that ghostly battle out there came to us faint and remote. Somewhere down the beach they were singing savage, barbaric songs, a sort of nasal caterwauling and wailing, a vocal tom-tom that stirred strange memories in me. It always gets me by the throat, that chanting. Sad, desirous, tormented! I was young, and there were desires in me. If it hadn't been for Archer I would have gone to watch the dancing, to placate my uneasy senses with the sight of voluptuous brown bodies moving in the glare of burning husks.

Suddenly Archer said: "Infernal racket! I'll stop them, if you like."

I rose hurriedly. "No, no."

"They'll do anything I say. I'm what you American's call 'boss' here now. The chief's a lazy old lizard." He smiled and waved his hand. "That girl you saw at dinner—if you say, I'll have her dance for you." And he added, in an unchanged voice: "She is mine."

The girl was sitting on the rim of the crowd. She rose to her feet as we approached, gave us a strange look, afraid and audacious, tossed back her coarse, shining hair with a quick movement of her head, and began to dance. After a moment I ceased watching her. Of the two, Archer was certainly the more interesting. Silhouetted against the heap of atoll dwellers, somehow quite at ease and unconscious of his incongruity, he watched the girl who was, so frankly, "his." Under the sun-faded brows his eyes were expressionless. But I have never seen a face so stamped with devastating passion, so lined and hollowed and put awry by obscure and terrible emotions, such a mask of despair, shame, and disbelief. I stared, fascinated by its ugliness and tragic brutality. I was suddenly grateful for his silence.

Whatever it was he was running away from, I didn't want to know about it.

In the morning he came out to the schooner again, bringing me a single letter addressed to his bank, to be posted in Tahiti.

After that I saw him once or twice every year for seven years and never got to know him any better.   Strangely enough, I grew to like him—or, rather, I liked the figure my imagination had made of him.

He was first and last a picturesque exile.   He told me that he dressed every night for his solitary dinner. He took meticulous care of himself so that at any given moment he might have been put down in Bond Street without attracting attention.

He "lived" native, but he never "went" native. There is a subtle difference, a delicate hesitation on the shadow line between being a gentleman and crossing into the beautiful savagery of the children of the reefs.

Archer spoke English perhaps twice or three times a year.   He knew nothing of the outside world.   He had to all purposes died and been buried.   And, if you are to believe my powers of observation, he was happier than any earthbound ghost this side of Paradise.   The girl who was so simply his had given him three yellow-skinned babies, to whom, in my presence, he never paid any attention.   He was a lordly father.

And then there happened a strange thing.

The *Anne Beebe* was in Papeete again, taking on

stores for her last voyage. I was thinking of selling her to a writer chap who wanted to cruise after local colour from Tahiti to Java. But first I had a cargo to deliver and call for. So he retired to the veranda of the best hotel to write a South Seas novel, and I started off on my last voyage around the Low Archipelago.

And again I had a passenger. A woman. I'll call her Lady Palmerston. She had come from England looking for adventure. At least, so she said. Oh, she talked, that woman! She over-balanced Archer's silence like a stone outweighing a feather in a scale.

She was beautiful. Small and rarely beautiful in a way that gets under the skin and into the nerves of men. She had short brown hair, a wide brow, grey eyes with changing black centres, a rather long, fine nose, and a cruel mouth. There were warm shadows in her flesh. Her throat was full and she was always throwing back her head so that you saw the beauty of that throat. I have never seen such hands. They were more alive than the rest of her.

She had heard of the atolls. She wanted to see them. That was not enough reason for me to be taking her, but in the end I did, giving her my quarters and making myself thoroughly uncomfortable for the voyage. But I reminded myself that for nearly three months I could be looking at her. That was something. She was never two days alike. She was as nervous as one of those gay little fish you see shimmering down in the coral gardens. Emotions ran over her like water. On deck she wore a long silk coat over silk trousers, and her pretty bare feet in heelless slippers. She was up at dawn, and often I saw her sitting with her arms clasped round her knees and her head thrown back to watch the stars streaming across the sky like sparks. You know how they do, like white sparks from a falling rocket.

"This is a lark," she'd say to me.

She told me about her life. She had been married to an Englishman and divorced from him. "He was a stick-in-the-mud," she said. "As adventurous as a garden snail! I was bored to death. I loved the world. Not just London and teas and dinners and an endless gossiping about little people. I wanted to flavour the universe—taste it, smell and touch it from Liverpool to Timbuktu. My husband tried to tame me. Oh, we had an awful time—a terrible time! I led him a dance."

I believed her, I have never seen so tantalizing a creature. But from the beginning I suspected her of being civilized, over-civilized, beneath the surface. She was always scented and powdered. Hours she'd spend brushing that mop of short brown hair with ivory-backed brushes and polishing her pointed nails and rubbing stuff on her face.

My cabin aboard the *Anne Beebe* began to smell like a cosmetic shop. Her silk clothes hung on the pegs where my things had always been. She had thrown an embroidered scarf over the bed and a whole army of little satin pillows. This was no savage woman, roving the world, sunburnt and flea-bitten, if you'll excuse me. There were so many cushions—it was rather too elaborate a *mise en scène*.

"I've been cheated," she told me. "I married for love. I loved as I live—with—well, recklessly. And I've been left empty-handed. You see me—cheated."

I asked her why and how.

It seemed that she had fallen in love with a face, a shut-in, mysterious, terrible face, that had baffled and fascinated her.

"And there was nothing behind it! Not even brains! The man was an imbecile, and he looked as though he had passed through fire. He was as honest, as innocent, as shy, as empty as a child!"

She put her hand on my own. "My dear Captain, I married him with delicious forebodings. That face! Scarred and incomprehending, tragic and fascinating. Oh, fascinating! I shut my eyes and leaped."

She shuddered. "I had married an amiable, domesticated simpleton! He hated the things I loved. He expected me to settle down in Sussex and go in for gentleman-farming. He wanted"—that beautiful, dishevelled head of hers went down on her knees—"a family! I was like a mad woman. I said to him: 'Why, in heaven's name, were you born with a face like that?' He couldn't understand, of course. He never understood anything. Don't you see, he was simple. And he loved me!"

She lifted her head again. "I had taken him for a subtle adventurer, a man with a technique! He had all the uninteresting virtues of a country cousin. He was afraid of life. So I ran away—ran away, expecting him to follow me. Any man of spirit would have followed me, wouldn't he?

"And what do you fancy I did to that ridiculous fellow? Apparently, I broke his heart! He tried to drown himself and was saved by the gardener, who picked him out of a fountain where he was lying face down in less than a foot of water. Then he tried to shoot himself and shot his secretary instead. That cost him a thousand pounds. I wrote him that I was fed up. He wasn't romantic, and never would be. I wanted a divorce. So he divorced me, and disappeared. Oh, quite vanished! And was never heard from again—not from that day to this. It was the first dramatic thing he'd ever done."

A strange thought came to me: "Suppose it were Archer?" But I held my tongue.

Lady Palmerston stretched her arms over her head and lifted her chin so that I could see her throat.

"I believe you're in love with him," I said.

She closed her eyes. "I am. I want him back."

And one afternoon the *Anne Beebe* drifted down upon Archer's island. It was a still, polished day. The palms stood upside down in the water. You could see the pink coral on the sea bottom and little shivering clouds of fish and swaying weed. A canoe came out from the lagoon, and I sent Archer's mail ashore with word that I had as passenger an English lady who would like to see his "place." Archer's boy came back, bearing a formal invitation to dinner.

I didn't show the written words to Lady Palmerston. You understand, I wanted a proper climax. And I could see that she was taken with the suspicion that haunted me. She looked off at the gaudy island, her eyes aslant with her own peculiar mischief; then she went below to dress for this unique occasion. I expected a toilette, but when she came on deck again she was dazzling. The *Anne Beebe* had never seen the likes of her before. She wore a sort of slip girdled with a gilt ribbon. For the rest a band of brilliants around her hair, a flame-coloured scarf, and little gilt slippers strapped over her instep. For the first time I saw her bare shoulders whiter than the surf breaking on the reef. The crew was goggle-eyed. So, for that matter, was I.

It was dusk when I lifted her out of the whale-boat and set her down on the beach. She had the English way of being unconscious of her incongruity. moving through the crowd of Paumotuans as if they, not she, were out of the picture.

"The women are ugly," she said once.

The hanging lamp had been lighted in Archer's veranda, and as we came up the shell walk we saw him waiting to receive us, impeccable as ever. There must have been something familiar in the figure at my side, for he opened the screened door and came down the steps. Then she advanced into the circle of light, and I saw what it was he had run away from. He was still, as if his very heart, his very soul, listened for the familiar music of that woman. His face, scarred by hidden passions, seemed more than ever impenetrable, but there was a look in his eyes of a thirsty man who sees a pool of cold water, a dying man who glimpses Paradise, a sleeping man awakened.

"This is Lady Palmerston," I said.

They stood motionless, held apart by amazement.

"Palmerston," she said.

Her hand went out to him and he caught it, drawing her forward until he could look down into the audacious face she lifted. She was smiling.

"Are you glad to see me?"

He bent and whispered: "No, no!" Then he caught her close to him and kissed her, as I'd often wanted to kiss her, with hate, with passion, with disdain.

Her hands on his shoulders, she pushed him away and they stood staring at each other. Incongruous, there in the striped shadows of the coco trees, in the bottomless cup of silence. . . .

"You're not being polite, Bobs," she said. "You asked us to dinner——"

I stayed. Things like that don't happen every day to a trader.

Lady Palmerston explained lightly: "My—my ex-husband. You probably guessed. It's all very amusing. Poor old Bobs! He fancied he had lost me."

"I ran as far as I could," Archer said.

I saw him behind ten thousand miles and more of empty sea. This time she had him!

She sat at his table, the light from the candle set in an inverted coconut husk striking little sparks in the brilliants that bound her hair. The Paumotuan woman offered her unpalatable dishes, but she never seemed to encounter that mystified, shy glance.

She chattered of places and people, throwing her little barbs into his skin. He winced and said nothing, his eyes burning when they rested on her. She spoke of Paris and London and Sussex—drawing-rooms, theatres, personalities, English summers—wooing him. Oh, decidedly wooing him! Little wretch! Little humbug! She liked him now that he had eluded her, you see. I, who knew the formulæ of her magic, pitied him. It must have been so deadly stale, so deadly familiar.

And Palmerston listened, tempted. I dare say he could smell his Sussex hedgerows and hear the dear familiar music of his London streets. I dare say every word she said fell on his heart like a blow. But he knew her for what she was. No talk of adventuring now! She wanted him back again at any price, even Sussex and life on a gentleman's farm.

Coffee finished, Archer—or Palmerston—lighted a cigarette and, holding it carefully between thumb and forefinger, said: "Now that you're here, Margaret, you'd better stay."

She got up and walked about the veranda, slowly, turning her head this way and that. She stood by the screens, seeming to let the silence flow about her, while we stared. She examined the mats, the ugly furniture. Her eyes were quick and scornful. She made all that childish savagery, that happy simplicity, seem trivial and absurd.

"Stay here?" she demanded. "Impossible!"

She came back to him and touched his hair lightly with the tips of her fingers. In his eyes I saw what a tumult this fugitive caress had caused.

"You're coming back with me."

He shook his head.

"You're coming back with me," she said again. "This! You'll die of remembering, here. Oh, my dear! I'm so sorry. . . . My fault. . . . I've wanted you."

"Have you?"

Their eyes met, and I tell you his look made me shiver.

It was too much for me. I got up, breaking in with a polite, "You'll excuse me, perhaps?" and left them there together. I don't believe Archer saw me go. He opened the door for me and pretended to watch me until the shadows swallowed me up.

I went at once to the schooner. The *Anne Beebe* lay just beyond the lagoon, two or three hundred yards from shore. Looking back, I could see the lighted veranda. God knows what went on there between those two.

Perhaps I was jealous. I remember being uneasy, overstrung, shaken by that bitter kiss I had seen and the look in Archer's eyes. I waited on deck, pacing up and down, peering over the side, straining into the darkness—there was no moon—until after two o'clock. I heard nothing but the persistent thunder of breakers. I listened for Archer's hail and the dip of his paddle along side.

Finally I heard it: "Hallo!" A patch of white appeared on the smooth blackness of the water. A canoe slipped up to the side-ladder and, looking over, I saw Archer in his shirt-sleeves. He was alone.

"*Anna Beebe,*" he said in a guarded voice.

"Captain Armstrong," I whispered.

He came up, head and shoulders appearing over the rail suddenly, like an apparition. Then his whole body, dripping wet. He was in his stockinged feet. His hair was plastered down on his forehead. His mouth hung open. While he stood there, a pool of water formed around him.

"What on earth has happened?" I demanded, still whispering, as if we two were conspirators.

He grasped my shoulders with both hands and dug his fingers in.

"She's dead," he said, and began to shiver.

"Who?"

He bent his head, fighting for control.

I knew, of course.

He pointed. "On the reef. Over! Both of us. I couldn't save her." He drew himself up and added: "I tried!"

Stepping back, I shook myself free of his hands and ran to the side. His canoe had drifted clear and was circling in an invisible current.

Suddenly, behind me, he said: "I'm alone again."

That's all. Not a word of explanation. No defence. He stood there shivering until I brought

him a drink. Then I got him to my cabin—her cabin
—and he lay on the embroidered coverlet, his face
pressed into the scented pillows, his hands clenched
over his head. After a while he slept and sobbed in
his sleep. I woke him and questioned him again.
She was dead. That gaudy little fish had been carried
away from him and broken on the reef, broken and
perhaps tossed up clear on the beach. Perhaps.
He would look in the morning. It was, he whispered,
terrible—unavoidable—abominable. . . . He asked
for whiskey and drank it, shivering and gulping.

Suddenly jerking himself upright, he laughed:
"Not romantic in London. . . . Everybody—dresses
for dinner."

"Here," I said sharply, "talk sense."

"That's sense," he assured me. "Sense. Profound. The whole reason. Oh, my God! Terrible."

At dawn he got unsteadily to his feet and began
stripping off his clothes, the water-soaked ruin of that
famous dress suit. Naked as Adam he went on deck
and stood there, blinking at his Paradise. I have no
doubt—not a doubt in the world—that he had tipped
that devilish Lilith out of his canoe. He was going
back to Eve and the yellow progeny, to mediocrity,
to security. Oh! he was the most romantic man I've
ever known, that innocent murderer with the face of
the devil! All he wanted, I'm sure, was a peaceful
home life.

He slipped into the water, shook his head and
stretched himself. The sun was coming up, flat and

golden as a king's dish.   Archer swam away with slow strokes, and I saw the blue shadow of him, foreshortened and contorted, moving along the bottom of the sea. . . .

THE BRIDGE

THE Kinneys have run through my life like a scarlet thread across a grey tapestry. Theirs was one of the "great romances," and it was my luck to see the beginning, the middle, and end of that famous, that infamous, affair.

Kinney I knew before the encounter at Cortina d'Ampezzo which brought us together, if not as intimate friends, at least as conspirators. I had seen him in and out of London for several years. He was fairly young, very dynamic, almost, if not quite, an intellectual, with the most charming manners in the world and everything on God's green earth to live for. He was the seventh son of an earl's seventh son, or something of that sort. Not titled, but quite top-notch, with an easy familiarity with good things and an amiable assumption of careless superiority. Nice fellow. He had made a name for himself in the engineering world, and in that society which crowns the builders of bridges he had already won his laurels. He was "made," not in the making. It was well on the books that he would marry the seventh daughter of an earl's seventh son, and die eventually with many great bridges to his credit and no stain on his excellent name. But there was a queer streak in him, an unexpected eccentricity, a wilfulness that was almost "artistic." He ran off with the beautiful wife of an .M.P.—Lady Esther Milward—and most everlastingly blighted that career of his. I crossed his path at the moment of the blighting.

I had gone to Cortina a little in advance of the tourist season, in order to climb unmolested by amateurs and to enjoy the undivided attention of Simone, who was the best guide in the village. The Faloria was open, and a few guests came into the dining-room on the night of my arrival. Kinney was sitting at a table by the window. He nodded and flushed when he caught sight of me.

"Webb! Glad to see you!"

We shook hands. I thought he seemed in very high spirits. "Bridge building?" I queried.

He laughed. "Hardly. Walking."

"The Stelvio?"

"Not this time. We're going through the valley."

"Ah! Then you're not alone?"

He flushed again. "Yes. That is—I'm expecting some one."

I went on to my table, thinking: "Then he won't want to share Simone. I shall be left in peace."

During dinner I watched him, amused by his air of distraction. I knew nothing about Lady Esther Milward then; had never heard of her or of Kinney's infatuation. Up to this point they must have been singularly circumspect. Fifteen years ago married women were rather more circumspect, to begin with! As Kinney sat there in the big, half-empty dining-room of that Austrian hotel, he was very "typical," very English, very correct, bearing the unmistakable patina of generations of correct behaviour. You could no more imagine him doing a shocking thing, tearing the conventions into tatters, than you could imagine him kicking a dog or beating a child.

After dinner we met on the terrace and strolled up and down in a transparent twilight, smoking, our feet crunching pleasantly on the gravel walks. The Tre Croce kindled in the glow of the sun even then setting behind the Venetian lagoons. But the valley was as full of purple shadows as a cup of wine, and little lights twinkled down there in shops and *châlets*.

Kinney took a deep breath of the sweet air scented with clover, crocus, and larch. "Glorious place. Beautiful." He stopped short, and with his hands in his pockets stared off at the mountains. "I may as well tell you," he said. "You'll know it sooner or later. Lady Esther Milward, Frank Milward's wife, is coming out here to join me. We're going to walk into Italy together, and then we're going to Florence to settle down."

"Just like that?" I asked frivolously.

"Well, yes—just like that."

"My dear fellow, why do you feel it necessary to tell me?" I inquired, suddenly serious.

"Because she's coming tomorrow and there'll be the devil to pay—the newspapers, and all the rest of it."

"Oh, if you think I'd have scruples——"

He glanced quickly at me. "After tomorrow, I won't have to make explanations. But you—why, you're rather caught unawares. I thought I'd give you your opportunity."

"To snub you? Thanks awfully." I scrutinized his face, gone white with a sudden emotion. "You're not very sure that it's going to work, then—I mean, for your own happiness?"

"Absolutely sure," he said sharply. He nodded, tossed his cigarette away into the dew-laden grass, and stalked off.

I saw him hesitate in the lighted doorway of the hotel. Then he went in, his thin, tall body silhouetted —very English, very correct. I paced the terrace an hour longer, wondering what forces had driven him to this stupendous piece of folly. It is easy enough to imagine a Latin carried away by passion into the maelstrom of social defeat and professional failure. But Kinney's passions were so far below the surface that one doubted their existence; he was Anglo-Saxon in the essence; yet here he was, doing the sort of thing that isn't done, and doing it as if there were an unalterable justification. There was. I felt sure of it when I saw Esther Milward. . . .

It was raining in the morning, so I regretfully dismissed Simone and, getting into the camel's-hair cape and feather-ornamented hat which it amused me to affect in Austria, I swung down the steep hill to the village and followed the high road along the valley. Just this side of Alta Croce, to my surprise, I overtook Kinney and the woman who had come out from England to "go down into Italy" with him. They were walking slowly, one on one side of the road, one on the other, splashing through puddles, laughing; I thought, until I came abreast, that they were a German honeymoon couple off for a lark. Both wore packs and carried sticks. Their shoes were already caked with mud, their clothes dripping. Kinney turned when he heard my footsteps, and I saw his eyes alight with some magnificent resolve.

"Webb, again!"

The woman stopped, too, easing her heavy pack with a quick shrug of her shoulders. She smiled, but did not offer me her hand at Kinney's introduction. I was embarrassed. They were not! I fancy Kinney must have told her of our conversation on the terrace the night before. And since I could not decently turn back, I went on with them, walking between them, a caped and hatted serpent in their Paradise. There was no wind; the rain was like a heavy mist; it clung to our clothes—big, white drops, clear as quicksilver—and wet our faces and powdered our hair. Particularly did it powder Esther Milward's hair, like crystal sequins on spun gold. She was beautiful, as indeed she had to be to justify the look in Kinney's eyes. Small and light, she walked like a young girl, swinging from the hips, with her shoulders back and her head high. Her eyes were dark brown, hiding her thoughts. But her mouth told all her secrets— she was fearless and passionate, thoughtless and fascinating, generous and perhaps not quite honest. Her mouth, I saw, was what had come between Kinney and his respectable laurels.

"Did you follow us?" she asked impetuously.

"No," I said decidedly.

"Then it's all right. You know we're doing an unusual thing."

"I know."

"You'll hear a lot about it, I dare say. I telegraphed my husband this morning. Oh, there'll be a horrid scandal."

"Probably."

She laughed, with a sidelong flash of her beautiful eyes. "You're not very pleasant, are you?"

"Do you want me to disagree with you?"

"No. Only I feel strangely moved to explain myself to you. Coming upon us like this, in the first moments of our adventure."

"But, my dear lady, I'm not curious! I'm only being polite. Now that I've gone a little way, I'll turn back."

She put out her hand. "I'd like to tell you——"

"Please don't."

"Oh, not the whole story! I'm not such an idiot. Only this: I'm *happy*." She reached across and took Kinney's hand, their eyes meeting with a sort of triumph, a light, as if a flame had been kindled. "It's going to be a success. . . ."

"I hope so," I said, and bared my head to the mist. "Good-bye, and good luck."

I stood in the muddy road, watching them go, hand in hand, towards Italy. They climbed a short hill between rows of long-branched larch. Beyond them the mountains were black and soaked, deprived of ruby and coral and gold. Once they turned and waved. Then the hill dipped under them and they were gone.

I did not see them again for ten years. Then one day I ran into Kinney on the Lung 'Arno, in Florence —the same Kinney, grown a little grey, but thin and springy and typical as ever. He recognized me in passing and stopped short, flushing, as he had flushed that evening in ′Cortina. He need not have stopped, since I had, by glancing aside at the river, given him first choice. But he seemed genuinely glad to see me, as if the sight of an Englishman in deserted mid-summer Florence were an exciting event. It never occurred to me that he might be socially starved. He had married Lady Milward, and ten years had worn off the rough edges of their scandal. I had not heard them spoken of in London for five years. Milward had risen to fame—like the dear old proverbial phœnix leaping from the ashes of his dead love—and had never remarried. That, at least, I could under-stand. There could not be two such mouths as Esther Milward's in the world. Milward kept his son, since it was manifestly impossible to send a ten-year-old boy out to that Italian Paradise where his mother lived in flagrant happiness with the second man of her choice. . . .

I thought of Milward and of Milward's son as I stood talking to Kinney on the sunny Lung' Arno. How had Kinney managed *them*—imaginatively? After all, the Milwards *père* and *fils,* were keeping Kinney out here where he didn't belong, where he never would belong.

He was wearing an easy suit of tweed clothes and smoking a pipe. There was not a trace of ironic modern Italy in his face. The same well-controlled romanticism in his brown eyes; the same sensitive and proud mouth. . . . An exile!

"You'll come out to our place, of course?" he asked eagerly. "We're not far from Settignano—a small house, but an astonishing view of the city and some fine old cypresses."

"I'm leaving Florence tomorrow," I said.

"Then come tonight. I've got lots to talk about. You know I'm not bridge-building any more. I've rather gone in for art collecting, and all that. Make a sort of study of the primitives. I'd like to show you what I've found."

There was such a begging in his voice that I said quickly: "I'll come, of course. How shall I find you?"

He explained in detail, drawing a rough map on the stone parapet to show me where the tram stopped and where I would find the path leading from the high road to their villa, Il Tramonto.

"Come before sunset," he said. "The view's magnificent."

I promised and he swung away, keeping, it seemed on purpose, the sunny side of the street, in defiance of Italian custom which hugs the shadow during the blistering white days of August. Kinney might have been strolling along a mist-soaked Devon down between fragrant hedgerows. Yet all about him the heat fumes quivered and shimmered, and the stone pavements burned beneath his feet. He was making the best of a bargain, but I had no way of telling whether it was good or bad, lean or fat. And I was, I admit, curious.

I spent the day in the damp galleries of the Pitti, tiptoeing down shining acres of polished floor—a lonely tourist gaping at serried rows of indifferent masterpieces. Then, seeing that the sun was already gathering about itself the golden mists of the Arno, I crossed the city and took the tram to Settignano. Kinney's map had been very explicit—he had always been a superlative draughtsman!—so that I found the path to his villa just where he had said it would be: "Behind a farmhouse, through a gate painted green and then follow the cypress alley."

I thought, as I climbed slowly up between the sombre, flanking trees: "Beauty! That, at any rate, they have." The dark green tips, very far above me, gilded by the light of the setting sun, seemed to trace invisible spirals upon a sky the colour of turquoise, opaque, and flawless. The house stood upon a double terrace and was approached by wing-shaped stone steps. Glancing up, I saw Kinney and his wife leaning on the terrace railing and staring off at the valley. The sunlight was on them, too, and as they stood there shoulder to shoulder, they were like gilded effigies, perhaps a god and goddess of love or happiness. His arm was around her and they were still, as if listening to the beating of their own hearts. The perverse thought came to me: "Ten years of this! Good Lord, how awful! . . ."

Esther Milward had changed. At first, when I clasped her hand and saw that fascinating mouth again, I couldn't be sure—she wasn't visibly older; darker, perhaps—Italy had done *that* much. I had seen her first in an Austrian mist, with her face stung by raindrops and her hair a-glitter with them—a muddy, radiant, daring woman face to face with love. Now she was wearing a black velvet dress girdled with jet, and long jet earrings set in gold dangled from her ears. It was charming, stunning, but a shade too artistic for Lady Milward. As Mrs. Kinney, she was playing a new rôle—she, too, was a lover in exile. And in the meeting of our eyes she challenged me: "I'm happy! I told you I would be. I told you I'd make a success of it. I have. I have, d'you hear?"

Well, outwardly, it was perfect. We stood on the terrace, politely unconscious of the "drama" again, staring off at the Dome, the towers and the palaces, beautiful stone flowers dusted with the pollen of yellow twilight. A cuckoo was singing in the young cypresses of Vincigliata, and somewhere in the shadowy garden beneath us a fountain gushed and rippled over the worn, stone lips of an old basin.

"Splendid, isn't it?" Kinney demanded. "Beautiful! Eh?"

Mrs. Kinney turned away with an abrupt gesture. "Let's go in. It's rather too beautiful."

"Esther prefers England," Kinney said.

She gave him a quick look. "But I don't!"

"My dear, have you forgotten——?"

"Oh, I said this was *obvious*. Even sunsets can be rococo. . . ."

They laughed, and Kinney caught her hand, giving her fingers a long pressure.

She had outdone herself in my behalf. The dining-room was full of yellow roses. The table had been set with strips of crimson brocade and purple glass. I had an unpleasant feeling that I personified her world, and that Esther Milward, Mrs. Kinney, meant to dazzle me. All this brave show of form and finish was to prove that there had been no backsliding, even in exile. Even, I would better say, in Paradise! And they didn't know, poor mortals, poor lovers, that the rest of the world had forgotten them!

I would have been surer of their victory if they had dined me according to their custom—on the terrace, very *al fresco* indeed. The Italian maid-servant was scared and awkward. The cook came to the door to peer in at this unusual elegance. And the food was a bad imitation of English food.

Kinney, very erect and, I think, uncomfortable in his evening clothes, watched the bungling servant, wincing visibly when she passed behind his chair. Esther ignored everything and every one but me. Tense and watchful, with burning eyes, she strove to hold my attention away from the details, to hold me down to the facts of her triumph. She had Kinney; she had Italy; she was still beautiful. . . . In the candle-light her shoulders and arms were flawless, cool as ivory, and her brown eyes were provocative and her mouth smiled. She wasn't a great woman, but she was a plucky one. She seemed to be balancing her happiness in both hands for me to see. "I have this, and this, and this. . . ."

After dinner she wandered away into the big, shadowy sala, and with a cigarette between her lips sat down at the piano. Kinney spoke irritably in Italian to the servant and she went out, banging the door.

"Damned nuisance, food!" he said. "Let's look at my treasures."

He had them in the library—an immense, un-carpeted room, without windows, which must have been built quite recently. The walls were lined with books, papered with them, from floor to ceiling. Only one wall was reserved for the paintings that came and went for Kinney's inspection. He had, it seemed, become quite an "expert." He could, in the mysteri-ous manner of such experts, tell a bogus from a real Piero de Cosimo by the mere brushing of his Anglo-Saxon nose over the surface of the canvas. He had "discovered" a new Botticelli in a farmhouse some-where; had pounced upon the skull of Santa Chiara and declared it a substitute for the real skull, which he maintained was hidden within a terra-cotta bust of the saint at Sienna. He owned a veritable and quite marvellous Luini. Framed in black and gold, it stood on the mantel-shelf, and he took it down to show me the exquisite surfaces, letting me run my finger over the Madonna's face and trace the faultless outlines of fruits and leaves and twisted tendril vines.

"You must wonder," he said, "that I could interest myself in this sort of thing. I don't take gracefully to idleness. When we came down here I cast about for something to do. I was through with engineering for good. Couldn't stick it." His eyes wavered and he put the Luini back, standing a little away to stare at it while he talked. "I fell in with an American who lives here—an enthusiast. He knows more about the early fellows than the Italians themselves. I used to walk with him up into the hill towns and little villages, stalking masterpieces. By jove, it got me! I began to study. Found I had a sort of *flair* for it. After all, success is only a matter of enthusiasm. . . ."

His voice trailed off and he stood there sucking at his pipe, staring at the placid Madonna. I saw him in his early days, watching the growth of great bridges that straddled hills and waded rivers, with the rattle and shriek of cranes and winches, donkey engines and riveters in his ears, and his little army of workers turning to him for the word, and pride in his heart.

He moved away and unlocked a cabinet to show me a dish carved, he said, by Benvenuto Cellini. "Found it in a reduced nobleman's china closet," he explained, dusting it off. "These Italians will sell anything."

"Don't you like them, then?"

He frowned. "I don't understand them," he said. "Funny beggars! The new school is arrogant, mad, decadent, and modern in a breath. The old school is conservative, pious, stupid. I fall between two stools here. I've made few friends. To begin with, I speak Italian abominably, and I despise their English

—somehow I can't respect a man who speaks with an accent." He lifted his head suddenly. "By jove, I'd like to get back to England!"

"Why don't you?"

"Go back?" he asked with a startled look.

"Yes."

"Oh, I couldn't——"

He hesitated, seeing his wife in the doorway. She came towards us, smiling, one hand on her hip, the other still holding a cigarette. "You couldn't what, dear?" she asked.

He faced her. "Go home to England."

She looked from his flushed face to me, the smile unchanging, as if she hadn't courage enough to alter her expression. "But I thought that was settled," she said. "This was to be home. We weren't to go back, ever."

"We aren't going back."

"But you said——"

She caught her breath, as if she felt herself on the brink of a precipice. A look of sickness passed across her face, an almost visible shiver of the spirit. She slipped her arm through Kinney's and leaned against him. "I thought, for a minute, you were unhappy," she whispered.

"Nonsense!" Kinney's voice was loud and re-assuring. "I have just been confessing to Webb my complete, my triumphant, happiness."

She met my eyes. "I came in to tell you," she said, "that there's going to be a moon. Shall we go outside?"

Kinney followed us reluctantly, lingering to put out the electric reflectors that blazed upon his treasures. A moon had indeed come out of the mountains, very yellow and a little one-sided, after the manner of old moons. And now there were nightingales in the woods.

"I'm very proud of him," Esther said, leaning on the stone railing and tossing her cigarette down into the shadowy garden.

"He seems to have done awfully well."

"I want them to know—the people who hurt him, because of me."

Kinney came to the door and, seeing us, seemed to hesitate. Mrs. Kinney whispered to me: "Are you going straight back to England?"

Surprised, I answered: "Yes."

"Will you take a letter to my son?"

"My dear Mrs. Kinney, surely there is some other way?"

She shook her head with a sort of desperate anger. "No, no! They won't give him my letters."

Kinney had gone into the house again. Mrs. Kinney covered her face with her hands and for a moment shivered uncontrollably. Then she straightened and I saw her face, changed and old, no longer watchful but distraught.

"Did I startle you?" she asked. "I'm sorry. Only I was afraid I hadn't time to ask you, so I bolted. Don't think I haven't written my son. I have. And twice he answered. Once from his school; a funny letter: 'Dear Mumsie,' and a lot of school gossip, and, 'I hope you are well.' Then, again, a year or so ago. He was in Switzerland with his tutor. Lately —nothing."

She lifted her beautiful head and met my eyes. "He's twenty, you know. A darling. He must be a darling."

"Of course. But aren't you asking too much of him?"

"You mean——"

"He has his allegiances. After all, he's there, and you're here, in Italy."

She looked beyond me, her expression changing. Kinney was coming out again with her wrap over his arm. And what she did for him was miraculous, magnificent. Literally, she grew young again, as if she were forcing her pain and bitterness back into her inner consciousness, out of Kinney's sight. Her lips smiled. The old love swam into her eyes, caressing him as he came towards her. Her body was mysteriously triumphant, dedicated to him. I have never seen a more insolent gesture. She meant to say, and said louder than words, that she, at least, had not failed. Oh, she held him to it! I thought, as he put the wrap around her shoulders: "She wants her son and he wants his bridges."

They had, instead, the Italian moon. It topped the hills and sailed low in the amber sky, filling the valley with a sort of ghostly moonlight, dim and strange. Esther Milward slipped her arm through Kinney's, and we walked up and down the terrace, our voices sounding very loud and out of place in that spot made for lutes and whisperings, that alien loveliness.

When I left, Kinney walked to the tram, carrying a primitive *contadino's* lantern to light us safely through the sombre tunnel of the cypress alley. To the last he was very gay, very friendly. I'll be hanged if I know whether he was aware of his own tragedy or not. Once he said: "I dare say there's been lots of talk about us?"

"Not recently. After all, there's nothing more to be said."

"Ah!" He flourished the lantern. "You see, we proved it!"

"Proved what?"

"Why, that every one has a right to happiness! A right. Incontrovertible! Only people don't dare. They prefer to be unhappy in safety. Cowards." He caught my hand and shook it violently. "Here's your tram. Good-bye. It's been jolly, seeing you again."

As the lighted car rumbled back towards the city between high villa walls and olive groves, I thought of Kinney stumbling up the path between the cypresses, his shadow, cast by that capering lantern, looming gigantic and grotesque by his side.

Esther would be waiting on the terrace: and he would lean there, close to her, staring off at sleeping Florence, old Florence, secretive and elusive Florence, city of stone flowers.

And the damnable part of it would be that no one would know and no one, not even Sir Frank Milward, M.P., would care!

I am not trying to prove anything. To me it is a matter of supreme indifference whether they did right or wrong. I am only interested in recording, for the benefit of romantic women and sceptical men, my own impression of that "great affair." Undoubtedly they did a shocking thing. Esther Milward shrugged her lovely shoulders and turned her back on a faultless husband and a charming child—she herself said, you remember, that her son *must* be charming—to take what she wanted of happiness. Kinney betrayed his code and smashed his idols and tore off his gilded laurels. Neither of them had seemed particularly desperate; they were not even dramatic in the manner of their going. Remember, I saw them, plodding hand in hand through the rain, with that look in their eyes of a smouldering light. . . .

And then the deluge! Her family summoning her back, demanding her back, threatening, denouncing; Milward's family preserving an icy silence and snatching his son, Esther's son, away to their Kentish seat, where they intended to hold him against "that outrageous woman," his mother. Kinney's family vaguely apologetic and eager to mend matters. A deluge of letters sent post-haste to Italy—letters from bishops and curates, lawyers and friends, business associates and relatives. Milward, M.P., being patted consolingly on the back in the House. Talk, talk, talk! And all the while those two were at Venice, at Verona, at Florence. . . . How shall I say what beauty they had? What kisses flavoured with the bitter-sweetness of long denial? They had made their choice, and perhaps neither of them thought about, or cared, for the future.

There are times when the present is complete enough. . . . I can see them dining in little restaurants on the lagoon—August, in Venice—with a bottle of red wine between them and a soft-eyed Italian waiter tending them with a sort of worship, and their gondola outside, the gondolier asleep, waiting patiently for the time when he should take them across to the Lido, smiling in the dark at their secret laughter, winking at their silences. I can see them, later, in Florence, where their letters and telegrams must have caught up with them—for even happiness cannot outstrip offended morality. They probably laughed at the breakfast table; Esther excited and secretly pleased at her own audacity; Kinney silent and flushed, with stormy eyes.

"Confounded impudence, all of it. As if our lives weren't our own!"

Esther would make a little grimace. "Let them talk. We can afford to be generous—even with our reputations."

"But we have done nothing."

I can imagine her running around the breakfast-table to put her hand over his mouth. "Don't begin to question *now*, my dear!"

And then together they probably read Milward's dignified epistles, offering forgiveness, promising to "overlook" what so patently loomed larger than either his goodwill or his charity.

I can imagine them holding their heads high, rather

stimulated by curious stares and whisperings. I dare say there were people who envied them, and people who imitated them, and people who felt a morbid delight in their revolt. And while the scandal lasted they must have felt very superior and enlightened— prophets, standard bearers, brave martyrs to the cause of personal liberty. . . .

Strangely enough, as I had read the first page of the romance, so I read the last.

I had gone to the Italian lakes for a brief vacation —quite out of season, for Como is hot as blazes in August. And, of course, I encountered the Kinneys in the garden of my hotel. I say of course, since it is a trick of destiny that we never taste the wine of life that we do not drain it to the last drop. All the loose ends are gathered up; all the bow-knots neatly tied. Existence seems to revolve like a wheel; sooner or later we complete the revolution. I was not sur- prised to see the Kinneys, only amazed at what five years had done to them. . . .

Kinney was apparently very ill. He was sitting in a wheel chair with a rug thrown over his knees— the shadow of that springy, brown self! Esther was scarcely older, but she was too bright and eager to be convincing.

"And here we are again," Kinney said, giving me his hand. I felt the faint pressure of his thin, cold fingers. "I've been ill," he explained. "We had to leave Florence."

"I want him to go higher—to Switzerland," Esther said quickly.

Kinney shook his head. "No, no. Not out of Italy."

I stayed with them until dinner-time, when a servant came and wheeled Kinney away to his room. After dinner Esther followed me into the garden again. She had removed her hat and thrown a filmy white scarf over her hair, twisting it around her throat. In the twilight I thought she seemed younger than ever, almost beautiful—not simply but feverishly beautiful, as if she clung to her loveliness with defiance, as if it were the only symbol of her triumph, the only proof of her rightness.

"Well," she said, "this is the end."

"Are you sure?"

"Quite. There's no hope. Not a vestige. And he won't leave Italy."

"Is that your fault?"

"My fault?" Her eyes met mine with a flash of fear and anger.

"Haven't you insisted on exile?"

"You mean I should have let him go?"

"Shouldn't you?"

"To England?" She shuddered and turned her back, staring across the dark lake at the diamond-strung lights of Belaggio. "No! He was happier here." She faced me again with a violent gesture. "You don't believe it? Then ask him! Ask him!"

"My dear lady, he would lie to me."

"But not to me!"

"To you most of all."

"I gave up everything for him—position, friends,

security. My son. My son, d'you hear? I haven't seen my son for fifteen years! He's twenty-five now. He fought in France—oh, splendidly! And I couldn't even be proud of him. What's that to——" She caught her breath.

"To bridges?"

She turned away from me again, pressing the tips of her fingers against her closed eyes.

"Yes," she whispered, after a moment, "to bridges."

I did not answer, and presently she said, with a sharp laugh: "And I loved him so!"

That was all. She brushed aside the rather perilous moment with a sweep of both arms and let me see that I had said, if not too much, at least quite enough. I might never have heard that bitter summary at all, she changed the subject so adroitly, so expertly. She asked for a cigarette, and, puffing it, strolled up and down the narrow garden paths at my side, the warm wind fluttering the ends of her scarf. I felt suddenly poignantly sorry for Kinney, lying upstairs in that hotel bedroom, face to face with the pigmy shadow that had been such a magnificent illusion. For a moment the Alps seemed to blot out the sky, an insuperable barrier between Kinney and England. . . .

"He'll have to build a bridge," I said aloud.

"What?" Mrs. Kinney demanded.

I stammered, confused by my pity: "I beg your pardon. Nothing."

But that exactly is what Kinney did.

The next morning, coming down to a solitary

breakfast of coffee and rolls, I learned that Kinney had died during the night.

"The poor gentleman got out of his bed," the waiter said, "and went to the balcony. They found him there an hour ago. Just like in life. His eyes open—so—and looking, or seeming to look, at the mountains."

Later I saw Esther Milward. Her eyes were hard and bright. She held herself erect before my sympathy.

"And what," I asked, "will you do?"

She met my glance without flinching. "I am going to England," she answered, " to see my son."

"Ah!" I said quickly. "Kinney built you a bridge."

Esther Milward shrugged her shoulders. "I'm sorry," she said. "I've no idea what you mean!"

But she had.

THE LOTUS AT MITCHELL HOUSE

MITCHELL inherited the plantation from his grandfather, a South Carolinian planter of the old school who had outlived his own sons, as he had outlived his own times.

Mitchell was globe-trotting when he got the news. To be exact, he was in Tibet, the least likely place you would have expected to find him. He was a restless man given to long fits of abstraction, not always good company. In his rare moments of expressiveness he attached to himself all sorts of devoted friends. If this won't "give" him to you, I will try, later, to make him clearer.

The story begins with the plantation. A letter from old Blaisdell, Mitchell's lawyers in Charleston, caught up with young Mitchell in Lhassa. The envelope was a brilliant mosaic of cancelled stamps. The sight of it recalled Mitchell to a world of facts. He was staying at the moment with a Tibetan gentleman of varied culture and high caste, who had promised to disclose to him the mystery of the Dalai Lama, the true story of Mangu, the intricacies of Buddhistic monasticism, the extraordinary tale of the British invasion, and other manifold, absorbing things. It had taken Mitchell some time to fashion himself into the confidant of a Tibetan gentleman. He had been patient, painstaking, tactful.

And now, into the languor and excitement of the moment, came the letter.

The plantation was his.   And, secondly, his grandfather was dead.

That meant he must hurry to Hongkong, and get aboard the first ship that would take him back to America.   He knew that his wandering days were over.

He had begun to feel himself a modern Marco Polo, lover of China, holding the half-furled lotus bloom between his hands.   He was drowsy with so much beauty; the ringing of bells, the aromatic sweetness of incense, temples, images, priests, sunlight—a pageantry not wholly beyond his comprehension, for he loved strangeness above all things. At thirty-five he had already had more than the usual allotment, perhaps because he had gone in pursuit of the strange with more than the usual enthusiasm.   He was a great adventurer.

He bade the Tibetan gentleman good-bye, and went at once to Hongkong.   Characteristically, he felt that the moment had been spoiled.   To peer into the heart of the lotus required time; all of life, perhaps.   He would not pry the leaves back!   At Lhassa he left his curiosity and, like Polo, his affection, his belief in something hidden, miraculous, illusory, wonderful—something only guessed at.

At Hongkong there was a wait of a few days. He spent the time very comfortably in a first-rate hotel, where he had a shower and as many whiskey-and-sodas as he needed, but rather too many tourists.

In order not to break rudely into his mood, he prowled about the town, sniffing China. He was saying good-bye to an old enthusiasm; for all he knew, he would never come back. The Mitchell plantation—Mitchell House—was more than an inheritance, it was a tradition. He would grow and sell rice, as his fathers before him. And the future involved more than following in his grandfather's, his father's footsteps; the roots of the affair reached into his consciousness, tangled and complicated— religious, social, romantic.

Well, he was ready! Only he felt that something had been denied him. He had counted on his grandfather's living until he himself was forty. He saw, now, that he had been too leisurely.

The little streets of Hongkong were as fascinating as little stories; Mitchell followed them eagerly, turning corner after corner as you turn page after page. He was going to Manila in the morning aboard a Chinese steamer of dubious reputation. But at Manila, he knew, he could get a decent passage to America.

Mitchell was swinging through an alleyway in an unsavoury quarter, when he became suddenly conscious that he was the only person in sight. This was unusual enough to startle him. The shifting greys and blues had melted into other alleys, into doorways, and he was advancing alone down a muddy, malodorous cañon between stained and toppling walls.

Then he saw the reason. A murder was being done.

Two men were beating a third man to death in the open doorway of a shop. Mitchell saw the brutal fact and all the details at first glance. Before he could turn back he was a witness, and, as a witness, considering his type, implicated. He could have scuttled back to the "foreign quarter." He could have melted, like the grey and blue crowds. But he saw what he saw.

The man who was dying was little and weak. He made feeble efforts to live; his clawlike hands struck out, clutched, at nothing; his mouth was open and his tongue protruded, black, swollen. Mitchell was not armed, but he flung himself at the two who were doing this ghastly business, and, using an art he had learned in Japan, tied them in agonizing bow-knots, flung them into the mud, dragged the little man inside the shop and closed the door.

He was half an hour bringing him to. He had to wheedle the life into that feeble body; inch by inch to beckon it back. A Chinaman dead. Just like a Chinaman alive, Mitchell decided! Yellow cheeks, deep lids, emaciated neck, hands like the skinny, tapering hands of a ghost—mysterious people! He supposed that he'd be mobbed when he opened the door again. But now, as he laboured to blow the flame into that handful of bones and parchment, there was no sound outside save the usual pad and shuffle of feet back and forth and the gulping, bubbling sing-song that in China is speech. The door remained closed.

The shop, if such it was, came out of the shadows, corner by corner, a place stuffed with junk, a warehouse of rags, tags, bottles and God knew what.

Presently the little man opened his eyes and gathered himself back into animation. His dull glance recognized, accepted, flickered for an instant with an inner conflagration. He fumbled in his sleeve, sucked deep with the ecstasy of some discovery, and gave into Mitchell's keeping a small, cold, smooth object. The gesture, his offering, was furtive; it had in it, as well, a trace of gratitude, of award. And Mitchell, accepting, because he was both curious and touched, put the gift into his pocket without looking at it.

To his amazement, the resuscitated victim rushed to the door and opened it, waving him out. He must go, he gathered, and as quickly as possible.

And no one turned to give him a glance. The bow-knotted assailants had vanished. From the enigmatic walls the crowd had flowed again. He passed with them, out of the quarter, where he didn't belong, into the quarter where, supposedly, he did. All the way he kept his hand closed round the token of gratitude. It seemed to fill his grasp, to be of strange shape, to be made of some stone, or glass of wonderful texture. It might prove to be anything, of no value at all, or again, something precious, something very strange indeed. It pleased him to imagine.

In his room at the hotel again, he sat down on the bed and drew the gift out.

Buddha.

A little figure, carved from a single green stone, of a colour so marvellous, so intense, that the light falling through it cast a glow all about, a pool of green. It sat in the palm of Mitchell's hand and his fingers, his wrist, were stained as if he had thrust them into green water. Undoubtedly, this was an emerald, some relic of the Boxer thefts, some precious jewel from the Forbidden City smuggled from hand to hand into his, at last. Because, he thought, he had wanted a sign from China? This was perhaps the answer to his questioning, the beauty for his desire, one more mystery insoluble and tantalizing.

Buddha.

The face was not characteristic. The image of Gautama had none of the inscrutability associated with such images. Mitchell himself, in all of his rather aimless wanderings along the Aryan Path, had never encountered a Buddha so devoid of claptrap. He felt an immediate interest, a lively sense of recognition and kinship, as one serious man looking into the face of another. These eyes looked out with an expression both penetrating and benign; there was no malice about the mouth, no smile suggestive of cherished secrets. The face was not Mongolian but, as it should have been, Aryan —long, thin, bony; the nose high, with flaring nostrils; the mouth sensitive and ironic; the head generously modelled.

The carving was so delicate, so painstaking, that Mitchell felt certain that it was the work of a Chinese craftsman, but, he decided, a craftsman of unusual intelligence, brave enough to see the man behind the idol.

As Mitchell sat staring at this curious and arresting thing, a shadow fell across his open window—a flash, like the darting flight of a bird. A knife entered, pierced the wall behind him and hung there quivering.

Mitchell plucked it out, examined the thin blade and went to the window. No one was in the hotel garden twenty feet below save a gardener who methodically brushed the gravel paths with a European broom. No face was visible beneath the wide coolie hat and no glance was lifted, while Mitchell stood there, to his window. The trick had been so theatrical that Mitchell laughed. He felt, at the moment, a sense of disappointment, that China should make a gesture both melodramatic and futile.

He slipped the green image into his pocket and went downstairs to dinner.

In the morning he set out to board the steamer which was to take him to Manila.

It is no part of this story to tell in detail the things that happened to Mitchell between Hongkong and Charleston. He knew unquestionably that he had no right to the little Buddha. But he had given a great deal of himself to China—his desire to know the secret heart of her, expecting to find it beautiful. And this gift had been given him.

He cherished it at the risk of his life.

Three times aboard that evil-smelling, wallowing steamer his room was entered and his things turned inside out. Twice he was attacked late at night on the deck and desperate efforts were made to throw him overboard into the South China Sea. Mitchell is reluctant to talk overmuch about his own part in all this. By day he was unmolested, the object of suave and unflagging courtesy. At night he stood, literally, with his back to the wall, playing with all his wit a game of obtuse chances. He was the only European on the ship except for a fear-smitten, sea-sick German Jew, a Hamburg sales-man who stood in abject terror of the yellow race. Mitchell ignored him and with a sort of reckless enjoyment played the game alone. He admitted, afterwards, that he hardly expected to reach Manila. It was quixotic, to say the least, to fence with death because he had taken a fancy to a hand-high "heathen idol." An emerald, yes. Invaluable, yes. Fabulous, of course. But Mitchell wasn't interested in material values. His attachment was intellectual. This, he believed, was the real Gautama, rice-grower, gentleman, dreamer, prophet of India.

Mitchell might have placed the emerald in full view of his tormentors, and, in surrendering it, have saved his own skin. But he chose instead to keep it, and, by a lucky chance, he kept his skin as well. He never knew whether the officers and crew of the steamer were aware of what went on. The eyes that met his were bland and indifferent. His enemies—and there were four of them—materialized out of the shadows, at odd moments, in odd places, to strike swift blows. He was quick; he was skilful in that art already mentioned. Nothing else could have seen him through.

He landed at Manila still in possession of his treasure. It was part of the game, amusing enough, to tip a man, whose left arm he had broken the night before, for carrying his kit ashore.

He was followed from Manila to San Francisco by an Australian in Chinese pay; from San Francisco to New York by a yellowish man of doubtful racial inheritance who never slept and whose teeth were perpetually bared in a smile of anticipation. Mitchell lost this shadow by doubling on his own tracks in the columbarium mazes of a New York hotel. But the negro porter of a Pullman car, between New York and Washington, fumbled through the curtains of Mitchell's berth and drove a penknife into his shoulder. In the morning there was no porter to answer the angry buzzing of electric bells. He had dropped off, empty-handed, nursing a broken wrist.

All of which sounds very portentous. To Mitchell, it was a simple proof that China is not to be won easily. Inwardly, he was gratified by this attention, as a man is gratified by a smile from a fastidious woman.

He waited long enough in Washington to be sure that he was no longer followed, and then went to Charleston to claim his inheritance.

Six weeks later, a planter at last, in possession of his future, he moved into Mitchell House. It was summer. The rice fields steamed beneath a white sun that whirled in pale vapours, a pin-wheel of hot light. When Mitchell arrived, his negro labourers gathered on the lawn. The meeting made him inexpressibly shy and inarticulate. Profoundly he envied his grandfather's control over these people, his paternal authority, his manner, inimitable, wonderful!

All those eyes, rolling sideways as he came up the drive, the shuffle of feet, the unexpressed, haunting doubt of him as master of their fate. . . .

Good lord, he wasn't equal to it! He should have felt pride, a certain inevitable arrogance of possession. Figuratively, he did. Actually, he was embarrassed. All those blacks—the Mitchell blacks— looked to him for something he couldn't possibly give because he both understood and pitied, where his grandfather had loved and despised them. Mitchell felt that there was a gulf of difference between the two attitudes. His grandfather had been born, had died, a Mitchell. He himself had been born a Mitchell, had first seen light in this very house, yet he had been other men as well, had somehow exchanged his identity for a dozen identities. Between himself and mastery of these blacks there were selves that shrank from authority. He would never hold the whip-hand.

He spoke to them from the portico and they drifted away again, back to the watery fields—he imagined, disappointed.

The year that followed was full of questioning. Mitchell was alone. None of his friends belonged in that period of re-adjustment; they were, most of them, too settled, too sure of things. And Mitchell wasn't sure at all.

It was a time of inward searching, when he doubted the rightness of his past; it seemed to him that he had overlooked the essentials in a feverish pursuit of trivialities. In every man's life there comes a time when he must know the reasons for his being, when he must find out for himself whether or not he is a link in a spiritual chain or animal man let loose in a world of matter.

Mitchell had never permitted himself to love a woman, considering that his loves were too manifold to admit of one passion. He was afraid of surrender, of losing for a second his awareness of himself and the world. Since he was not a father, he had missed the pride of creation. His experience, colourful, unique, had not, somehow, satisfied his heart. He had arrived at that interval of discontent and staleness, when, for the lack of a sharer, his possessions meant nothing to him.

He had accumulated beauty, he had many things to say and no one in particular to say them to. He felt, without being able to analyse his restlessness, that the past and the future were equally futile.

He had often turned to the image of Gautama during those lonely months. He had had the rear "gallery" screened; his desk, a few comfortable chairs and a table were put out there and the cool, open place became his office. The little green god sat upon the desk facing him. Looking beyond, in

moods of abstraction, Mitchell could see the rice
fields, pale and feathery, where pickers waded in the
shallow irrigation ditches, bent in the eternal attitude
of garnering. He knew every feature of that
strangely un-American landscape—sky and earth
swimming; the sun sucking up bands of moisture;
the rice, sown, in growth, plucked, sown again.
To the left, low down, a cluster of sheds and houses.
To the right, far off, the wood. Running straight
ahead, long, converging ditches now clogged with
growth, now reflecting the pale contours of clouds
or the bodies of workmen, bent, making eternally
the identical gestures, sowing and reaping.

So, Mitchell reflected, Gautama must have watched
his workmen in the rice-fields beneath the Himalayas.
And he would glance at the green image, and turn it
about, so that Buddha might for a moment face
the old, forgotten realities. It amused Mitchell
to speculate upon the history of the carved emerald,
its shrine, its power over men, the desperation of the
hired thieves who had tried to recover it.

It was a natural step to a deeper study. Mitchell
sent for books, surprised that there were so few,
and went as far as he could, alone, into the Aryan
Truth, Gautama's precepts for the peace of the
soul.

It was, he discovered, primarily, a religion of
self-forgetfulness. To Mitchell this was enormously
difficult, immersed as he was in a sea of self-doubt.
He could think of nothing but himself, his part in
the world-play; it was vitally important what hap-

pened to him, to Mitchell! The rest of humanity could go hang—it was wallowing in its own discontent, anyway. This fellow Buddha wanted you to gather to yourself, impersonally, all richness, only to spend it, impersonally, on mankind. Reward, serenity, lay in self-abnegation. But to Mitchell this seemed to exclude the intensity of life without which no man can hope to gain wisdom—to surrender self was a sort of shrinking from experience! Who wanted serenity at the cost of happiness? Yet Gautama said that happiness was cut across by the shadow of the wing of death. . . .

Mitchell turned the god about, one day, and left him, disgusted. He had seen too much, in China, Tibet, Siam, of Gautama's priesthood. He could not separate the man from the deity, the truth from the superstition. He remembered too well where this man's ardour had carried him—it was, Mitchell supposed, the fate of all such teachers to see the kernel of truth at length magnified, distorted, gilded, enshrined, made into a lumpish idol hung with jewels and triple-crowned—man cheating man, man blinding man, everlastingly. Gautama's faith was a whirring of water-wheels, a procession of symbols, a ceaseless genuflection before fantastic altars. The miracle was lost in the gaudy pageantry. . . . As always. . . .

Mitchell rode every afternoon, making the traditional tour of inspection. Sometimes the world was beautiful and he rode like a man in a crystal goblet between sky and water. The marshy earth sank beneath the horse's hoofs, making a pleasant sound. The rice was pliant in the breeze, bending down and standing again with a soft, dancing motion. The workers sang, ankle, knee deep, black, in torn, sleeveless shirts and trousers rolled up to their thighs.

Again, it was sulky, sticky with heat. Mitchell's clothes plastered his body; foam flecked his horse's breast. The rice was leaden, motionless, rooted in mud, and the sullen, bent workers moved slowly beneath heaped thunderclouds, fabulously tall, rising tier upon tier in smouldering cupolas and fiery pinnacles, as if kindled by a remote, infernal flickering.

On such days Mitchell longed for companionship. The plantation was inland, away from the usual avenues of communication, approached only by a single-track miniature railroad and a highway deep in dust, practically impassable during a drought.

Mitchell was surprised, therefore, to come back one afternoon to find a guest.

"A gentleman, sir. A foreign gentleman," old Frank explained as he took Mitchell's horse. " 'Bout an hour ago. Come on foot. I ast him to wait on the gallery, sir."

"That's right."

Mitchell hurried indoors with an eager anticipation. The portico opened directly into the large hall; on either side, the doors of the drawing-room and dining-room remained closed, since Mitchell rarely used them. An excellent stairway spiralled out of the hall to the upstairs sleeping-quarters.

Mitchell went directly to the gallery, wondering why a visitor should have come afoot on such a day of burning heat and stifling calm, but more particularly wondering who had come, and why. Mitchell had overdone his period of exile; he was, after a fashion, being forgotten. . . .

A smallish, thin man rose to greet him as he entered the gallery. He saw at once that the emerald faced the rice-fields, undisturbed, and this relieved Mitchell since his guest was a stranger and, as Frank had said, a foreigner.

He was dressed in white linen; afterwards, in recalling the man, Mitchell could not remember the cut of his clothes, or whether there was dust on his shoes, if indeed he wore shoes, at all. Mitchell had the impression that he was greeting some one of authoritative personality. In the clasp of their hands the stranger was established in Mitchell's consciousness as a man unique and unforgettable, a man who had crossed many turbulent mental streams into calm country. He was, Mitchell felt, in control. And this elusive yet penetrating command gave the American planter a shock of pleasure, of relief.

"Won't you sit down?" Mitchell said. "I can offer you cigarettes and a cold drink—julep, if you prefer. Or a Daiquiri—my servant is not unskilful. It is very gratifying to welcome some one from the outside world—I live somewhat in exile, as you see."

The stranger glanced about the gallery. The

wire screens, enclosing all three sides, blurred the landscape. Yet the long ditches were very lovely in the glow of the setting sun, and a flight of wild birds in formation passed, fluttering, like a kite, down the sky. Old Frank appeared with the juleps, green and fragrant, in tall glasses beaded with cold moisture. And with the lighting of cigarettes, the moment became, inexplicably, an occasion. The little Buddha flashed in their crossed glances like the beam struck from a square-cut jewel turning in the sun.

"You are very comfortable here," the visitor said presently.

"I have everything," Mitchell agreed, "except serenity of soul. Nirvana eludes me. Strange, in a place like this! I have just come here, after a life-time spent in the accumulation of experience —very personal experience. I am, if you care to put it that way, a storehouse of beauty. I have soaked up the sevenfold splendours of the earth until I am like a saturated sponge. I am full of things to say—with no one in particular to say them to. The sensation is unpleasant."

"Perilous! I speak from experience."

"Ah. You do?"

The stranger made a gesture of apology. "We speak at once of ourselves. Very human. Very reprehensible. Very necessary at times, when the soul must be cleared at all costs of what you just now called its accumulation of experiences. To speak to a stranger—of ourselves! I think we both can understand the spiritual value of confession. Absolution is another matter. I am not qualified——"

Mitchell interrupted. "Who are you anyway?"

The stranger leaned forward and glanced into the pool of light cast by the image of Buddha. "My name is Siddhattha. I come from Benares in the North of India. A curious coincidence. This little figure——"

Mitchell laughed. He felt uncomfortable and a cold shiver passed along his spine. Now he knew this man was another agent of that vengeance which had pursued him across the world. But why an Indian? And why one who would so brazenly assume the personal name of Gautama? The joke was, to say the least, rather thick.

"A coincidence," he said. "How do you mean?"

The Indian touched the god with the tip of his finger and turned it about so that he could stare into the carved face. "This god was once a man, Siddhattha Gautama of the Sakya clan. Behold him now! A squat deity sitting on his haunches, withholding his secret. . . . A bitter and terrible irony. What behooves it a man to look into his soul for the truth if the truth he finds be carved into precious stone and set up as an idol?"

"The coincidence——" Mitchell insisted.

"That we should be here together!"

"You and I? Or you and my Buddha?"

"You and I."

"I don't think I understand."

The Indian had not tasted the julep. Now he

lifted the glass and turned it against the smouldering sunset light and set it down again.

"Our personal experience," he said, "is so nearly identical. We are both planters and, if I am not mistaken, nearly of an age. You have, you told me, every reason for happiness and are unhappy. You have lived violently, and death seems abominable because it will find you still unsatisfied. You are too intelligent to turn to gods like this, too proud to turn to any god at all. Am I right?"

"Exactly," Mitchell confessed.

"Men! Identical, here, in the jungle, in the wastes; white, black, red and yellow! Always seeking, always cheated, always baffled, and groping on their hands and knees in the darkness! They say prayers. They cut their fear into stone. They write it upon banners. Such dim sayings as *Om Mani padme hum*—what does it mean? Their fear! Death! Extinction! They beat their foreheads in the dust, make strange music with drums and tom-toms, build temples, fashion charms, go upon their knees, wipe their foreheads in the dust. . . . Do you think, if all this were made, for a single moment, visible and audible, that it would bring mankind nearer to peace? All this ugly posturing, this filthy effort to placate the powers of darkness. . . . Absurd, isn't it? To be born, to live in fear, to die ignorant. . . .

"When the dreams of adolescence have dissolved, leaving the outlines of reality hard and clear, the unendurable questioning begins. In some of us the need to know is more acute because the first dreams were more beautiful. Only a great lover can know great loneliness.

"The time comes when we see marble as granite, flowers as parasites, clouds as jets of infernal steam —the vision vanishes and we behold a hideous, encrusted, purposeless planet. We ourselves are infinitesimal atoms of life that flicker for an instant and are gone, serving no purpose. A world among worlds. Man on his belly before his dread. Alone. Eternally alone. Love itself only another defeat, since lovers' eyes are only another enigma. . . ."

After a pause, he went on again to say:

"I remember. . . . I was a boy, in a beautiful world. Imagine a country where fruit grows in clusters like precious stones, there for the hand that reaches out. Sunlight thick and yellow as pollen dusting the shiny leaves of shade-trees and the roofs of palaces and temples. Elephants in gilded trappings moving along forest trails. Pools of clear water framed in marble. The sweet, clear voices of girls singing to the frail harmony of lutes. . . .

"I saw her first when I was no more than a boy. She was, I thought, the purpose of my seeking. So beautiful! White, perfect, with red lips and heavy eyes, a little nose, a throat like the stem of a lily. She was a lute for my playing; a bird to nestle in my hand; the fragrance of flowers; happiness. My blood ran with delight; I saw Paradise waiting for me in this cool young body; I saw tranquillity, water to quench my thirst for ever. A dream of woman like the tinkle of a fountain and I, drinking, drinking at the source.

"I married her."

Mitchell interrupted sharply: "I have no wife."

The Indian smiled. "It would be the same with you, as with me. Unless——"

He leaned forward: *"She was not the answer!* How could she be? Consider. She was like myself. She reflected me. No more. At times I saw fear in her eyes. She, too! I thought: A child will satisfy us.' "

Mitchell said: "I have no child."

"No. But the answer is not there. They told me: 'A son is born.' My wife was lying asleep, my child in her arms. I crept in to look at them, my wife and my son. Asleep, with their soft lids closed over their eyes. Had I been able to look into their eyes—who knows? But they were asleep. And for a long time I stood over them, watching their breath, the delicate breath, coming and going. Their secret was shut away from me. Helpless, tender, both of them! And the shadow of death lay across them even then, in spite of my love! Can you understand?"

Mitchell nodded: "It seems that misery is reality, happiness an illusion. Why this should be is beyond my understanding. It cannot be perversity, for all of us are honest enough in our quest."

"So I told myself. Since I had everything,

why then should I miss what I wanted most? There, in my grasp, actual, visible, alive—mother and son, asleep, my own! My rice fields touched the flanks of the Himalayas, even as yours run down beyond the horizon.

"Yet I questioned. And my heart was burdened with pity and shame. These things—old age, disease, lust, betrayal, cruelty, ignorance and death.

"I left my wife and my son and went away alone, to seek the answer to this enigma."

"So, they say, did Gautama," Mitchell remarked.

"And how many others? Are you and I alone in our curiosity?"

Again Mitchell felt that odd shiver. The sun was low, balanced on the rim of the woods, a great copper disk. It cast a baleful light, a steady pouring of rays. And off to the right, towards the shanties, the negroes began to sing: "Had a hard time— worked so long—But I done got over, Done got over, *Done got over at las'!*"

"Well," Mitchell asked sharply, "what did you find?"

"At first, nothing. I tried, by certain physical means, to lose myself. It seemed easier to lose the things that belonged to me—my wealth, my house, my family, my dress—than to rid myself of preoccupation with self. We men walk in a prison, and that is not the least of our difficulty. Whenever we glance down, we see our bodies—ugly or beautiful, old or young, well or ill. There is no escape so long as our bodies are only dwelling-places; they must become, before we can escape, instruments of our will."

"I don't understand."

"I cannot make myself clearer."

"I take it that you believe in self-abnegation?"

"There is no other serenity."

"Oh, if you mean withdrawal from life——"

"No!"

"Then what?"

"I found a way, so clear, so easy, so open that any child or ancient or beast can walk it—into Nirvana."

Mitchell lifted the julep-cup and drank unsteadily. "If this is so, why don't you preach up and down the land? Why don't you go before the multitude and shout from the housetops and in the market-places?"

"I have."

Leaning forward, the Indian lifted Mitchell's Buddha and held it in the palm of his hand.

"This is what they have done with my teaching. . . . I told them to work for the good of men. To plant trees. To build roads. To dig wells. To heal the sick. To teach the young. To educate women. I told them to lose themselves in something greater than themselves. To forgo gratification of the senses, personal immortality, personal possessions. To serve. . . .

"Consider for a moment your opportunity—here, and now!"

"Good heavens," Mitchell cried, "I have none!

A farm.   A few hundred negroes——" He flushed.
"I beg your pardon.   I think I understand.   Only
it's confounded difficult to bring yourself to the point
of surrender.   I am not a Buddha, coming into divine
wisdom beneath a spreading Bo tree."

"Why not?"

"Well, for one thing, I like what I've got.   All
my treasures, pottery, books, swords. . . . Call it
gratifying the senses, but there's something very
precious in the 'feel' of this thin, etched glass and
the tinkle of ice.   Even the leather of my boots.
And this silk cushion.   Or, if you prefer, our conversation, playing about the peaks of human thought.
Companionship.   The daily, lovable homely trivialities.   My black servant bringing coffee on a silver
tray.   The touch of cool water on the naked
body.   My horse's ears, velvet, hot, flicking away
from my hand. . . ."

The Indian smiled: "I did not intend to preach
to you.   But you said, in the beginning, that these
things had failed you.   Now that I suggest taking
them away, you discover a vast affection. . . ."

He put the Buddha down again and the thought
flashed through Mitchell's mind: "He is playing
with me as a cat plays with a mouse."

It was dusk now.   The sun was gone, leaving
the sky a sheet of copper light.   No breath of air
seemed to penetrate the wire screens.   Mitchell felt
suddenly that he had been too casual in his acceptance of this man.   If he was a thief, he was a cool
one.   Was he waiting for darkness, to snatch the

prize and make a dash through the hall to the portico and a waiting motor down the road? He couldn't escape by way of the gallery—the screens were steel and offered no loop-hole.

The suspicion was replaced by a feeling of shame. And Mitchell asked again, striving to read that curiously eager face: "Well, then? What must I do?"

"Surrender."

"It would be," Mitchell objected, "like dying! For I am made this way—what I do, I do thoroughly. I have lived—to the hilt. If I throw myself away, I shall be thrown away for ever. I shall be like a snake that has shed its skin."

"You will be happy."

"Who knows? In that thin, cold atmosphere of complete forgetfulness! Attentuated. Ghostly. I am afraid."

"There is no other serenity."

Then Mitchell pointed at the god, the focus of their thoughts: "So he preached! And what has happened? Wherever his thought has penetrated —China, Tibet, Siam, Burma, Mongolia, Japan— there are altars, incense, lamas, white elephants, Buddisatvas. Hariti, goddess of pestilences. Kwannon. Celebrants, exorcisms, fasts, litanies, witchcraft, hells and transmigrations. All the stuff of fear and damnation! This god—this little green demon —is he a symbol of freedom today or of eternal servitude?"

The other leaned forward, and stretched out his

hand. "That," he explained, "is why I have come——"

" 'Scuse me, sir," old Frank said from the doorway behind them. "Another gentleman. Seems like I can't just 'sactly remember his name. A China gentleman——"

Mitchell rose. "I'll come at once."

He was so much a man of his particular world, that it did not occur to him to take the Buddha away. He put it down again on the desk, within reach of the slender, outstretched hand. Then he turned his back squarely, and went into the hall, where a small, strange figure in black waited.

It was, he saw immediately, the gentleman from Tibet, the ironic scholar, the mystic misanthrope of Lhassa, he who had offered to pry apart the sacred leaves of the lotus.

He offered Mitchell his hand and then a sheaf of papers, sealed, signed and countersigned by many embassies and ambassadors—unnecessary proofs of his authentic self and his authentic purpose.

Dust lay thick on his ill-fitting European frock coat, his patent shoes, his shiny silk hat held in the crook of his arm. But his face was serene and untroubled, only puckered with fine wrinkles—a face ancient, inscrutable, wise.

"I have come a long way," he explained, "to ask of you a favour. I ask in a few words, for I must not delay. The car that brought me from Washington is waiting outside to take me back again. You have in your possession a small carving of inestimable value, stolen two years ago from the inmost heart of the great temple of Lhassa. To be exact, an image cut from a single emerald, the largest in the world. As your friend, I was commissioned by the proper authorities to recover this stolen treasure. The Buddha was famous throughout Tibet as a worker of miracles, a healer of the sick. You understand—the simple people. Faith. As for myself, I distrust the miraculous. But we must consider our children—the ignorant, the sick, the simple. . . . The thief was traced to a small shop in Hongkong. Our agents, sent to recover it, encountered you, my dear friend. Unexpectedly. Ignominiously! You accepted the precious booty. Unknowing, of course! Now, I request, courteously, as one gentleman to another, its return."

"Certainly."

Mitchell turned and the Tibetan followed him across the hall, where old Frank was lighting the candles, to the door of the rear gallery.

It was almost dark out there. But Mitchell saw at once that the stranger was gone.

The chairs, the desk, the glasses, one empty, one full, were undisturbed. No one had passed through the steel screens; no one had passed through the hallway to the front door and the portico.

But the image of Gautama, Buddha, prophet of India, lay on the table a shattered, crumbled heap of emerald dust.

Then Mitchell, standing bewildered and dismayed on the threshold, became conscious of a strange and delicate odour, an odour, fresh, exquisite, suggestive of infinite loveliness. And a murmur of amazed voices rose outside. He heard the shuffle of feet as the negroes came from their quarters and spread over the lawn beneath the gallery, whispering.

Peering through the screen, with the Tibetan gentleman at his side, and old Frank faltering and chattering behind them, he saw a miraculous thing.

As far as the eye could reach, down the straight, shallow ditches where the rice had been, there was lotus growing, lotus tall, immaculate, in full bloom, great flowers that lifted above dark leaves like pale moons, mysterious, glowing—miles and miles of them, clogging the fields, filling the still, hot air with sweetness, swaying a little as dancers sway to a slow melody, dipping their heavy heads and rising again, lotus and lotus as far as the eye could reach.

EXHIBIT B

THE Austins lived in an old brownstone house on Murray Hill—the house was Martha's, inherited from her conventional forefathers. The interior was Austin's. Martha moved against that sombre background of trophy-hung walnut like a transparent, yellow butterfly seeking its way out of a jungle. It was her poor fortune to have to live there, while Austin roamed the world. He would go off to forest and swamp, to delta and veldt, to steppe and range, caring not a hang that Martha waited on Murray Hill. She was always there when his cab drove up to the door again.

His return from outlandish places brought her to life. Her pale loveliness glowed. For him? No one knew. The dark house would be full of people —Austin's scientific crowd, with a scattering of Martha's loyal friends. "Murray Hill blackbirds," Austin called them. His boxes were unpacked and, in a litter of excelsior and cotton, glassy-eyed specimens lay staring back at the curious—brilliant birds, mountain sheep with curling horns, beetles, butterflies, delicate antelope, owls, jaguars, and silky monkeys with pointed faces. And canvas cases containing carbines and rifles, rods, strangely fashioned nets, cameras, typewriters, microscopes. Austin's equipment went into the far corners of the earth on the backs of an army of native bearers. The cab that brought him back to Martha and Murray Hill from these adventures was always encrusted with duffel—behind it, an express wagon transported his trophies from ship to doorstep.

The house was narrow and deep. Martha would have liked clear, grey walls with English chintz at the windows. But Austin had his way, and Martha served tea in black Canton cups from an ebony table, herself balanced uncomfortably in a chair made of reversed elephant tusks and alligator hide. The panelled walls bristled with beautifully mounted heads. The floor was strewn with skins—leopards, polar bears, fox, bison; creatures that had perished by Austin's ready right hand; had gone down in the dust, plugged through the heart as neat as you please.

Martha was the only live thing in the house. She grew paler with the years until, at thirty, she seemed quite transparent. But she lived. There was strength in her, what Austin called an "unconquerable feminity," twisting his mouth as if he rather meant an "unconquerable littleness."

He was sure of her. He had never missed a shot —how could a woman elude him? He had married her (when she was twenty) with a visible stoop of condescension, a smile that claimed her even while it rebuffed her. He was now famous and fascinating —far too fascinating to make any civilized woman happy—dark, wrinkled by exposure to blazing suns, thin as a pipe-stem, with a prowling, soft-footed gait.

Why he married Martha in the beginning puzzled her friends more than is usual in such cases. He left her in the middle of their first married year to join an expedition into the heart of Papua.

"He didn't need a wife," some one remarked. "He is married to orchids or beetles or jungle mud or something inhuman. He has installed Martha on Murray Hill as Exhibit A. Or B. She wouldn't be A. He prefers armadillos."

Ten years. No one knew what went on in Martha's heart until Arthur Merrill tried, deliberately and tirelessly, to find out.

Austin was in Africa, sending monthly bulletins to an illustrated magazine in a style faultless and magnificently resonant. He was a great naturalist because he was a debauched lover of Nature. His descriptions of birds and sunsets had the lingering tenderness of a caress savoured and cherished, a caress prolonged, sustained, made epic. He loved every minute, living particle in the swarming jungle. Yet he could leave Martha for two years, with nothing to hold her save illegible, scrawled messages sent back by runners.

"My love. I am well. Bridges will send you advance proofs of the articles. In them you will find all the news of me. I hope you are amusing yourself. Admirable lady.

"HARRY."

No one guessed all this from Martha's behaviour. She wasn't the sort to tell her secrets to those Murray Hill blackbirds Austin referred to. She entertained, sitting alone at the head of an enormous walnut table; behind her, a portrait of Austin looked down at her guests with an amused and mocking smile, creating an atmosphere of self-consciousness.

She was so lovely, Arthur Merrill thought, watching her face in the candle glow—a dauntless, reassuring creature, straight as an arrow, plucky, proud; the sort of woman a man would cherish. Well, apparently, Austin didn't. Austin was taking advantage of her "quality," rare enough in modern women, when he trusted and deserted her so flagrantly. A lovely, gold creature, all ivory and warm skin— shadows and grace—her gestures were an unmixed delight. Arthur Merrill found himself watching her hands, unconsciously trying to link their promised tenderness to that painted personality behind her. It occurred to him, with a shock of horror, that she might have loved Austin. A woman like Martha to have loved a man who laughed at her!

Very adroitly, Merrill asked questions. He was one of those Georgian young men who seem, without trying to, to know every one. After that first dinner party, when he sensed her tragedy, he set about to untangle it, to pick out the knots and to hold the unravelled skeins himself. He meant to marry her. Austin was in Africa, being photographed astride murdered elephant cows and crumpled wildebeests, a creature remote, inexplicable, romantic.

His "crowd," scientists and curators, sporting men and litterateurs, spoke of him with a sort of astonished reverence—he was as sonorous a stylist as Conrad; he was, besides, an original, scientific genius and the best raconteur in America. Merrill gathered that there had been an unsavoury episode—an episode only—in his past; somehow he had touched bottom and had come up again, rather more romantic for the experience. It was mentioned simply as an indication of his "capacity." His marriage, it seemed, had anchored him to windward of dangerous shoals. Merrill began to see Martha as a brave little ship standing by a picturesque derelict.

Her friends, and she had a good many, detested Austin. Ten years before, she had come back from a trip to "some jungle scmewhere" already married to the gaunt and taciturn naturalist, whom she had met out there. For six months he sulked on the rim of Martha's dinner parties and teas—Mr. and Mrs. Harry Austin at home—watching her with a strange look in which hate and a grudging admiration were mixed with jealous passion. He made no effort to be amusing, or even civil. And Martha, feverishly excited, played her own game and his—putting him forward as a genius, a being unique and dedicated. No one had heard of him then, but Martha saw to it that professional ears were cocked in his direction. She fed him well, and that famished look gave way to a dark and ironic distinction. Then, one day, he borrowed money and sailed, under contract to write a thrilling biography of the Papuan beetle or something of the sort. Martha was left, listless, rather tired, with a growing habit of watching the door and of listening to bells. Two years and a half, before he came again to claim her.

Arthur Merrill had heard enough. He wanted her with a very particular longing, since he knew that a love thwarted and defeated so long would come with a rush of wings through an open door.

He found her obdurate.

There was no easy way to her heart; all the barriers were up save her loneliness; he sought to enter that way. Merrill wasn't clever—he was a very healthy and happy man with average good taste. He couldn't tell a Botticelli from a Franz von Stuck or a Scarlatti *étude* from a Bach fugue, but he did know a good Airedale when he saw one, and his taste in friendships was faultless. He didn't love Martha because she was tragic, but because he knew how deliciously gay she could be—well, with him!

He saw to it that his Georgian good looks brightened Martha's tea hour five afternoons out of seven. After all, he was better to look at than a gallery of glass-eyed brutes! He talked to her of things he liked to do—and Merrill didn't like jungle ooze and the black madness of Africa. He liked pleasant resorts, country houses, polo, theatres, green golf links, laughter and sanity. To Merrill, Austin wasn't romantic; he was a ghoul, a madman, a very poor sport indeed.

Martha began to glow again; a faint pink flushed the transparency of her skin, as if the sun had penetrated the gloomy walls of her house, transforming her. One late afternoon when she and Merrill were left alone, isolated in the firelight, her hands went out to him without any reason save her longing, and they kissed over the Canton cups, breathless, both of them, ashamed, exalted, tremulous.

Then he told her how long he had loved her and offered her happiness and knew the exquisite sorrow of holding her while she wept in his arms. In the middle of it, with that lovely yellow head just under his chin, he caught sight of Austin's portrait smiling at them from the dining room.

"You didn't love that—that hyena, did you?" he demanded.

She seemed to hold her breath.

Presently she lifted her head and let him see her eyes.

"Yes, I did. I still do. I'm sorry. I still do. You see—but you won't see! You see—he has been mine."

Merrill learned his first lesson in love at that instant. His impulse was to push her away from him; seeing her hands holding fast to his lapels, he thought better of it. Merrill was an old-fashioned man in that he respected women—he had none of Austin's amused acceptance of them. Austin would have mocked at his own mother. Merrill loved Martha because she was Martha, but also because she was a woman. He braced himself and said:

"If you love him, you can't love me."

"But I do."

"All right. But how?"

It was like Merrill to take her word. Austin wasn't so simple.

She tried very earnestly to explain.

It seems that she had met Austin at the time of his one lapse from character. She had gone with typically conservative friends to the Belgian Congo or the Dutch East Indies or some impossible backwater of civilization. Merrill didn't hear and didn't care—all he knew was that it was a savage place full of fever and creepers, naked natives, dirt, discomfort and brutality. Martha's friends, a professor and his wife, travelled into the interior and left her at some outpost on the extreme edge of civilization.

She lived in a missionary compound, a clearing set in a circle of white-hot sunlight and surrounded by a tangled forest full of prowling beasts and greasy black men with spears, tom-toms and top-knots. Into this oasis came Harry Austin, a very unnatural naturalist, white as clay, stumbling like a drunkard, with fever in his eyes and some terrible memory driving him out of the forest towards the sea. Martha first saw him beating one of his carriers, shouting things that aren't mentionable and threatening to shoot any one who interfered with him. But the missionary silenced Austin with a single, neat blow behind the ear—he was a practical man of God—and then carried him into the mission slung over one shoulder like a bag of flour.

Austin did not open his eyes again for two weeks. Motionless in a canvas hammock in the shade, he lay like a dead man, and talked! And Martha, hovering over this beaten, fever-ridden, tormented being, listened with horror to what he said.

Oh, he had fallen very low indeed.

Martha could not be sure how much of what he said was true and how much of it was perverse mental acrobatics. She gathered that he had suffered a damnable collapse of the nerves—that love of Nature which had always burned in him, clear and unfaltering, had been dimmed by scepticism. He saw the world as a fungus-encrusted planet, himself a parasite, beasts and birds no more than the feeble sparks of an inferior life force that got nowhere. He moved through the choked forests searching for the lost illusion. He was sick. Sick to his soul. Sick to death. There was no colour, no grace, no beauty—only a crowded, purposeless repetition of species. He had lost his hold on spirit.

Then began the decline towards physical surrender. Terrified, he prayed, seeking God in the silence, in the vast, unconquerable, hidden activity of the jungle. It was a theatrical gesture and got him nowhere—he found himself on his knees beneath an empty, white-hot sky.

Unleashed, his mind darted down forbidden trails. He suffered, but he was too weak to fight. He thought: "If some one were here who knew the truth, and could reassure me! I'm going mad, or worse." He would sit for hours studying the brilliant forest birds through his glasses, but the flashing wings made no more than erratic shadows across the sensitive retina of his mind.

Martha heard in detail the processes of his disintegration. He had stopped at a native village where he was well known and there set about deliberately to drink himself to death. He could *remember* sanity, but strangely enough he could only reproduce it in intoxication. Then the blurred outlines became clear; the atrocious confusion of his thoughts reassembled, became a familiar pattern. He could have written magnificently then, only that he was too weak. He was, for a time, a superman, shaken with the sense of his own power. Then drunken sleep and stupor shot through with exhausting struggle—the forces of darkness gathering for a new assault. Always he opened his eyes to a world drab and monstrous, a world swollen, stark, unbearable. On their heels about him his bearers squatted and stared, uncertain whether to kill him or not, afraid of him, despising him.

Martha listened, fascinated and revolted. Here was a strange creature, a lion in a net. It occurred to her, with a shock of a revelation, that she might be the mouse to gnaw him free again.

She told Merrill that she had had no definite plan. When Austin's babbling stopped, she used to lean over him and whisper things—just odds and ends of thought. Some instinct told her that he needed a clean, cold draught. His eyes remained closed, his face impassive. She had no way of telling whether he heard. She would speak of laughter, beauty, friendship, the easy, pleasant ways of childhood. She was not a psychologist, but a woman instinctively maternal.

At last he opened his eyes.

He saw a healthy, golden creature in a white dress, where he had expected a ring of steaming, black bodies.

"You are better," she said.

And Austin answered:

"Yes, I think I am."

After that, she fought for his soul with the zeal of a mediaeval Saint Catherine snatching brands from the fire. She did not shrink from holding his hand or touching his forehead with her cool palms. She gave him back, one by one, the precious things he had lost, meeting mockery and rebuff with patience, with divine patience, Merrill thought. He would have let the fellow go down in the welter! But Martha shook her head.

"He was great. The world needed him."

"Romantic poppycock, my dear! He sacrificed you on the foulest altar of all—he offered you up to his vanity."

She shook her head again:

"You don't understand. I found him an ugly wreck, all bleach-boned and rotted—I made him whole again. He clung to me. He wept, pressing my hands against his face. 'Don't leave me, Martha. Don't leave me!' I promised him. The missionary married us and we started back to the sea before my friends returned. I didn't love him as I love you

—it wasn't happiness. But I was proud of him. At night, before the fire, he'd talk of things he intended to do, once he was well again. And he'd go to sleep with his head *here,* as if he lived by the beating of my heart. Have I hurt you? I didn't mean to. It was like watching a miracle. One night he woke me, laughing: 'Martha, look. The stars! I see them again! Beautiful! Reasonable. In their places! In order! You don't know what that means—it is as if I had found God. Or, is it myself I have found?' "

"Himself, of course."

"Perhaps." She gave Merrill a strange look. "He began from that hour to laugh at me," she said.

Merrill heard later, not from Martha, that Austin's mental struggle in the forest had involved him in worse excesses than she dreamed. Austin had been running away from more than whiskey when he stumbled into the missionary compound. Knowing this, and disgusted beyond words, Merrill urged her to write Austin the truth, and then, as soon as possible, to divorce him. Martha seemed dazzled by the prospect of happiness. She let Merrill lead her to the door and point out the bland beauty of the future.

"I'm going to get you out of this confounded natural history museum into a house of mine in Connecticut. Wait till you see it; gardens all round and a pool where the river bends. You'll be lovely there, my dear."

Martha touched his hair; it was black and thick, very smooth. His eyes were clear; they offered her security. No danger there!

"Very well," she said suddenly, "I'll write Harry tonight."

But her letter never reached him. Austin had finished his series of magazine articles, and, with a ship's hold full of unmounted specimens, was on his way home. He would enjoy dropping down on New York, a sunburnt wanderer returned from delectable adventures, and, with a gesture, resuming his place as chief planet in that little system of his. He would enjoy finding Martha there. He would enjoy exploring her soul while she retreated before him, afraid and fascinated.

His cab drove up to the door through a November drizzle, a fine rain that slanted out of a yellow sky full of scudding vapour. Martha, sitting within the circle of Arthur Merrill's arms before the library fire, heard the clop of horses' hoofs and then the loud, triumphant ringing of the bell below stairs. She stiffened and the blood drained out of her face.

"Harry! I cannot tell him. Not *now*. Help me—take your arms away—don't you realize?—it's Harry. He's back."

To Merrill's everlasting credit, he paid no attention to her, and when Austin opened the door he found his wife leaning against a strange young man's shoulder, her face hidden, her whole body quiet, as if she had died.

"Well," Austin said, pausing. His eyes played

over them. He smiled. "This *is* extraordinary, Martha!"

She lifted her head, made a weak gesture, said faintly:

"It's true. I love him. I want to marry him."

Austin closed the door on a confused entrance of bags and boxes into the hall behind him. His expression was watchful as if he had caught sight of a very desirable quarry.

"I haven't met the gentleman you love, my dear."

Merrill introduced himself and, putting Martha gently back against the sofa pillows, came into the open. He had a feeling that Austin could have shot him there and then—he was a fair target for either bullets or insults. He explained that Martha was promised to him and that he intended to have her; she had been notoriously neglected and rebuffed; she was worthy of the best the world afforded, and he meant by that the very things he himself could offer her—love and devotion, protection and happiness; he had no foolish notions about the sanctity of an unsanctified marriage; he rather expected that Austin would surrender quickly and decently what he seemed to value so little.

Martha interrupted him.

"Go. Please. I'll talk to Harry myself."

And so Merrill went, stumbling over Austin's luggage and an astounded houseman who had had to settle with the cabby and was out of pocket.

Austin remained where he was until the front

door had closed with a decisive and defiant bang behind that audacious young man.

"A lover," he said in a dry voice, "in my absence."

Martha would have surrendered then and there had Austin persisted in his irony. But his voice changed suddenly—a break came into it, a whining indication of self-pity:

"You can't mean it. Martha, you aren't going to leave me?"

"Why shouldn't I!" she demanded.

He flung himself on his knees beside her and she felt his nervous hands pulling at her dress.

"You can't. You won't. I need you. You'll stay. Everything I am, you made me."

She said contemptuously:

"Get up. Don't make a fool of yourself."

She opened her eyes and leaned desperately sidewise to avoid him. Now, at last, she hated him because he wept and pleaded. She could deny because he asked so desperately. She was as inflexible as steel.

"Don't make me ashamed of you," she said.

At that moment Martha believed that she was hurting him; she had a sense of power, of ascendancy over his tyrannical possession of her spirit. There was no glamour about him now—a man begging for pity. She rejoiced that she could be pitiless. Crouching at her feet, a suppliant, he aroused her contempt. She heard him saying that without her he would fall back into the pit where she had found him; everything he had done the past ten years had been for her; his scientific achievement had been a love offering; he had thought her capable of a great impersonality—and she had preferred kisses! Well, he would give her kisses; he would play lover; he would kneel at her feet—science could go hang—kisses, kisses without end——

"This is intolerable," she said.

She stood up quickly, loosening his grasp, and ran out of the room.

That night she left the Murray Hill house for ever.

A year later Martha and Arthur Merrill were married. Heaven knows why Austin chose to get himself talked about on that particular day—but he behaved scandalously. Locking himself into his room at the club, he shot himself—not dead, but rather unpleasantly near it. For a crack shot, he missed it, one might say, miraculously! In the morning, together with the announcement of the divorced Mrs. Austin's marriage to Arthur Merrill, there was a two-column account of Austin's attempt at suicide. He had been taken to the hospital and lay there wrapped in gauze bandages, silent, with eyes that had in them a gleam of his old sardonic mastery. He seemed to be enjoying himself. And when it looked as if he might, after all, die, he asked for Martha. She came, a bride tear-stained and shaken, and spent the first ten days of her honeymoon sitting at Austin's bedside, stroking his thin hands as she had stroked them that time when he lay unconscious in the missionary's canvas hammock.

"I am sorry," he said, "I missed it." And he added: "You see, I need you. *My dear.*"

Martha went back to Merrill and the garden in an uncertain state of mind. Merrill was patient. He rode with her over the hills; he romped with her between the long beds of phlox, clove-pinks and hollyhocks; he sat at her feet in the shadow of the willows by the river pool; he tried conscientiously to be what Austin had never been—a friend and a sweetheart.

That winter they moved into Merrill's town house and there Martha let her fancy go gaily mad on chintzes and pink geraniums in apple-green boxes. The Murray Hill blackbirds flocked to see her. One and all of them had lugubrious croakings to make about Austin. Austin was living alone, it seemed, in his doleful, black-walnut museum. He never went out. He never entertained or even took the trouble to be entertaining. His scar made him more strangely fascinating than ever. "Poor dear Austin" had been at some pains to make himself sympathetic.

"I suppose," they told Martha, "his heart is broken. And no wonder, with you—his sunshine —gone."

Merrill laughed.

"Don't mind them, my dear. They're human. And we're so much more than human—we're happy."

Martha wasn't sure. She tried very hard to be happy, but happiness responds reluctantly to the will;

Martha's imagination was stronger than her desire. Austin was not writing. He was not planning an expedition anywhere. He was not, in fact, doing anything! She had brought him to life, and now, it seems, she had killed him. For Merrill's sake, she hid her mourning beneath reckless trappings of chiffon and satin—floating *negligeés* that made her look like a butterfly in a field of flowers. She loved Merrill a little too recklessly, rather too prodigally, as if she knew that she must go back out of the clearing into the shadowy jungle.

Austin's friends came to dinner and fixed her with an accusing eye. Sooner or later the talk always fell on the naturalist's literary defection. They rather put it up to Martha. "Poor Austin" was down and out again. He acted strangely—had been seen prowling up and down Fifth Avenue at midnight. Couldn't she do something about it?

For Merrill's sake she could not. And Merrill was not familiar enough with the hidden places of the soul to help her. To him Austin was simply a rotter, a very ordinary coward. Rather bored, he kissed Martha's tears away.

"I didn't marry your former husband, dear," he said. "I don't care what happens to him. If he wants to sink and we want to swim, why shouldn't we?" Martha was alone with the spectre.

Then Austin changed the angle of attack. He appeared at the club, very humble about himself, and announced that he was going away. Things were too difficult—happiness wasn't in his mood.

He wanted to be generous, God knew. He thought that he'd drop out of sight for a while.

Why in Heaven's name Austin behaved in this manner, no one took the trouble to explain. The reaction was subtle and, strangely enough, damning to Martha—Martha, who knew every nuance of his peculiar cruelty! Martha who knew that Austin hated her! Martha who knew that Austin knew how much she had given him!

When he had gone, she was, for a time, at peace. Then for three years stories kept turning up like bad numbers at the game of *petits chevaux*. Austin was globe-trotting, trying, he said, to cement his broken heart. He reached out across space to Martha, calling her back. "He needs me," she thought. And there was, somehow, a romantic insinuation, a subtle flattery, an imperative summons to her most potent self. Merrill was sufficient unto Merrill; he loved her with a light heart, since love, he argued, was not a matter for tears, but for rejoicing. But Martha, strangely moved, tormented, uneasy, seemed always to be listening, as though she expected the clop of horses' hoofs in the street, and then the loud, triumphant ringing of the door-bell.

Austin wrote no more. In literary columns he was spoken of in the past tense. She heard of him in Surabaya, in Bali, and later in India, where he talked wildly of her to every one he met. She had, it seemed, been his reason for living; without her, he had lost "the excuse for creation." To whom, he demanded, could he make his offering? Once she received a letter from him, written on soiled paper in his small, neat writing that always moved slightly uphill. He intended to return to the forest where he had met her, to recapture, if he could, the inestimable gift she had denied him. And if he should find only darkness again, he would do better what he had done badly on the day of her marriage to Merrill. The rest of the letter was in his old ironic strain. Holding the crumpled sheets with trembling hands, Martha felt the fear and the fascination of her love for him. This was her masterpiece, and she had wilfully destroyed it, to give her feminine magic to Merrill, who had no need of any magic save life itself!

She glanced out of the window—they were in Connecticut—and saw her husband preparing to mount his horse. A white dog frisked and barked at his heels. The sun touched Merrill's smooth, black hair like a benediction. Decidedly he had no need of her. Martha felt suddenly old and tired. Still clutching at Austin's letter, she went to the mirror and stared at herself. Not a butterfly for Merrill's garden—a grey moth, to flutter in the shadows—grey eyes, grey flesh, hair already greying. She would go. With the last of the flame that was in her, she would light the quenched brand again.

Merrill listened patiently that night, holding her quietly, saying little. He was very sorry for her; she trembled in his arms. But he had the great good sense to say: "I'll be waiting for you." And he didn't laugh at her; he did not even smile in the dark.

Nor did he kiss her tears away, but let them fall, fast and furious. And she heard the beating of his heart, loud and steady, loud and steady, against her own that fluttered. But she would go. She must go.

She found that Austin had disappeared into the forest. The practical missionary had been supplanted by a thin-lipped fanatic who could tell her very little except that Austin had stayed for a month at the compound studying the inexhaustible mysteries of the jungle. The missionary was hostile and inquisitive. It was not safe for a lady alone to penetrate farther into that wilderness, and he himself could not leave his post. Why had she come?

Martha found it difficult to explain. The heat, the blinding sunlight, the stench and disorder of the place sickened her. She said: "I don't know."

Late that night, sitting in a flood of white moonlight on the mission veranda, she heard the hostile man of God behind her. He cleared his throat.

"I feel I must tell you. Mr. Austin was not— alone. This is very embarrassing. A woman came with him and they went on together. She was pretty and young. Perhaps a lady, perhaps not. But very gay. A Hollander, I understand, from Surabaya in the Dutch East Indies. She and Mr. Austin had been married more than a year ago. She was helping him to write a book of some sort. They were, if you will excuse my saying so, very happy together."

"I didn't know," Martha said.

She lifted her eyes to the moon.   Somewhere in the forest a native drum was beaten rhythmically.   It was like a heart, a human heart, calling her back.

Suddenly she laughed.

"Damn Austin!" she said.

"Madam!"

"Oh, yes, damn him!   Let me say it.   I'm free. You've set me free.   Oh, jumping Jupiter!"

At dawn, gold as a dancing butterfly again, she started back to the sea.   And what she had to tell New York about Austin settled Austin, good and proper.   Settled him for ever.   She did it humorously, with a nice irony, a nice understanding of her own folly which was very disarming.   She could, you see, turn the laugh on Austin.   So that when Austin got back from his jungle with his beetles and boxes and his Dutch East Indian wife and his sardonic fascination all intact, he found that his star had dimmed.

And Martha, divinely magnanimous, invited them both to dinner.

Still, Austin had the last word.   Leaning over Martha in the firelight after dinner he whispered:

"If I had known that you loved me—if I had dreamed that you would follow me out there—I wouldn't have married this woman.   I wouldn't have hurt you so, my dear!   I ask you to forgive me. After all, it appears that I was destined to make you unhappy."   And he added: "My poor dear Martha!"

ODELL

ONLY one thing of importance has ever happened at Odell's landing. It happened about ten years ago, and since the place is probably obliterated by this time, wiped out by the devouring forest, knee-deep in tangled grass, rotted, burned by the sun and forgotten, the story can be safely told.

In those days Odell's landing was an ivory station. If you were going out there from London, for instance, you had to take a steamer to Port Michael and then wait for a coast trader, one of those itinerant pedlars that poke their noses into every harbour and river where there is a native settlement or an isolated post. Odell's landing—named after the first Englishman who risked his sanity in that God-forsaken spot—was within reach of these vagrant steamers. A clearing had been made on the banks of a river which poured towards the sea out of the heart of the continent—a clearing won by sheer courage from the grasp of the forest, maintained by cunning, violence and desperation. A crazy wharf braved the swift current for a few feet. The house itself was built solidly enough then—Heaven knows what it is like now! Odell had planned a comfortable bungalow, one-storied, with broad verandas, large, airy rooms and many doors. When young Michelson came out, he added distinctive American touches— a bay window, for one thing, from which he could look down the rushing, foaming river towards the sea.

About once every five or six months the panting steamer fought her way two hundred yards beyond the landing, then drifted into the current, blowing whistles and ringing bells hysterically, bringing up against the wharf with a crash. She never stayed more than a day. The captain, who was an unimpressionable Dutchman accustomed to silence and desolation, nevertheless shrank from going ashore at Odell's Landing. He went, because it was undoubtedly good policy to be polite to the agent, but he always slept aboard the steamer and departed in the thick white mists of dawn, taking with him what ivory there happened to be, and a bag of letters and reports to be posted at Port Michael.

When Odell died, succumbing at last to fever, the post was vacant for some time. A tall, sombre negro, Odell's servant, kept the books and lied to the natives. Odell was not dead, he said, but asleep. All white men slept five months every third year. In this way the canny native saved his own neck and his job. When young Michelson came out, it was Sambo who taught him the primitive, simple and unalterable rules of existence at Odell's Landing. . . . The little steamer turned downstream again, borne at furious speed on the brown current, and left Michelson to silence.

Silence—silence in that small clearing hemmed in by a whole continent of unbroken forest; silence in the shadowy storehouses, Sambo's quarters; silence on the river, where the vast stream, clogged with the up-tearings of the forest along its banks, swept forward without a sound. Much farther down it was to break into murmurings, and at the bars into a joyous thunder of amber-coloured surf; but the water swept past Odell's Landing a compact mass, like the rapid motion of a serpent, smooth, inaudible, resistless. Now and again, as some great uprooted tree travelled towards the sea, a black arm would rise from the river, beckon grotesquely and disappear in a swirl of foam. Michelson liked to watch the human antics of these logs. He found, after several months of it, that they were strangely companionable. When Sambo wasn't about, he'd shout at them and wave his hand.

Michelson succeeded Odell because the Dutch branch of the company had no one in mind and telegraphed to the English branch, which was equally embarrassed. Michelson's fate became temporarily embodied in the person of the family lawyer, who happened to hear that the Dutch-English Company had an excellent vacancy for a "young man of courage and initiative," and who rather put it up to young Michelson.

"Two years out there, and you will have proved your worth. When you come back there will be an opening, either in London or Rotterdam. It's the best thing I can think of now."

When Michelson accepted he had very little idea what he was being let in for. He was a big, shy, likeable fellow, taciturn but not moody, poetic in an inarticulate way. He had Dutch blood in his veins, and it had stamped him with the Hollander's fair skin, blond hair and blue eyes. All his life he had followed the amiable path of the well-to-do. When his parents died, leaving him nothing, he woke to the realization of his utter worthlessness in the world of business. There was literally nothing that he could do.

"Odell's Landing," he said to the family lawyer, "sounds quite harmless."

The lawyer glanced at the English firm's letter again and wrinkled his brow. "I don't imagine there will be any one there except an—an assistant of some sort. A chap called Odell established the post."

"What happened to him?"

"He died," the lawyer admitted.

Michelson smiled and tapped his brown boots with his cane. "It happens," he remarked, "now and then. I think I won't let that stop me. It's a chance to travel again. And I must have been a source of anxiety to you. Thank you—I'll go out there."

Before Michelson left New York he asked Agatha Wrightson to marry him. She was young and well-bred and fearless—a little too young to marry him, a little too well-bred to risk two years in a jungle wilderness, not quite fearless enough to face silence and hardship with Michelson. But she promised to wait for him and gave him her heart and her lips before he left. Michelson went away exalted. The post at Odell's Landing seemed a dignified, a magnificent thing, a place worthy of a big gesture, an open door to illimitable opportunities. He would improve the place, put American business methods on trial in the wilderness. When he went finally to England, or better still, to Holland, the company would receive him with respect.

He had no thought for his predecessor, Odell, the Englishman, who had been foolish enough to die in the arms of his great opportunity. But when the wheezing tramp-steamer had waddled away, leaving him at last alone in his silent kingdom, Odell appeared beside him, voiceless and featureless, but unavoidable. The Englishman's things still hung in the bedroom closets—tweeds, ulsters, a dinner-jacket, overcoats and several suits of dirty linen clothes.

Michelson took them all down to make way for his own possessions, and from them reconstructed the agent's life. He found a sprig of heather in the side-pocket of one of the overcoats. It crumbled into grey dust between his fingers—relic of some upland pasture, the smell of fresh earth, mist from the sea and buoyant winds. The dinner-jacket was redolent of camphor, good cigars and an indescribable odour of the river-mist. Michelson felt through the pockets and discovered nothing save a woman's letter, written on a single sheet of white stationery, asking

Odell to write often "from that outlandish place of exile, wherever it is you are going, obstinate dreamer that you are."

Well, Odell had died in exile! Michelson tied the clothes together and gave them to Sambo, that inscrutable "assistant" mentioned so hopefully by the family lawyer. Sambo accepted them without comment and carried them into his quarters behind the house. Presently he emerged again, still wearing his dazzling loin-cloth, but carrying one of Odell's walking-sticks between thumb and forefinger. Thereafter he was never without it.

No one had taken the trouble to put Odell's desk in order; there were neat packages of business letters, a year of the *Graphic* carefully arranged in a pile, a pipe and a jar of tobacco, the photograph of a woman. The tobacco had gone musty, Michelson discovered; it, too, was flavoured with that penetrating odour of jungle and mud, wet, sticky, super-sweet, disgusting.

It took Michelson a week to settle himself in the house. With Agatha Wrightson's photograph on the desk, and a new supply of pens and paper, the place looked quite ship-shape, ready for business. Sitting there, far into the beating silence of the nights, he poured out his heart to Agatha on the stationery of the Dutch company. His letters piled up—one a day for five months—a mountain of love to be called for and carried away by the erratic steamer when it came again. His reports he left entirely to Sambo, who understood Odell's way. Whenever the native hunters slipped out of the forest into the hard-won clearing by the river-bank, it was Sambo who bargained with them, paying for the ivory in that exchange of calico and canned goods, umbrellas and beads, cheap ribbon and wire, known only to his kind.

Twice Michelson showed himself to a watchful half-circle of hunters while Sambo explained in strange speech that here was the white lord, refreshed and rejuvenated by his long sleep, friend of the people, son of the Great Queen and enemy of thieves and liars. Michelson felt decidedly uncomfortable beneath the unblinking gaze of all those eyes. He went into the house and opened one of Odell's books, but his attention wandered. The indispensable Sambo was entertaining guests out in the clearing; a fire blazed, there was a low, unceasing murmur of voices and, grotesque and indescribable, the ribald piping of a mouth-organ blown upon by some naked savage.

Michelson had always liked to believe that the picturesque formalities of life would cling to him even in exile. At first he dressed scrupulously for dinner. It distressed him that Odell had tried and had failed. Whenever he sat down to his lonely evening meal, washed, brushed and wearing a fresh suit of linen clothes, it seemed to him that the dead Englishman in dirty linen, crumpled and torn, sat down facing him, his elbows on the table, his pipe in his mouth, a gleam of unpleasant humour in his sunken eyes.

"You won't last."

Michelson started. "The devil I won't," he said aloud.

"You spoke?" Sambo asked, coming in from the kitchen with the tea.

"No."

Talking aloud became a secret pleasure. Whenever Sambo was clear of the house, Michelson addressed Agatha's photograph, as if his voice could penetrate the wall of silence and make itself audible above the brazen clamour of civilization. The days were more endurable. He pottered about the house, hammering and painting; when the feverish sun touched the rim of the forest, he stripped and launched the heavy native canoe belonging to the post. At first it gave him a good deal of trouble. The paddles were unwieldy and he could make no headway against the impetuous downrush of the river. Little by little he conquered the craft. His white body was burned in the sun; he rejoiced in his strength, his skill and his sanity. Also he was fever-proof. Odell had not been so lucky.

When the little steamer came again, it brought three letters from Agatha, an official confirmation of his appointment from Rotterdam and a letter for Odell.

"Is no one watching out for this chap's affairs?" he asked the Dutch captain at dinner.

The captain shrugged his shoulders.

"A man living in a place like this has no affairs," he said.

"This letter——"

"Some woman! My dear sir, women are tenacious creatures—tenacious. I have had some little experience with the sex. If a woman once makes up her mind—— But why don't you read the letter see for yourself?"

Michelson put his finger beneath the flap of the envelope. Then he shook his head and tossed Odell's letter aside. "No. There might be instructions later. I'll hold it."

He kept the captain as long as he could, made drunk by the sound of words. The Dutchman was sullen and uncommunicative. At ten o'clock he got up, stretched his short arms above his head, yawned and waddled back to his steamer.

"See you in the morning," he said, shaking Michelson off at the gangway.

Michelson was left again within the beating, tangible silence of his house. He went to bed without having opened Agatha's letters; they were to be saved for the coming months. Tonight he must taste to the full the presence of white men. He lay awake, listening for the loud clatter of ship's bells.

In the morning Sambo appeared, quiet, efficient, carrying Odell's walking-stick. He attended to the unloading of stores, the weighing and loading of the ivory. Whenever Michelson interfered, he felt that he was being brushed aside by an invisible hand.

"Why don't you come back with me to Port

Michael?" the captain asked. "That nigger of yours knows more about this job than you do. You can play around Port Michael for five months and come back with me. Pretty women there."

"Did Odell do that?" Michelson asked quickly.

"No." The captain squinted and stared at the intolerable brightness of the river. "He stayed. And the damn fool died. Fidelity! He had some idea of duty to the company. Duty—bah!"

Michelson went back into the house. He stared long at the photograph of Agatha Wrightson. Presently he put his head down on the desk and clenched his hands and cried. One year and seven months more of it!

When he got to his feet again his mouth was set. He said good-bye to the captain with ostentatious good-humour. "I'll want a piano," he said. "Bring it down next trip."

"A piano? God in Heaven! Why not an elephant?"

But five months later the piano came, strapped to the pedlar steamer's broad back and covered with straw matting. Michelson went down to the wharf to get it. He was burnt black by countless days of implacable sunlight; his eyes were unnaturally wide open, as if he had stared too long at the invisible. His clothes were dirty, and he wore a pair of straw sandals that flapped loosely against his bare and blackened heels.

"Here's your piano," the captain bawled from the bridge.

"Ah!" was Michelson's answer. "Now I'm safe."

He did not explain himself, then or later; all that afternoon and late into the night he laboured to get the piano into the house. It gave him a tremendous amount of trouble. The tackle broke; the muddy bank gave way beneath the unaccustomed weight; at the steps it seemed as if the whole rotten fabric of the dwelling would crumble into strips of sodden wood. When the thing was finally in place, Michelson threw his hat into a corner and sat down to play. All that night, until the white mists of dawn rolled down the river and enveloped Odell's Landing, the grumbling crew of the steamer heard the tinkle of that precious instrument. It stopped only when Sambo appeared to take the stores ashore. Then Michelson stood on the veranda, haggard and listless, to watch the feverish activity of loading and unloading. When the pedlar had dropped down the river, he rubbed his dirty hands across his eyes and went into the house to read his letters.

There were two envelopes addressed to Odell. Michelson compared them with the one which had come five months before—the same stationery, heavy, white, with the single word "Blythlea" printed on the back; all three bore a Devonshire postmark; the handwriting was identical.

"A tenacious woman," Michelson thought, with a pang of envy for Odell. Unconsciously he glanced at the place where Odell's shadow always seemed to be —a forlorn shadow with burning eyes.

Agatha had written frequently. He read her letters hungrily, one after the other, with a fury to know what she felt, whether her love had outlived the numbling silence of the months. She chattered about her crowded life—theatres, dinner-parties, personalities. "I am very happy," she wrote, "because you love me. And I want you to stay out there for as long as you promised. Then no one can accuse you of failure—failure would hurt me more than anything that could happen to you." Which was all the comfort Michelson got. "I am very happy because you love me!" Little enough! And he had given her full measure!

In the months that followed he became convinced of his own worthlessness. He left the administration of the station entirely to Sambo, and spent his days lounging in a hammock on the shady side of the house. He was a failure, always had been. It was a simple matter to believe that he always would be. He had thrown two years of his youth into a pit of mud and burning sun, into a pit of silence. There was no escape. He counted the days, the hours, the crawling and interminable minutes. Hopeless! Time hung stationary.

Presently Michelson became unaware of the difference between night and day. He slept through the blistering progress of the sun from forest to forest; prowling at night up and down the river in the canoe, he watched the flickering bowl of the sky, listened to the grunting and coughing of animals in the thickets along the banks, drifted aimlessly, tempted to let the current carry him to the bars and shatter the canoe in that thunderous encounter of river and sea at the mouth. Always he turned back to the landing, beached the canoe with a savage plunge of the paddle, and threw himself into his hammock, sleepless, disgusted.

Sambo he despised. The big negro moved about the clearing, attending to his own business. Either he had companionship in the forest, or else he knew the secret of happiness. Once Sambo brought Michelson a bottle of whiskey from the storehouse. "It was the English lord's," he explained. "There is more."

"The fellow wants to destroy me," Michelson thought. But he drank. Thereafter the bottle stood always at his elbow. With it there came dreams, lassitude, a penetrating languor, content, broken by hours of passionate self-hatred. He no longer thought of returning to the world of white men and responsibilities.

The steamer came again, bringing a letter from the Company offering an increase of salary if he would "continue, for two years, to administer the new post with the wisdom, accuracy, and devotion displayed during the contracted term." His reply, pledging himself to two more years of despair, was the only letter carried back to Port Michael by the Dutch pedlar. Michelson came to himself a few days later to find that Agatha Wrightson had not written, and that four letters, postmarked Devonshire, had come for Odell. He tore them into strips and threw them at the shadow which nowadays was always there.

That night he spoke to Sambo. "When the steamer comes again," he said, steadying his hands with a perceptible effort, "I am going away."

"Where?" Sambo asked softly.

"To America. I have had enough of this."

"Will Mr. Michelson recommend me as agent of the post?" Sambo asked in his precise English.

"The Company will decide," Michelson answered without lifting his eyes.

"Very well. I have been faithful."

"Faith. Humbug! There is no reward. Failure —failure and silence." He looked up, caught the negro's eyes, and shouted: "Get out! I am master here."

Sambo glanced aside. "Odell is master here," he said in a clear voice. "I serve him, not you. You are a shadow; he is a man. It is well that you are going when the white steamer comes again."

Michelson clenched his hands and rose to his feet, shouting incoherently. It seemed to him that the negro glided backward out of the room, smiling a sweet smile full of malice and disdain. He felt himself clawing at the closed door. A great light burst before his eyes. His knees were weak and gave way, letting him down on the floor. He was alone again. He was cold—cold for the first time in two years. Shivering—weeping like a woman! As he lay there, face down, with his hands clenched over his head, he heard Odell say distinctly: "Fever! You will have died too late!"

But Michelson did not die. One attack of fever rarely kills a man of Michelson's sort. But he forgot the passage of time completely, so that when the steamer came again he was not even standing on the crazy wharf to watch the landing. From his hammock he heard the whistle—three sharp blasts which splintered the silence. The Dutch captain, seeing no one about but the inscrutable Sambo, shouted from the bridge: "Where's Michelson? Where's that fool agent? There's a woman here who wants to see him."

A woman! Michelson heard and sat straight up as if electrified. He ran his fingers across his unshaven face, tried to smooth down his hair, groaned, then got unsteadily to his feet. "I am coming," he shouted in a desperate voice. He could not find his straw sandals; so after feeling about on the floor of the veranda vainly, he went out barefooted and hatless, blinking in the white-hot glare of the clearing.

"Agatha!"

He ran down to the wharf and pushed Sambo aside, staring up at the deck. There was a woman, but she was not Agatha Wrightson—a tall, dark woman whom he had never seen before; that much he realized in that terrible moment of disappointment, when their eyes met across the narrow strip of muddy water between the steamer and the jetty.

When Michelson again became aware of things he was in bed. Consciousness came like the rolling-up of a curtain, and he saw the strange woman standing by the window with her back turned to the room. He spoke, and she turned, not quickly, but with a sort of expectancy, as if she were about to encounter a friend she had not seen for many years.

"You're better?" she said.

Michelson made an effort. "Real?" he asked.

She came over to the bedside and put her hand briefly òn his forehead. "You're wondering who I am. I came out here to see Odell. I didn't know, until I got to Port Michael, that anything—what had happened." She lifted her head. "I was going to marry him," she explained simply.

"The steamer——"

"Gone—a fortnight ago."

"Good God! What happened to me?"

"Fever—and worse."

"What d'you mean?"

"Conscience — self-hatred — blighted life. Oh, you've talked a lot."

"Why on earth did you stay?"

"Because you needed help and so did I. The captain wouldn't take you aboard—he isn't amiable, is he? And I hadn't any money. So I stayed."

"I might have died."

"But you didn't."

Michelson felt again the appalling weakness. The woman's face wavered; he caught at her hand, seemed somehow to have missed it, and was whirled away on an amber current of silence. When he opened his eyes again she was still there, but it was night, and a candle burned dimly behind her. She did not see that he had come back, and for a long time he watched her, deeply conscious of her as the sick are always conscious of those who are well. She had grey eyes, black brows with a curious downward sweep, white skin and shapely hands.

"You won't go away?" he whispered.

Her eyes turned slowly. "I can't, very well," she said.

"What's your name?"

"Lilah Stevens. I wish you'd call me Lilah. We have five months of this ahead of us."

"You're English, aren't you?"

"Scotch, but Devonshire bred. I live among the hills of Blythlea."

"I know."

"My letters?"

He nodded, and she said: "Odell didn't get them?"

"I'm not sure."

"What d'you mean?"

"It takes a long time to kill a man out here."

She drew in her breath sharply and averted her eyes. Then she gave him a look both beseeching and inscrutable. "It is a shadow," she said.

"It is Odell," Michelson answered.

She laughed. "You are ill, and I am overwrought," she said. "Neither of us has seen—anything. Some day I'll tell you why I came away out here alone. It's a long story."

"I don't care why you came," he said. "I'm only glad you're here."

He held out his hand and she took it, her fingers closing around his with a firm, strong pressure that seemed to envelop his sick spirit, his exhausted heart. He closed his eyes. And still clinging to this strange woman's hand, he presently fell into a heavy, smothering sleep.

He woke to a sense of unreality. He had dreamed. There had been no woman. The house was entirely empty. White slivers of sunlight cut through the closed blinds. The air was flavoured with the sticky sweetness of mud and decaying vegetation.

He got out of bed, dressed, and staggered into the corridor, keeping himself erect with difficulty. Despair seized him with the conviction that Sambo had followed the roll of the native drums farther into the shadows of the forest, leaving the station to its fate.

"Sambo!" he shouted, setting in motion a fusillade of echoes. "Sambo! Where are you? I'll see that you pay for this, you——"

The answer came from the office. A woman's voice, startlingly loud and steady, said: "I am in here, Mr. Michelson."

"You!" he shouted, and ran forward. She was standing by the desk—Odell's affianced. Michelson swayed in the doorway, staring at her. The blinds were drawn, but the hostile sunlight entered the room and lay across the woman's white dress like chains made of some dazzling and fluid metal. She had thrust flowers into the thick strands of her hair—scarlet flowers without perfume, waxen things that had blossomed in darkness. In the look she gave Michelson there was no hostility, only a sort of frightened patience, and he thought: "She is a woman made for love."

Aloud he said: "Did I startle you?"

She moved, the chains of light falling away as if struck off by an unseen hand. "No."

"Is he here?"

"Who?"

"Odell."

She put her hands over her eyes. "Odell is dead," she said in a tragic voice. "They told me at Port Michael——"

"What did they tell you?"

"That Odell died two years ago." Her head bent forward, her face twisted. "Is it true? Tell me! You've got to tell me!"

Michelson shivered. He took her hands in both of his and looked at them, turning them over so that he could examine the soft palms, the strong flexible fingers. Holding his breath, he listened with awe to her breathing. He leaned forward and brushed his lips across her hair. Then he knew that he was no longer alone. Dropping her hands he stammered: "I beg your pardon. I'm not myself. Of course Odell is dead!"

Saying this, he felt suddenly secure, as if in denying that detestable shadow he had banished it forever.

She lifted her head and smiled. "Did you know him?"

"No."

"He was romantic—not a great man, you understand, but a man of ideas, a man of dreams. And this was the end of it all. This river—silence—and death."

"Why didn't you come out here sooner? A woman like you—you might have saved him."

"I wonder if you'll understand? My family didn't like Odell. He was something of a mystery. I met him one summer in London—at some one's house. I've forgotten. I remember nothing except that I loved him—at once, without question, without reason! We talked very little together. I knew nothing about him except that he was poor, that he had great ambitions, that he hated struggle—what he called the ugliness of life. He believed that wealth and accomplishment would come to him under romantic circumstances, in such a place as this. He could not bear failure, criticism, or rebuffs. I think he loved me because I had such faith——"

Michelson, who had flung himself down in a chair, shouted suddenly: "Faith! Where did it get you?"

"Here," she said simply. "A long way, if you stop to think of it. When I met Odell I was only twenty. He wanted me to run away with him. I didn't. There were so many things. . . . I went

back to Blythlea, and he followed. When my father
saw him he said: 'Dammit all, Lilah, you can't
marry that fellow. That chap! That sombre idiot!
Odell of all men on God's green earth! No, my dear
girl, I'll save you from that.'

"Odell couldn't understand. He raged. Once, I
remember, he wept. We were walking in the moor,
and the wind was powdered with fine sea-mist. Odell
looked at me and said: 'You will come. No one will
ever love you unless I do.' When I shook my head,
he pulled me down in the heather beside him and put
his head in my lap and wept.

"The next day he went away. And my father
said: 'You will forget him.' I didn't. He wrote
to me from Rotterdam: 'I am going out to
Maylasia. I will send for you when I can. Be
ready.' When I showed the letter to my father he
said what you said to me just now: 'A woman like
you—going out to a backwater, a pit of darkness.'
A woman like me? Who knows what it is that makes
us do things, makes us feel, here in our hearts?
Odell had touched my imagination. He belonged to
me—all, his dreams, his madness, his desire for an
easy triumph, for power without struggle. He called
me, across the continent, across two seas. Do you
believe that?"

Michelson thought of Agatha Wrightson. "No,"
he answered sharply.

She laughed. "Well, here I am! I came!"

"Without knowing——"

"He sent me money. The letter reached me a year after he had written it. 'Come,' he said. But there were no instructions. I had no idea how to get out here. I wrote to Rotterdam. 'We should not advise you,' they answered, 'to make the attempt alone. The station is isolated, and there are peculiar difficulties.' Then I received another letter from Odell. I must wait. He did not say why. I waited —a year. I wrote. No answer—no sign! No word, until six months ago, when a letter came—one sheet of paper, stained and torn, on which was scrawled: *'Come.—Odell.'* "

"Six months ago?"

She nodded. "My father said at the last: 'Go. The man is indestructible. But you are flinging yourself away.' And I left. At Port Michael they could tell me nothing of Odell. No one there had ever heard of him. I waited for three months. I heard the silence for the first time—I wondered if I could make my voice heard against it. Then your Dutchman turned up and told me. Odell was dead! 'They all die, sooner or later,' he said. 'What is one Englishman in this place?' A mad dance of black men! Ooze and silence! He advised me to turn back. 'There is another fool at Odell's Landing,' he told me: 'Michelson. Came out two years ago, full of ideas. You should see him now—a barefooted spectre kept alive by rum. Afraid to come away, afraid to die.' "

"He lied!"

"Perhaps."

Michelson got unsteadily to his feet. "Why, in God's name, did you come here?"

"I couldn't go back to England. I coudn't face the future in Port Michael—not then." She lifted her head. "Besides," she said, "I had promised Odell."

"So there are two of us," Michelson said bitterly.

"Are you afraid?"

He put his hands on her shoulders, holding her erect so that their eyes were level. The flowers in her hair had faded and lay crushed against the smooth braids. She trembled a little beneath his hands, but her eyes did not waver. "Are you afraid?" she whispered again.

"I am afraid of no one but you," he answered.

He saw her eyes dilate. Looking beyond him, she said quickly: "Sambo! He is watching us."

The black man stood in the doorway. Behind him a flood of white light poured in from the clearing. He was wearing gaudy clothes and had added a nose-ring to his other adornments. He leaned against the wall, his attitude indifferent, as if the gestures of the white man and woman were incomprehensible and unimportant. He seemed to be staring beyond them at some one who remained in the shadows of the room, and the illusion was so perfect, of communion and understanding, that Michelson waited for speech between the negro and Odell.

Sambo stood there a moment, silhouetted against the blazing daylight. Then he turned and stalked across the clearing, absurd, black, pompous.

That night there were drums in the forest, and a fire burned before Sambo's quarters. Looking from the windows of the house itself, Michelson and Lilah saw outlandish shapes passing before the flames. A forest of spears leaped and quivered. A chorus of insane shouts drove back the encroaching silence, so that Odell's Landing was a bedlam in the centre of immeasurable stillness.

"Ivory," Sambo said in explanation the next morning, "much, fine quality." And he added, with a note of malice: "The English lord will be pleased."

Michelson said: "Remember, I am the agent. Show me the ivory."

He followed Sambo to the store, pretending to make inspection. But he knew nothing about ivory. He knew nothing of the manner in which Sambo collected it, paid for it, guarded it against the covetous attacks of hostile savages. While he fumbled with the tusks in the half-shadow of the mud hut, he was conscious of Sambo's eyes upon his back. Something prompted him to say contemptuously: "A poor lot. You must do better than this."

He crossed the clearing again as slowly as he dared. When he reached the dilapidated steps of the house, he heard a little whispering sound, and an arrow struck the panels of the door before him, quivered and dropped at his feet. He turned. Sambo was leaning against the wall of the store, pensive, indifferent.

"What does it matter?" Michelson thought. "He will get me sooner or later."

And, stepping across the arrow, he went into the house.

Time passes slowly in such a place. But at first Lilah and Michelson had so much to say to one another that they lost the illusion of suspended existence. They were actually happy. Michelson shaved and put on a fresh suit of clothes and wore shoes. He felt decent again.

"Five months," he said. "We'll make it. No man, alive or dead, can hold me here when the steamer comes."

They saw Odell's shadow no longer. Sambo cooked for them, and when they could forget his naked body and filed teeth, did very well indeed. He seemed absorbed in some dream of his own. Michelson, watching the big black with half-closed eyes, could detect nothing hostile or threatening. He slept with a loaded revolver beneath his pillow for some time; then he used it to fire at a hippo that had wandered into the clearing, and thereafter left it in the desk drawer. If the fellow contemplated any mischief, he, Michelson, was helpless. No use taking precautionary measures against a death which might strike from the darkness at any moment.

"These natives are all cowards at heart," he told Lilah. "Sambo knows that if anything happens to us, he will lose his job."

They talked a great deal those first days, striving to keep the silence at bay—Lilah lying in the canvas hammock, her white arms over her head, her grey eyes veiled sleepily, Michelson sitting tailor-fashion on the veranda floor. He told her about Agatha Wrightson. He spoke glibly of going back to an "assured position in London or Rotterdam." Made drunk by empty phrases and easy evasions, he told her all his dreams, his plans, his faith in the essential sanity of civilization. He assured himself that he was not in love with her. He was not even afraid of her. Escape was in sight; he was going away from this unclean silence, away from the everlasting spectacle of his own degradation, away from terror of the unseen.

Lilah listened. She seemed strangely contented to swing idly in the hammock. She braided her hair in two long plaits that hung over her shoulders; in them she placed exotic flowers and leaves.

"Where are you going when the steamer comes?" Michelson asked.

She shook her head and smiled. "I don't know."

"I will see that you get to England."

She frowned. "Never! Never there!"

"But what on earth are you going to do?"

"I don't know."

Her indifference irritated him. He got up abruptly and went into the living-room, where he wrote assiduously for more than an hour—a long letter to the Company. In it he assured them at length of his ability and fidelity, as if the matter of his success were of vital importance. He had forgotten his own insignificance. It seemed to him that all the energies of the Company were being applied to save him from the terror he had glimpsed and by some miracle had escaped. He felt sure that he could not escape a second time.

When the steamer was expected he began to pack his clothes, deriving comfort from the neat appearance of his trunks and boxes; he folded his shirts in exact piles, coiled his collars, starched no longer but still recognizable, in a leather box stamped with his initials, and put his overcoat near the top. He dreamed at night of cold winds, human voices, the sound of feet passing and repassing on paved streets, of bath-tubs with nickel fittings, laughter, theatres, restaurants, trains—all the familiar, sane, recognizable facts of civilization. He had had no idea of how he loved them. More than anything else he wanted noise—raucous, ear-splitting, constant.

Lilah made no move to pack her few things. All day she lay in the hammock, her eyes fixed upon some invisible tapestry of dreams. A hundred times a day Michelson rushed to the landing to stare down the river. He imagined that he heard the whistle and would start from his bed in the middle of the night to listen.

"Mistah Michelson goes with the steamer?" Sambo asked.

"Yes."

"Ah!"

"What d'you mean by that, you black scoundrel?"

Sambo's flaring nostrils dilated. He gave Michelson a scornful look. "The white woman stays," he said.

"She is going, too."

"She stays," Sambo repeated. He lifted Odell's cane and made as if to hurl it at Michelson's breast. "She is Odell's."

Michelson did not flinch. "If I hear any more of that from you," he shouted, "I'll see that the Company knows of it."

He went back to the veranda feeling angry and shaken. Lilah opened her sleepy eyes. "What's the matter?" she asked.

"That darky! Pompous fool! Keep away from him."

"What has he been saying?"

Michelson gave her a quick look. Something malicious and alien prompted him to say: "He has an idea that Odell is only waiting for me to go away."

"Why?" she asked, sitting suddenly upright.

Michelson laughed. "He is waiting for you, it seems."

"For me?"

"Alone."

She got unsteadily to her feet and looked wildly around. "I cannot! I cannot!" she cried. "It is too much!"

Michelson was profoundly ashamed. He put his arm around her shoulders, holding her fast until she had ceased to tremble. "I'm so confoundedly sorry," he said. "This place isn't safe—my mind's no good —rotten, like the mud! I didn't mean to frighten you. Tomorrow the steamer will be here, and we'll go back to decency."

The steamer did not come that day or the next. Somewhere down the coast she had gone ashore, and the irate Dutchman was engaged in pulling her out of the mud inch by inch. Michelson's plight never occurred to him. What was one agent, or even two? The fool couldn't expect miracles.

A month passed. Michelson had permitted Sambo to be reckless with the stores, and there was nothing fit to eat at the station save a few meagre and discouraged vegetables which grew in a garden Michelson had scratched on the edge of the clearing. Michelson was too weak to hunt and too lazy to fish. He was seized with despair.

"They have forgotten us," he said bitterly.

He became again dirty, unshaven, and sullen, and sat all day with his arms around his knees, staring at nothing. Into Lilah's eyes there had come a strange brightness—she no longer swung in the hammock, but wandered about the clearing and even into the forest. In the house she went barefoot and wore a wrapper, frilled, faded, a little too long in the back. When she walked it flapped against her pretty bare heels. Sometimes she sang—a low, crooning tenderness. Sometimes she laughed.

"Keep out of the sun," Michelson warned her.

"I am not afraid," she said.

Michelson watched her. Without warning of any sort, he forgot Agatha Wrightson. This woman, grey-eyed, white-skinned, mysterious, doomed like himself to eternal silence, filled his thoughts. He began to feel a fierce jealousy of Odell, the man she had loved and still loved. It seemed to Michelson that he himself had changed. He no longer knew what his standards were, what he was capable of, what possibilities of violence and madness lay within him. He became suspicious of that fetish he had worshipped so long—civilization. He was alone in the world, beyond restraint, beyond criticism, beyond faith. He believed that he was beyond remorse as well. He reasoned with immense cunning that nothing mattered —success, failure, justification. The days would pass and bring nothing but death. Everything was illusion. He had tried to keep faith with the world of reality—love, accomplishment, dignity—and it had cheated him.

The steamer was not coming; there was no doubt of that. They lived on rice, dried beans, the dregs of their scant supply of coffee. There was no salt, no sugar, no bread. All about them an immense wilderness, the wide river which never ceased to flow between the lush banks towards the unattainable freshness of the sea. Down there, ships were passing, cutting north to crowded cities, to things understandable and safe. But there was no way to get there unless——

Michelson went down to the river's edge and contemplated his canoe. He jumped in and lifted the paddle. It was heavy. He had not gone ten feet from the shore before he felt dizzy, weak, shaken by chills. So he went back and squatted on the veranda, his head in his hands. There was no escape.

That night he saw the shadow again.

They had lighted the last of the candles sent out by the Company. It flickered unsteadily on the table between Michelson and Lilah, and in the narrow circle of light behind them Sambo moved about, serving the eternal boiled rice. His hair was twisted into oiled ringlets; the brass ornament in his nose glittered. He stepped softly, his bare feet brushing the floor with a curious whispering sound. Outside, the darkness had come from the forest and had flowed over the clearing like a palpable tide. Lilah was sitting with her elbows on the table, and her hands clasped under her chin. She had kicked off her slippers. The sleeves of her wrapper fell back, showing the whiteness of her arms.

"You are beautiful," Michelson said suddenly.

Lilah said nothing. She sat still, staring beyond the pool of light into the shadows of the room. Michelson turned his head and looked. Odell was standing by the desk.

"Intolerable!" Michelson shouted. He pushed back his chair, seized a glass and hurled it. It splintered against the wall, leaving a splash like the imprint of a hand on the plaster.

"What on earth is the matter?" Lilah cried.

"Odell!"

"I can see nothing."

Sambo had paused, his eyes flashing. Now he crossed the room, picked up the broken glass and went back to his quarters. Michelson thought: "Ah, I frightened them! They will know who is master here."

He laughed. His hands were shaking. "Do you still love that man?" he demanded.

"Yes," she said simply.

"It is impossible. I love you."

"You should not have told me."

"Why? In God's name, why?"

She moved her head from side to side and whispered: "It isn't safe. Believe me. It isn't safe for you."

"And you?"

"It doesn't matter. I am happy."

"Happy?" he shouted.

"I am here. I have kept my promise. What happens to me now cannot matter."

"You are mad."

"No." She fixed him with her eyes. "I would rather die than go away from here."

"Black magic!" Michelson cried. "That scoundrel Sambo is to blame."

She shook her head again. "No."

"Then why——" He stopped short and stared at her in the flickering and uncertain light of the candle. He heard again that palpable and degrading silence, pressing against the very walls of the house, invading the room, obsessing his spirit. "You are too beautiful," he said in a low voice. "You have bewitched me."

"Take care!"

"Of what? I love you. I tell you now, I love you. I have loved you—for an eternity. There is no shadow, no absurd phantom, no romantic ghost that can come between my love and you. They are bound up in each other, inseparable."

"It isn't true."

Michelson rose unsteadily and went towards her "I am master here," he said thickly.

Lilah watched him with a look of profound sorrow. "Take care!" she whispered.

Michelson grasped her hands and lifted her to her feet. Their eyes met and remained fastened together, with fear, like the gaze of accomplices. The violence of the tumult within him had not touched her. She was remote and mysterious as ever.

"This is the beginning," he cried exultantly.

"The end," she said in a despairing voice.

She leaned against him, relaxed and white; Michelson's arms tightened. He caught his breath sharply, tipped her head back against his shoulder and kissed her. Her breath died against his lips.

"Odell," a voice shouted in the clearing. "I have kept my word. She is yours!"

Michelson raised his head and looked into the woman's face. Her eyes stared beyond him. She shivered, sighed, slipped slowly out of his arms and lay at his feet. A spear, flung from the darkness, had struck between her shoulders into her heart.

Michelson stood above her for a moment. While he stared, the last candle flickered and went out. He shouted, leaped back and furiously searched for his revolver in the darkness. Finding it, he became suddenly calm.

There was no sound in the clearing. Creeping on

all fours to the open window, he lifted his head and peered out. He saw Sambo standing about five feet away, a motionless shadow in a world of shadows. Michelson chuckled aloud and fired.

He heard a deep sigh—then nothing more. Silence—silence complete, stifling, suggestive. He got to his feet and rushed out of the house, down to the bank, stumbling in the thick grass. He heard with relief the cough of an alligator in the thicket.

His canoe was there. Pushing clear, he plunged the paddle into the invisible water and turned the prow towards the sea.

Three days later the tramp-steamer floundered slowly up-stream, like a puffy old woman climbing a hill. Fifty miles below Odell's Landing the laconic Dutchman came upon an overturned canoe.

"Impatient fool!" he remarked.

But when he found the others at the station he discovered unexpected eloquence. "A tenacious woman," he said, shrugging his shoulders. "Tenacious."

THE PRECIOUS CERTITUDE

THE two men who shared the first-class compartment of the Harwich express were not alike save for a common reluctance to appear inquisitive. Yet they had managed to encounter each other rather obstinately for several days. They had come from Glasgow to London on the same train. They had stopped for two days at the same hotel in town. And here they were again, occupying the same compartment. Obviously, there was no reason to be surly. The Englishman nodded first, intending to be polite and have done with it; then spoke with brief courtesy.

"Beastly night."

The American glanced at the rain-spangled windows and smiled, as if he hesitated to criticize even the climate of a country he liked so well.

Presently they talked. The American came from Colorado. He spoke of Long's Peak with the tempered enthusiasm of a man for his god. The Englishman had his own god—a nameless mountain in southern Austria—and, pleasantly launched, the talk went from mountains to places, and from places to people. All the while they watched each other, surprised to find that they could neglect their papers and magazines for this casual exchange of ideas.

The train, like most post-war trains, was slow. There was a long delay in the suburbs, when for half an hour people bobbed up and down a strange station platform waving lanterns and shouting. The first-class compartment was pleasantly bright and isolated. The two men might have been on a desert island or sharing a prison cell. And the American talked a little more openly than he otherwise would have talked to a stranger. Somehow he liked the Englishman's way of seeming interested without in the least expecting to be confided in.

The American was a self-confessed feminist, not convinced but experimental. His feeling about women was frankly that of a sportsman. "I'll admit, I'd like to see them win!" The war had shaken him into this enthusiasm.

"I was married for fifteen years to an old-fashioned woman—the sort that leans on the male shoulder like a ton of bricks. She drove my feet into the ground. Charming woman. Very feminine, if you like that sort of thing. I didn't." He met the Englishman's eyes. "I'm being frank with you because I'm not likely to see you again. I've never said as much to any living being. . . . When my wife died, I began to totter a little—tired of being the supporting wall, I suppose. Cut loose and learned to weep like a baby on the broad breast of nature. I was tired of being a Little Lord Fauntleroy bravely gasping: 'Lean harder, Grandpapa.'"

The Englishman smiled. "You cut loose," he said.

"Well, yes. I'm something of a humanitarian. It wasn't the spectacle of woman enslaved that upset me; it was the reverse side of the medal—man, the poor Simon Legree of society."

"What did you do?"

"I agreed that self-supporting, self-motivating, self-thinking women were a heap sight less troublesome than a race of professional leaners. Remember, my shoulder still ached from the burden of that pretty little thistledown! I wore a purple and yellow ribbon in my coat and went forth to free my fellow-man."

The Englishman rubbed the window-pane and stared out at that stationary blur of lights along the suburban platform. "Don't you like women?" he asked.

"I have the illusions of a boy of sixteen—at fifty. I am always ready to believe in the existence of the unique, impossible She. Why, yes—I like them. There are times when I am base enough to believe that they were created for our delight."

"Delight? I doubt that."

The American let this opening pass unnoticed. Rather deliberately he looked away from the flash of disdain in the other's face.

"Don't imagine," he said, "that being their champion has won me their favour. To the contrary. Women distrust me, sensing in me the primitive enemy. And so I am. The more power I gain for them, the further I remove them from their need of men and the need of men for them."

"How about your own need?"

The American said simply: "I've never re-married."

"Lucky dog."

The Englishman laughed shortly, flushing. "There you have me, you see. A confessed failure in matrimony. Very neat! I've never said so before—not even to myself. Oh, I've had my doubts. . . . Women! I don't understand them. They get under my skin. I'm a slave to them. Always have been, from the cradle."

He leaned forward, clasping his hands and staring hard at the American.

"See here. I think I'll tell you something. That is, if you don't object. We're not likely to meet again. I'm anchored in England, and Colorado's a big place. . . . I'm going down to Harwich to meet my wife. The truth is, I don't know whether to go on, or to jump out on that platform—what's the place, Brentwood?—and disappear. Chuck it. Vanish. And never come back!"

He made an apologetic gesture. "It might make things clearer to think out loud. It's a queer story. Damned unpleasant. I warn you. You don't have to listen. Only I'd like to get it straight in my own mind—what's happened to me, why I'm on this train going perhaps to the most unpleasant reckoning of my life, perhaps to——" he hesitated, embarrassed by the phrase—"to heaven."

The American glanced at his watch, conscious of having made a national gesture, for he smiled.

"We're moving! An hour and a quarter, if we aren't held up again. An hour and a quarter in which to put your mind in order. If I'm bored, I'll go to sleep. But that needn't stop you. Get this woman into words. I guess it's a woman you want to talk about——"

"My wife. She's coming into Harwich from Rotterdam tomorrow morning. I haven't seen her for eight months. Eight months of my own particular brew of hell and damnation—doubt. I like the facts of life clear and recognizable. I like to know where I stand. Training, perhaps. Heredity. Neatness, bred in the bone. And for a year I've been dealing with spectres. . . ."

The Englishman broke off and began again: "I understand that it's not fashionable, in the States, to talk about the War."

"It creeps in," the American said, "now and then."

"You saw it?"

"Some. At fifty one doesn't see much. I contributed to the making of 'listening gear.' I am, you see, an amateur feminist, a professional engineer. I hope this won't antagonize you."

"We're agreed, I suppose, that the whole thing was a confounded nuisance?"

"A break in the lute, perhaps, for you youngsters. The universe out of tune. . . . I see you've got a scar."

The Englishman touched his cheek with the tips of his fingers and drew them away to stare at them as if he expected them to be wet and red with his blood. "At Loos. I'm not so young as I look; I was in it almost from the beginning. I didn't get out until after the Armistice. At first I liked it—it was jolly good pageantry. You see, I have the bad luck to love the beautiful, to need it in everything. I dare say there was beauty in 'listening gear'?"

"Well, yes. The first steps were backward into unexplored regions. Later, we made very intriguing beginnings—the C-tube, the K-tube, the MB-tube. We were too hurried—alchemists poring feverishly over our pots and kettles. But there was, as you say, beauty in it. I've listened to sound waves in a microphone, with my heart in my mouth—it's a mysterious orchestra. . . . You were saying. . . ."

"I'd better begin at the beginning. You are perfectly free to go to sleep, or to knock me down, or, if you prefer, to throw me out of the window. It isn't customary to skin one's innermost heart so that a stranger may contemplate it raw. The fact is, I haven't any family and very few friends; no one to go to with this story. I'll try to perform a clean autopsy. I won't spare you. And I'll say now, I'm awfully obliged."

The American nodded and closed his eyes, leaning back against the upholstered seat with his hands clasped on his stomach. He looked, the Englishman thought, like a complacent idol, impersonal, benign, with a touch of malice in his smile. All during that long, broken recital he did not once move or alter his expression, as if he had retreated from his amused survey of a topsy-turvy world into a remote temple

of his own.   The Englishman couldn't be sure that he
was heard.   He found himself growing more and
more eager to penetrate into that silence and to make
himself understood.

"I came back from France," he began, "happier
than I had any right to be.   I mean that I didn't
give a hang about post-war politics, or peace con-
ferences, or a League of Nations.   I was through
with struggle.   I hadn't had your luck.   Listening to
celestial harmonies through a microphone is one
thing; the trenches, another.   I had had enough of
drama.   I wanted an idyllic security—days on end
with nothing to do but lie on the crest of a green hill
and watch the clouds go over.   Safe.   Clean.
What is it Conrad says—'The precious certitude of
beauty'?

"I went to a village in Cornwall, a place off the
railroad, frequented by vacationing clergy and
athletic spinsters—and sheep.   It was very early in
the spring.   The cliffs were covered with a thick
carpet of pink daisies.   The sea was green and cold
as ice, but I managed to swim every day in a cove
about a mile from the village.   I had the local Mer-
lin's Cave all to myself as a bathhouse, and when I'd
done with playing porpoise in that deep smooth
water, I'd climb a little way up the cliff and dry
myself in the sun, with pink daisies as a bed and an
immaculate blue sky for a canopy.   I don't know
whether you can appreciate the quality of my content.   It was enough to feel the earth beneath me
—its contour, its warmth.   Sometimes I'd sing, or

recite pages of schoolday poetry. You might say that I was ripe for romance. There had been women enough during those four years of war, but not one of them would have done for my mood or the place. I wanted nothing familiar. This was a rebirth, if you like.

"The thing that happened was romantic enough. I was lying there on the cliff one day when I heard the sound of oars in the cove; splash and squeak, splash and squeak. It wasn't usual. Vacationing clergy are too timid to row out from the harbour, and athletic spinsters play golf. I sat up cautiously and took a look.

"A woman was rowing a small boat into the cove. She took three or four long pulls at the oars and then sat still, seeming to stare into the water, as if she were watching the red-brown seaweed on the rocks down there. She had the brightest hair I've ever seen, copper gold, shining, incredible. Then she turned her head abruptly, and I saw her face, quiet as the face of one already dead.

"It was perfectly clear what she intended to do. I thought: 'I'll shout. I'll frighten her.' But I did nothing of the sort. There was an unreality about her coming, her intention, her beauty. I held my breath, like a boy in the gallery of a theatre.

"She shipped the oars with a precise gesture and sat a little sideways, her face bent above the water. Then she stood up, stretched herself, pushed her hair back from her forehead with both hands and stepped out. Literally. One thinks of suicides as leaping to death, making a terrible, unwilling effort, screaming, perhaps. This woman sank under the water almost without a splash. The boat rocked and drifted in a circle, empty. . . .

"Then, of course, I remembered my relation to this shocking drama. Shocking, because the world was at peace, the day benign, and there were pink daisies on the cliffs! Incongruous!

"I slid down to the beach head first, with a rattle of small stones and a cloud of dust, and swam out to the centre of the great hoop of ripples that spread from the spot where that lovely copper head had disappeared. I did not see her come again to the surface. Peering down, as one looks into a crystal, I found her just below the surface, seeming to hold herself there by the sheer force of her will to die. I reached down and pulled her up—by the hair of her head, for all I know. I was excited and furious. What right had this strange woman to bring her despair into my brand-new, spotless place of dreams? I hated her. She had the strength of an octopus; she clung to me, struck at me, twined her arms about me, kicked, sobbed, dragged me down in a smother of hair. . . . I think at last I said:

"*'What ho! My pretty!'*

"Or something contemptuous and infuriated, and shook the breath out of her without caring whether she liked it or not. Then I pulled her in and spread her out on the pebbly beach to dry, sitting by with my arms clasped around my knees and the glitter of triumph in my eyes. I felt very much as one feels when he has landed a very devil of a devil-fish. She lay there, panting, her eyes closed, her white cheeks sucking in and out. Her hair had fallen down and lay tangled on her shoulders, little rivulets of water staining the blue pebbles a dark lapis beneath her head. Her fine hands opened and shut spasmodically. I think she was quite conscious, for as I grew to know her, later, I found that her mind never ceased to accept impressions, not even in sleep. She knew that I was there. She knew that I watched her and that I had no intention of letting her step off again into the pool. She felt resentment and shame—to have been pulled by the hair of her head out of finality into a world where the sun was too bright and the air too sweet and my eyes too curious.

"For I found her lovely, soaked and tattered and blue-lipped as she was. Strangely lovely. She did not fit my robust mood. She was too fragile, too—how shall I put it?—too beaten. As if all the winds of Heaven had buffeted her. A lady of Camelot, transparent and waxen. Only her hair seemed alive. The warm sun dried it, strand by strand, and it seemed to move, to twist itself into fine-spun copper coils.

"I sat there wondering what could have lured her away from the sun.

"Presently she opened her eyes and looked at me, steady as a man. And I've never seen such resentment in human eyes—if you imagined that she *thanked* me for saving her!

" 'That was very silly of you,' I said.

"She sat up, shaking her hair forward over her face. Then she took out the pins one by one to make a little heap of them in her lap. I felt somehow that I had insulted her. I stood up, but remained steadfastly near, shivering, because that second dip had shocked me, coming as I did out of my warm earthbed. I watched her twist her hair up again and fasten the shining plaits in place. Her white dress clung to her body. She was lovelier than any woman I had ever seen, because her every gesture was slow, plastic, harmonious; when she moved she transfixed you. Certain great actresses have had that power of making the most casual gesture seem poetic—Duse and your Mary Garden. But she was poetic without being in the least human, like Debussy on a player-piano, a very good player-piano. Something had happened to deprive her of the essence. At least, that's the way she struck me then. I don't know what to think of her, now that I have learned what harm had been done to her soul.

" 'My boat's drifted out,' she said suddenly; 'I'll have to walk back!'

"I looked down at my wet clothing. 'We're curious objects. Perhaps I'd better go to the house back there and telephone for a carriage.'

" 'Yes,' she said. 'Do.'

"I laughed. 'If you think I'm going to leave you——'

" 'That's very kind of you. You're perfectly free to go. I shan't try—again.'

" 'Why on earth——'

"She flung out her hands. 'Don't question me! I don't know. I tell you, *I don't know!*'

"It ended by our walking back to the village together in silence. There was a narrow path along the face of the cliffs, nothing more than a shadow of footprints through the daisies, and I made her walk ahead so that I might grab at her in case she tried —as she had put it—again. I was very polite about it, and she took the lead without protest, as one might humour a madman or a boor. She made me feel that I had interfered stupidly, cheating her out of her own 'precious certitude.'

"At the gate of her lodgings she offered me her hand, and I saw again those hostile eyes.

" 'Please——' I began.

"She shook her head, turned sharply and went in, closing the door. I had to go on, and in order to be doing something, found the fisherman from whom she had hired the rowboat, told him there had been an 'accident,' and saw him start off to rescue his property from the sea.

"This fellow wasn't a Cornishman but a Yankee, begging your pardon. I don't know how he happened to be angling for a living in the English Channel. He told me that he had watched 'that girl' for several days. She had a habit of rowing out into deep water in all sorts of weather. He guessed she had something on her mind. She hadn't a healthy look. Her eyes were queer. I could take his word for it that if she fell out of the rowboat she intended to. . . . In his opinion she wasn't 'all there.'

"The next morning I met her walking slowly towards the cove. She was wearing a dress made of woollen stuff, a short cape, and no hat. To my surprise she stopped and spoke to me.

" 'You probably thought me very casual yesterday,' she said. 'I've always imagined that drowning would be easy. It wasn't! And when you caught me, I thought you were part of it—seaweed or undercurrent, dragging me down.'

"I smiled and she went on, looking about as the clear blue and green of the world: 'I suppose I ought to be grateful.'

"I said eagerly: 'You ought.'

" 'But I'm not. I wanted to drown.'

"We walked on side by side. There was a faint colour in her cheeks and no hostility in her eyes, only a sort of defeated and patient look, something dumb and terrible. She was not a happy companion for a war-fagged soldier stalking his personal renascence in a wilderness of shattered faiths. She was a minor chord, if ever there was one. Lovely, strange, and confoundedly fascinating. I found myself trying to get at that hidden self of hers and to find out why she, of all women on God's green earth where such women are rare, should have wanted to drown in the coldest, deepest pool in England, with no one looking on, as far as she knew, but a lot of silly sheep. I should have left her to her suicidal intentions. I should have had a roistering flirtation with the barmaid at the 'Pig and Whistle,' something elemental and incomplex—the homely passion, if you under-

stand. Instead, I let myself in for it. I fell in love
with her that first day; I'll tell you frankly I'd never
loved before as I loved then. It was the best I had
ever given or ever will give.

"If she was aware of my inner tumult she gave
no sign. Most women are flattered when they inspire
love, or frightened or odiously eager. This girl met
my eyes with the calm impartiality of a child—no,
that's not quite exact. I want you to see her as she
was. If she was calm or impartial, it was not that
she had seen too little, but too much. She made me
feel like a vapouring adolescent; yet she was innocent. Glacial. That was it. I never thought of her
as being in any sense corrupt, only wise; but there
was a black ugliness at the back of her wisdom which
didn't touch, only haunted, her.

"I met her every day by the old church on the
hill or among the powdery ruins of King Arthur's
Castle above the sea. Or we'd sit on the pebbly beach
talking. Two weeks of this, and all my colourful
dreams and projects faded in the intensity of one
desire—to marry her.

"She told me nothing of herself. Oh, she had
worked in the 'munitions.' She had been 'bombed.'
She had joined the Waacs, had served in the Officers'
Club at Abbeville, and lived through four French
winters in a hut with a galvanized iron roof and—
mark this, you lost feminist—chintz at the windows!
She was as familiar with *les morts* as I, but she held
no brief for life. Life was all very well for those
who believed the legend of happiness. Well, she

didn't. Her obstinacy egged me on. I felt that I had to prove my vision, to pass it through the acid of her scepticism. I circled on her, very cautious at first for fear of frightening her away. I knew her name, but not where she lived or where she intended to go when she left Cornwall. Every morning I woke with a catch at my heart. She might have run away, you see! I had no hold on her. Her eyes never kindled when they rested on me. *Never!* Now, it isn't beyond the range of possibility that the barmaid's might have. . . .

"We talked of books. She had read more than I and with better judgment, but she got no joy out of poetry or romance. She simply didn't believe in them. I'd lie at her feet, stretched full length, staring up at her, babbling of beauty. Once, I remember, she picked a tall red poppy and put it in her hair, smiling a little. But with her arm raised and the petals between her fingers, the smile faded; she plucked the poppy out again and threw it away, as if, mind you, she were ashamed. And yet— with eyes like that and a mouth like that, there must be a soul in her! She was a sweet lute for the playing, and I thought to hear strange and lovely music. So, one day, I asked her to marry me.

"We were sitting in the church porch to get shelter from a rain storm that came up from the moors with a rush of cold wind. There was no one about—not even a sheep. Sorry and tender and curious, I got hold of her hands and stammered, telling her I couldn't let her go, that I'd do anything for her, no matter what.

"She said: 'You haven't known me a fort-night.'

"For answer I kissed her hands.

"She began to tremble, and that encouraged me. She was human, after all. She said: 'I'll marry you, but you mustn't expect too much of me. Not at first.'

"I told her I only expected her to be herself. That was the proper answer, wasn't it? She pulled her hands away and shook her head.

" 'No, I'll not be myself! From today I'm going to be some one else, or you can let me go. You probably want to know all about me. Well, I shan't tell you anything. Hasn't the War changed everything—England and society, you and me, religion, geography? Well, today begins *our* story. We've had no childhood, no youth—we're just born!'

"I thought: 'A pretty fancy. She won't keep it up. Sooner or later I'll find out that she is a green-grocer's daughter or the seventh daughter of a down-at-heel baronet.' Aloud I said: 'You are a sea goddess, come from the green cove to delight me all the rest of my days.'

"She leaned towards me, offering her lips, and her eyes, remaining wide open while I kissed her, had in them that look of hostility. But instantly she laughed and took my face between her hands and said all manner of disarming things, never letting me kiss her again but, instead, kissing me, now on this cheek, now on that, vivacious, flushed, suddenly delectably alive from head to foot. I admit I lost my head. It never occurred to me to question her. After all, you'll say, she wasn't a mermaid, she was a woman, who had tried to drown herself, you suppose, for a reason. Yet she was so fragile or else so devilishly strong, that she had her way—we began our life from that day.

"Not that I didn't go back along the past. A man likes to talk to a woman about his first wild oats and his first success and his little popularities. I told her about my Aunt Fanny who had such a fondness for bad Eton boys—the badder the better! I told her about my year out in your Texas. And about India—the glamour of being a 'sub' in Cashmir. But not about Loos. I thought that could wait until a quieter time of friendship.

"We decided to go up to London at once and be married there, and I saw her off on the morning train, going back to the village to pack my own things at my leisure. She was to 'shop.' I was to follow her in a few days and we were to meet, like ordinary lovers, in Hyde Park near the Serpentine. The day and the hour were set very carefully—rain or shine, she promised to be there! Yet I began to doubt, the moment her train pulled out of the station, that I would see her again. I had actually forgotten to ask her for her address! The woman I loved more than life—suppose she were late. Or ill. Or had given me the slip. . . . You see, I didn't really believe in her. I was beset with all sorts of fears, recalling, not her mood of acquiescence, but her hostility and malice. Her eyes, looking back at me from the train window, had for an instant seemed eager, as if she wanted to hold the memory of my face. But I couldn't believe that I would ever see her again. Instead of waiting in Cornwall I went at once to London, where I put in a week of miserable self-torment and jealousy, looking everywhere for her, expecting heaven knows what. On the appointed day I was purposely late—for the rendezvous. But she was there, waiting quietly, wearing a smart dress and hat and carrying a sunshade. She looked so unlike a mermaid and so like a woman of my own world that I came into her presence penitent and ashamed.

"I see you're smiling. I suppose you think that I was disarmed by my good taste in women. I couldn't be mistaken in her, because she was my choice. . . . You're not altogether right. I couldn't be mistaken in her, because I saw at once what a superior creature she was. As we walked out of the park I noticed that it wasn't the man of the street who turned to stare at her, but he who might be expected to recognize and take delight in distinction.

"She was very grave. Meeting this way made us both shy and inexpressive. We lunched at a tea-room where the waitresses wore brown linen and had brown ribbon bows in their hair. I remember looking at the girl I was going to marry and saying over and over, as if to convince myself: *'I'm going to marry her. I'm going to marry her.'*

"She told me about her purchases. She had bought very few things, because she imagined we would travel on our honeymoon.

" 'You want to travel?' I asked.

" 'Why, yes. Of course.' She gave me a curious look. 'I suppose you can afford it.'

"I told her that there was very little I couldn't afford—my family's various fortunes, great and small, had come to me. She smiled: 'That's very fortunate, because I haven't a shilling.' She opened her purse and spilled out the contents—sixpence, a few copper pennies and a key: 'Literally, this is all that's left.'

"A look of comprehension and pity must have come into my eyes, for she flushed and said. 'You're quite wrong. It wasn't that. I'm not a coward.'

" 'No,' I said, 'I'm sure you're not. You're a brave and beautiful girl, and I love you. I wish you'd say, just once, that you love me.'

" 'I don't like saying things. I'm going to marry you; isn't that enough?'

"Well, after all, it was a good deal. She knew nothing about me. I suggested that we call on my Aunt Fanny. The wonderful old lady lived in Bloomsbury, among the retired butlers and city clerks, keeping up a great Victorian elegance in defiance of time and change. 'You'd like her. She'd be uncommonly gracious to you. And you might feel that you knew me better.'

" 'I know you very well. Can't I judge a man for myself?'

"You see, she had her way. We were married in a little church of her own choosing by a clergyman who had no interest in either of us and who called in a verger and a char-woman as witnesses. It was, you'll admit, romantic. Afterwards, we drove out to Richmond for dinner and went a little way down the river in a hired punt. She kept smiling at me, as if to hide that look of defeat which had come into her eyes. I thought again of the Lady of Camelot. There was a vast purple twilight over everything, and the slow river was full of fallen lilac petals—an hour tranquil, benign, suspended. I should have been happy. I assured myself that I was. Yet I would have given anything to have been away from that white, smiling face and those restless hands. We talked, I remember, not of the moment, our wedding-day, but of the honeymoon trip. She wanted to go out to the Dutch East Indies, and I had engaged passage from Rotterdam at the end of the week, for us and for my man, Knott.

"I should have mentioned Knott before. He is my man Friday. He has always been my friend and servant, and you remember I confessed to being older than I look. I could no more do without Knott's counsel and criticism, his personal interest in everything I do, than I could do without food. What is it they say: 'Every man's a hero to his valet'? In Knott's eyes I am infallible. I am of the essence of gentlemen.   He is a queer old chap.   I don't know that I can recall what he looks like—I think you'd say that he was a cross between a missionary and an actor.   He is, as a matter of fact, a clergyman's son, but there's a servile streak in him inherited from his lady's-maid mother; he is a born servant.   If England crumbles socially, his heart will break.   I have to keep up a pretence of gaiety for his sake—he so enjoys 'laying out' my evening things!   The old boy loves luxury, but he served in France with the best of them, not as orderly, but as cook.   Three times to hospital, and he has a neat, little platinum plate in his skull, just over the left ear.   When I got back from France I found him already at my flat, wearing his black clothes and a brand-new toupee. I remember that he said: 'Well, sir, it's over. Shall I lay out the brown suit, or the grey home-spun?'

"I'm going into particulars about Knott because he has to do with the rest of this story.   He had not followed me to Cornwall, because my flat was being redecorated and I wanted him to supervise the job in my absence.   When I got back I told him that I was expecting to be married; I had met the unique, improbable She.   Knott's eyes filled with tears and his lower lip trembled.   Yet it was all too hurried and obscure to quite please him.   He wanted a wedding at St. Margaret's.   My being married in an unheard-of parish nearly bowled him over.   That he couldn't be there offended him to the soul, but he was very correct and said nothing. He was, he knew, going with us on that preposterous wedding journey to the Indies, and that kept him from boiling visibly. He shook his head over my marriage; there was a covert mental reservation in his eye; it wasn't 'quite right.'

"At Richmond I spoke to my wife again about Knott. He had filled the flat with flowers and expected us to come back there. She said: 'Very well. But must he go with us out there?'

" 'Not if you prefer to leave him in England. Wait until you see him, my dear. He's priceless. He isn't a human being; he's magnificent mechanism with brains. Cook. Valet. Lady's maid. Philosopher. He will be a sort of skipper; not at all in the way, I promise you!'

"It would have been natural for her to have agreed to Knott for my sake, but she said nothing, only put her white hand into the water and let her fingers drag among the million floating petals shaken down from wind-blown lilac bushes along the banks. It was growing dark; we drifted under the willows and, kneeling down before her, I put my head in her lap. I felt her hand in my hair after a while— a tentative, almost unwilling caress. She spoke eagerly of our trip. She had always wanted to go out to the East Indies—supposed that reading Conrad had brought this vague longing to the surface. The very name Java made her see the East, 'so old, so mysterious, resplendent and sombre, living and unchanged, full of danger and promise.' She could feel in her dreams the 'violence of the sunshine.' She thought that she would understand those brown people and that they would understand her. . . . It was good of me to take her out there. . . . I felt her hands trembling, and a strange humidity came into her voice: 'I hope I'm not going to cheat you,' she said; 'I don't altogether understand myself. There are queer things in me—moments when I feel that, no matter how I may try to be what you expect of me, I shall fail.'

" 'Be yourself,' I told her again.

"She said: 'You are very good.'

"But I knew then that she didn't love me. I had been led by my own passion into accepting her fugitive affection as a deeper feeling—her funny, childish kisses, her bursts of gaiety, her way of taking my arm and squeezing it, as I had squeezed my Aunt Fanny's arm in the Eton days. We had almost a week, remember, before sailing, and I discovered that my wife wanted something more than my love; she was bending me to some mysterious purpose of her own, not selfishly, but driven by a force stronger than her will. What it was I couldn't guess. The woman had turned mermaid in my arms. What should have been a sweet lute singing was no song at all. Perhaps I am a romantic fool, but I was profoundly sorry for her. Oh, it was a merry little tragedy! Five days spent in contemplating a bride who fluttered against my heart like a fish in a net! She had a way of looking at me a little askance. Once I came upon her combing her hair before a mirror and tangled my fingers in the copper-coloured strands. She shook herself free, striking at me with both clenched hands, panting. I remember shaking her, not gently, either, and then she nestled in my arms, kissing me in that rapid, frightened way she had, begging me to forgive her, she hadn't realized, she hated to be touched . . . and all the rest of it.

"There was a reservation in Knott's acceptance of her, because, as he explained, she was 'very sad, somehow.' But, strangely enough, he pretended not to see how askew things were. He bent over her at table like a middle-aged Cupid in a toupee, offering his best in the way of eggs and muffins. He filled her room with flowers. In the evening, when she played for me—and she played well—there would be a pervasive stillness in the pantry, and I knew that Knott was listening, too. Then I saw what things she was capable of, what things were shut away from me. She played by ear with a sympathetic touch— Strauss, Brahms, Schubert. *Aus meinen grossen Schmerzen*. . . . You remember that? *I fashion my grief into little songs*. . . . There is no English for it. She'd sing it with her head bent . . . no mermaid, then; no Lorelei; a woman tender and real. I got it into my head that she was not playing for me but for some one who wasn't there. I had the ugly sensation of not belonging in my own home, of being an eavesdropper, an interloper, a rank outsider. I was jealous of a shadow! I can't make this clear to you unless you see that, at all times delightful, only in her rare moments of warmth she was not mine . . . the touch of my hand or the sound of my voice would bring her back to a fixed politeness, a sort of spiritual grin, horrible because it didn't, it couldn't, deceive me!

"I would have been justified, you may think, in refusing to go on. I just happened to be in love with her. I felt myself confronting a rival, a definite antagonist, in that other—whoever it was that claimed her. I was too proud to question her; she had no personal belongings, such as photographs, or books, or family Bibles. I couldn't 'get' her, you see. Not content to accept her as 'new-born,' I became suspicious, curious, doubtful; I watched her; I followed her about. It must have been, now that I think of it, very hard to bear.

"I could not doubt that she had a purpose in going to the East. Towards the end she was breathless with her hurry to be off. She even forgot her rôle and locked herself in her room where, all night, she was busy with preparations of her own. With my hand on the door-knob, I found Knott just behind me, his face puckered with emotion. 'I wouldn't, if I were you, sir. I really wouldn't. She's all keyed up.' He led me back to the library and gave me a whiskey-and-soda, as one gives a rubber ring to a teething baby. 'I wouldn't be hurt, sir. It's only seeming.'

" 'Well,' I thought, 'if Knott sees, then the whole world can see. I'm married to a woman who hates me. I'm a damned fool to go on with it.'

"But I did go on with it. I wanted to see the thing

to the end, to stare the mystery in the face. We sailed from Rotterdam on a Dutch ship, Knott accompanying us. My wife was like a woman who has sold her soul to the devil and is going to the reckoning. I have no less crude way of putting it. She was desperately determined and desperately unwilling. And little by little, as we spun southward, through warm summer seas, a name emerged . . . she wanted to go to a definite place, a settlement in the tobacco-growing district on the coast near Malacca. I asked her why. At first she fended skilfully. There were literary reasons—didn't I remember Conrad's Captain Whalley and the delightful Mr. Van Wyk? She had been told of this place—a typical 'plantation' worked by coolies, fifteen days from anywhere. There was a 'rajah,' a forest river—all the stage settings! She knew exactly how to get there from Malacca. . . . Her eyes wavered and she clasped and unclasped her hands. She turned to get my answer and found me looking at her with a smile that must have been positively terrifying, for she got up and hurried along the deck without saying another word.

"It was that night, I think, that she shut the door of her state room against me. I had been wandering up and down in the moonlight, smoking, enjoying the soft, warm breeze that came from off-shore seemingly perfumed with flowers. I thought she ought to be there with me. It seemed that in that silver splintering of moon shafts on the black water there must be magic. Perhaps she would open her heart to me. I went below, rather unsteady with longing, and rapped on her door. She asked: 'Who is it?' I said gently: 'Won't you come on deck?' There was no answer and I rapped again, not daring to rattle the knob, for a steward lurked in the corridor near by. I heard a long sigh, profound and terrible. 'Let me in! I want to talk to you.' After a silence she answered in a dull voice: 'Go away! For Heaven's sake, leave me in peace!'

"I turned on my heel and went on deck again. At midnight Knott found me and, touching my arm, told me that my wife had sent him to fetch me—she wanted to speak to me in her state room at once. Knott's face wore a sympathetic, scared look, as if he, too, had heard that terrible sighing.

"I found her sitting on the plush sofa under the port-hole, wearing a silk kimono with long lace sleeves, her hair hanging down over her shoulders in two shining plaits. She leaned a little forward, staring at the floor, as she had stared into the water that day in Cornwall. There was the same sense of resolution and finality about her expression. She motioned to me to sit down beside her. 'I have something to tell you.'

" 'I think I can guess,' I interrupted. 'You don't love me.'

"She raised her head sharply. 'I don't know. At first, I thought I did. I thought, if I married you, I'd forget the other.'

" 'So there's another. And you can't forget him.'

" 'It seems I can't. I've tried. Perhaps I'd better tell you. . . .'

"She began at once, without faltering, the strangest recital I've ever listened to. I can't repeat her words, of course. Memory plays curious tricks, yet I think I remember exactly the details of the story. She made no special plea for sympathy, but she seemed to expect me to understand. And so I did. There was something about the quality of my longing that matched hers.

"She told me that she was twenty-six years old. She was born in an English manufacturing town—the daughter of a printer and small publisher. When she was sixteen, a girl full of romantic ideas, a sort of 'silly young colt,' as she put it, she met a man whose control over her was subtle and immediate. He was a Hollander, in his early thirties, a big, steady-eyed man who said very little except to boast that he always had his own way. He said that he was a tobacco-planter in the East. He spoke to her in his taciturn, inexpressive way of his house out there, the tropical heat and colour, the fat 'rajah' who was his only neighbour, his loneliness. Whatever picturesqueness there was in his story must have come out of the girl's imagination, for, as far as I could make out, he was not generous with details. He had an inner and outer reticence, a thing part of his very tissue, she said. He moved slowly with a steady forward pressure that got him things. He had come to her town to look into the matter of an inheritance, and he stayed there less than a month.

"She did not have to explain her sixteen-year-old self to me, nor did she try, except to say that she knew nothing of life, didn't want to know, kept knowledge off consciously, fearful of stepping out of the aloof territory of the adolescent spirit into the dull acceptance of maturity. It was a curious fact that while she knew what lay beyond, she went on deceiving herself, postponing, dreaming, cherishing Heaven knows what golden illusions, what shining, incredible dreams! Why should you or I expect to know how a young girl's mind tackles the problems of love and life? This girl must have been a strange little creature, undeveloped, yet imaginatively wayward. She confessed to having had a love of that strangeness of proportion which means beauty.

"The Hollander fell in love with her. His emotions, for being so far out of sight, were hard to recognize. Yet he loved her immediately, with all the passion and ruthlessness of that sort of nature. He didn't comprehend her in the least. She babbled to him of love—love out of books! Her own heart was behind the citadel, untouched, uncomprehending, the heart of a child of ten, not a girl of sixteen. Mentally, she had not glimpsed womanhood.

"Heaven knows how she happened to go on meeting him. She told me that they met outside the town in a copse on the edge of a stream. It was summer. She used to bring books and read to him. This went on for weeks, and her parents guessed nothing. Presently she noticed that the Hollander's eyes had begun to smoulder. They had been steady. Now they flickered at her. She was frightened because she knew. She tried to quench that flaming. It may

have seemed—we'll give the fellow the benefit of the
doubt—a sort of coquetry. She met him, she scolded
him, she talked to him of her gilded illusions. She
must have been very lovely. He had just come out
from the Malaysian archipelago and from unremitting
labour, at grips with the forest wilderness and those
simple brown savages. The women he had known
were 'harbour' flirts, white driftwood at the ends of
the earth.

"He lay at this English girl's feet watching her with
the fire mounting in his eyes. It licked at his heart.
It set him to trembling. He told her over and over
again that he always got what he wanted. One day
he put his hands on hers—only that, but she said that
her 'body seemed to grow still, as if listening.' Then
she blushed and ran away. There was a tumult in her.
She hated him. She recalled his eyes, his straight,
bony nose, his big mouth with the white teeth, his
broad, short-fingered hands. She hated. She was
pitiless. She called him a 'boor,' a 'beast,' an 'un-
couth barbarian.' She avoided him. She lay awake
at night trembling with fear of him. He wrote to
her; when his letter was put at her plate she felt her
whole being collapse under the weight of her revulsion.
But she said nothing to her parents about this letter—
a note asking her to meet him. What had he done?
He promised never to frighten her again. Nothing
was said about love; she was a little ashamed of her
panic. She saw him in the street watching her window, and he seemed so carelessly good-natured and

awkward that she was sorry for him and giggled and blushed behind the window-curtain.

"I cannot tell you this story as she told it, for it was an intimate record of adolescence—not ordinary, for she was not an ordinary girl.   She had read, for instance, 'Aucassin and Nicolette,' Goethe, and in French, of all things, 'Le Mariage de Loti.'   She thought of passion as belonging in another world; it could never touch her; poets would write of it and singers sing of it and painters paint it—you understand, she preferred her citadel, but she had looked over the wall into strange country.

"The Hollander, we suppose, knew nothing of this. Forces had been let loose in him that he was not used to curbing.   One day when she was alone in the house he came there, and not knowing who it was that rapped at the door, she opened and let him in.   He explained that he was going back to his tobacco planting, and, carried beyond himself by her presence, told her thickly that he loved her, he wanted her to marry him and go out there with him on the next steamer.   He was embarrassed.   There were beads of perspiration on his forehead, and he sat stiffly on the edge of a chair twisting his hat between his hands. It was as if he sensed suddenly what a high wall stood between that young girl and himself—a man who had seen life from all sides and had probably taken his pleasure carelessly enough.   Not a bad sort.   But a man unused to the feminine maze he found himself in now.

"She should have been frightened, but she wasn't. He was so humble, so abjectly at her feet, that she felt secure and excited, reckless. She wanted to hurt him, and out of her obscure consciousness came certain ways to tease him. He flushed a darker red and went on begging in a broken, ridiculous voice. She laughed at him. . . . She told me how she laughed, flinging her head back, enjoying his discomfiture. He stopped short, as if in doubt, and then laughed, too, leaning forward to grasp her hands. She saw his eyes, no longer humble, but excited, full of little dancing flames. His expression was odious. She snatched her hands away, suddenly furious. He said: 'I'll discipline you, you little devil! You won't forget me.' And forcing her to his will, for he was a strong man, he saw to it that she would not forget him.

"She never encountered him again. He went out, slamming the door, leaving her in the crumbled citadel, pale, shivering, distraught, remembering. She ran to look at herself in the mirror, expecting a different face. She looked at the quiet face reflected there and said aloud: 'I'll punish him by forgetting.'

"But she didn't forget. He was always there. A complicated and devilish obsession, if ever there was one. Instead of vanishing, he became more real with time. Her mother and father died, and she went up to London to earn her living, thinking to lose that man in the crowded streets; but he was there, sunburnt, taciturn, with his slow smile and his flickering eyes. He had taken possession of her spirit. She

was, if you can accept so bizarre a statement, his
slave. And I dare say he had forgotten her very
existence!

" 'Do you love him?' I asked gently.

"She said she didn't know. She was getting used
to him. Perhaps. Other men meant nothing to her.
Men had made love to her, particularly during those
years of war, when men spoke lightly of great things
and with respect of little things. But there had been
no response in her because the other was always there,
listening. In France, at Abbeville, she had lost him
for a while. She had worked until she dropped asleep
in her clothes. A mud-stained, greasy, dog-tired
Lady of Camelot! But when she got back to London
he had followed her. Then she began to fear for her
wits. She heard his voice. Often he spoke to her
and put his hand on her arm. She thought: 'If I
could see him, I could rid myself of him.' So she
made inquiries and found that he was still in the East,
unmarried, and that his plantation had grown con-
siderably. She could not go out there, so it seemed
more simple, considering that there was no escape
from him, to do what I had prevented her from doing.
And then, for a while, she had been free again, until
that day in Hyde Park, when side by side with me
he had come towards her, claiming her, body and
soul, for himself.

"Is this too peculiar for your comprehension?
Do I seem to be dealing with palpable absurdities?
She had not seen this man for nearly ten years. Yet
he had so impressed the delicate sensitive-plate of

her perceptions that he was photographed there,
odious, fascinating, mysterious and terrible—an
enemy and a lover, unreality and reality, stamped,
made irrevocable, yet for ever beyond her comprehension. . . .

"She was going out there because she could not
help herself!

"She lifted her head and at last met my eyes,
and in the look, searching and impersonal which
passed between us, we seemed to clasp hands. I told
her that I would leave her at Singapore. She was to
go on, with Knott, of course, who would look out for
her safety, straight to the coast where it would be
easy enough to find the Hollander and, if possible,
to lay his ghost. I told her that I wanted her to
come back only if she were willing and ready. In
the meantime she wasn't to consider me. I even gave
her leave to forget me. Magnanimous? I wonder!
She gave me not the slightest encouragement. She
was grateful, but she made no scenes.

"Knott of course, had to be told some of this
bizarre story, as I could not let her go on alone. You
will like my wife better if you know that it was she
who made the purpose of her journey clear to that
extraordinary old chap. Took him aside and talked
to him for hours!

"Afterwards he came to my state room, and for
the first time in his long service sat down in my presence uninvited. 'A wonderful woman,' he said.
'We're not worthy of her. Very likely I'll have to
leave her out there. I'll see to that. You can trust

me, sir. I won't bring her back unless her mind is free.'

" 'You are quite sure you understand, Knott?'

"He gave me a queer look. 'Quite. She didn't, I'm proud to say, spare me.'

"After that Knott seemed to have left my service to go into hers. He never faltered. It was part of the day's work to take his master's ghost-ridden bride. . . .

"I find it hard to talk about it. All I know is that I left them at Singapore and turned back, not knowing whether I did right or wrong, outwardly amiable and indifferent, inwardly torn to very tatters. If she were haunted, I was possessed. I prowled about the peninsula for ten days brushing imaginary spectres from before my eyes. I had all the normal reactions. Jealousy. Rage. Hilarity. Suspicion. Indifference. I got back to London with an excellent case of post-war shell-shock. The woman I loved had been swallowed up in that dark country, had disappeared, going to Heaven knew what strange and revolting fate. . . .

"Well, that is almost the end of the story. I received three letters from Knott. One from Malacca, saying that they were all right. They had traced 'that fellow' and were starting out to his 'place,' aboard a small coast steamer, the following day. It was infernally hot. . . .

"Here. I'd better read the other two. Confounded queer documents. He says:

" 'Dear Sir: We arrived here safely after some-

what of a stew aboard the s.s. *Gull*. No gull, sir.
Ten days down the coast in the whitest weather I
ever saw.' Now, what d'you fancy he meant by
that? 'Slow. Stinking dirty. Ship full of black
natives, pigs, and hens. Not at all a place for her
ladyship. Her ladyship was calm as always. I fixed
her a chair in the shade and stood by.' I'll wager
he did! 'I was sorry for the way her eyes watched
the sea. Once she said to me: "Knott, I'll be glad
to be going back." I don't make much of that, but
I repeat it for your curiosity. We were a long time
getting there. At night it was no cooler; there were
hot stars, and at times rain that steamed on the
decks. We saw mountains. The place was up a
river. We tied to a dock at five in the morning.
Her ladyship came on deck and stood looking down at
the crowd of coolies and natives with one or two white
men who stood down below staring up at us. She
said: "This is the place. That's him in the white
coat over there; the one with the beard." They had
put a gangway down, and she went ashore and spoke
to that man. I don't know what she said. But I
saw her face.' That old idiot doesn't say what the
look in her face was at that moment. I've puzzled
over that. He goes on: 'We are staying at one of
the plantation-houses, and the steamer has gone away.
They tell us that she won't come back again for three
or four months. I am cooking for her ladyship, and
twice a week that man dines here. It is not my
affair to listen to what they say. They talk. I have
heard their voices going on, out in the veranda, late

at night. Her ladyship has not explained anything to me. She seems happier than you ever saw her. I don't say this to pain you, for somehow it seems a good thing. I have heard her singing, and she sits staring out at the river, smiling. That man comes and they ride together. He has a fair-sized place here. He isn't a gentleman, but neither is he a man you don't respect. He might be dreaming for all he notices what is going on beyond this house where her ladyship is. He circles on us like a hungry wolf. He calls her ladyship by another name, and your ring is not on her finger. I am watching out. I have arms, and I sleep—although her ladyship does not know it —on the veranda outside her window. I have heard that man prowling, but I am not afraid of him. If you want my word for it, her ladyship can handle him. He has a real look about him. No ghosts there. And her ladyship isn't afraid of real things. She looks him straight in the face. I must close; this letter goes by native boat to meet the steamer on her way north in the Strait. I am your obedient servant, Knott.'

"That's all. Damned little! I tried to drag more out of the paper, out of space, out of my tortured imagination. I understand nothing. Nothing!

"Then a month ago, this from Malacca:

" 'Dear Sir: We are coming home. We are forced to wait here. Her ladyship is ill with a fever, but she instructs me to tell you that there is no ill in her spirit. I repeat her exact words, I have got a good English doctor for her, a Dr. Smith from Birmingham. God knows why he is out in a place like this, but he seems to know his business. I cannot tell you what has happened beyond certain facts. I will be brief.' The precious fellow will be brief, mind you! 'Six weeks ago her ladyship said to me: "It was all a dream, Knott. We can go home." After that she seemed not to want to see that fellow. His look of a hungry wolf went to my heart. If you will pardon me, I think I can recognize when a man is desperate. Her ladyship was free of him, but he wasn't free of her. He'd got her on his mind, like. One day she called him to her and told him what she told you, and, I'm proud to say, me, who am her obedient servant and can keep a secret. They were on the veranda, her ladyship's voice down, that man groaning and carrying on. I could hear him in the kitchen. It sounded as if she stabbed him in the heart again and again with her words. I ran out and he was stumbling away, walking fast and tripping over everything for all the world like a drunkard. Her ladyship looked after him and then at me with a funny smile. "It's all right, Knott," she said. "Now I can forget him. For ever." She put her hands over her eyes and said: "I'll be glad to see England." Then she began to shiver. "I've punished him," she said. Like that. Over and over. We got out of there the next week. That man never came again. He never came back to the place. An old man, a native man, found his hat on the beach. They say that he swam out of the inlet into the

Strait. In the dark. Not a safe thing to do. But he might have been swimming away from a ghost of his own. They call him dead, but they have no proof —only his hat and his footprints down to the river's edge. I will wire you from Singapore. Your obedient servant, Knott.'

"Well that's all."

The Englishman folded the letters and put them back in his pocket. "We seem to be getting into Harwich. Are you putting up there?"

"Yes." The American opened his eyes with a slight start. "I'm down here to watch some British undersea experiments. We *are* getting in! Excellent run."

The two men gathered together their travelling paraphernalia as the train, with rain-splashed windows, approached the town. They said nothing more, as if reminded of the strangeness of their confidence. But on the station platform, in a sudden, confusing bustle of porters and guards, in a strong wind flavoured with salt spray from the North Sea they rather awkwardly clasped hands.

The American said: "There is, after all, beauty. You have your precious certitude. . . . Indubitable."

A sort of tidal wave of hurrying passengers separated them.

But in the morning the American happened to see his Englishman again. They passed, apparently unrecognizing. For the American had seen, out of one corner of his humorous, interested eyes, his Englishman and a pretty woman with copper hair, buying post-cards at a book-stall! And he heard, with those ears attuned to strange microphonic harmonies, the lightest-hearted laughter in the world.   .

"I'll be damned," he said, as he went on, "if I'm not sorry for that Hollander.   After all————"

THE END